Tania de la Cantera

Suzy McCall

DEDICATION

To my Mom and Dad,

Homer and Kathy McCall,

for demonstrating throughout their lifetimes

that anyone in need is our neighbor, and that sometimes

a smoked turkey is more welcome

than an eloquent sermon.

May God show us, for each of His lambs, His way of Love.

Cover photo by Maria Leticia Sanchez Martinez, one of my many talented and beloved children.

FORWARD

I can think of no other person equipped to tell a story such as this than Suzy McCall. She has been walking alongside people like the ones in this book for more than twenty years in Honduras. Suzy doesn't just know *about* these people. She has brought them home to live with her, to be fed by her and to be loved by her and her many children. She has sat up all night with them. She has heard countless heart-wrenching stories from the children and young girls she has rescued from neglect, sexual abuse, and exploitation. She has stood up to corrupt judges in the courts on behalf of little ones with no parent in sight for protection. She has gone to crime and gang-infested areas to rescue young women from self-destruction over and over again. Her heart has mourned over the ones who would not or could not bring themselves to respond to the gift of a new life in God and who chose instead a life of enslaving addiction or rebellion. She has seen; she has heard. Now she is telling.

Suzy knows well the darkness of despair that drives poor mothers in countries like Honduras to make terrible decisions over tiny innocent children. Yet if knowledge of the sheer poverty and injustice all around was all she had, she could never bear the immense outrage of it all. You see, she believes in a huge God. She knows that this God was also hungry, beaten, rejected and then killed. So He can completely identify with horrible sufferings. Not only that, He can do something about it. Suzy is just brazen enough to believe that He might use her as His holy change agent. There is an unparalleled determination in this one single woman who left a comfortable life as a much loved English teacher in the States now giving her life with abandon for the people of inner city Tegucigalpa, Honduras. With the fire of justice alongside mercy found together only in Jesus, she will stand up to evil and fight for those lost in body, soul or spirit.

You might think with all of this heaviness of call, Suzy would be one down-in-the-mouth kind of person. She is remarkably joyful with a hearty laugh and a huge hug. She is known by hundreds of children in the poor barrio of Flor del Campo in Teguc, as "Mami Suzy!" They will yell it out to get the turn of her head and a taste of her warm spirit in their direction. She is loved by the young and old alike, easily able to lift the heart of the wayward and struggling. Yet, watch out, she will not hesitate to speak stern words straight to the heart of those of us who may be very well taken care of and not really getting it that we ought to be doing something about the needs of others. I know of no one else who can quickly bring me to a true estimation of what my life is about. Suddenly a host of things I am very concerned about just don't matter a hill of beans. What matters is whether I am about Jesus' work while I am here on this earth. And He is especially concerned that the sick, the oppressed, the lonely, the orphaned, the poor and forgotten of this world know His love and are cared for by His Church.

An unassuming person, Suzy McCall, had never been out of South Carolina before she moved to Honduras. She rebukes the notion that she is anything special, but rather very ordinary. We certainly need more "ordinary" Christians like Suzy! What started as a tiny missionary training school, The LAMB Institute founded by Suzy in 1999, has become a stunning expression of God's love for the people of Honduras, caring for and about many hundreds of children and their families in the inner city.

The telling of this story is thrust out of Suzy's lifetime desire to express the devastating plight of a child born into poverty, the limited choices of women who live in these crippling situations and the opportunity all of us have as Christians to make a difference in their lives. We need to *read* this unbelievable tale. We need to *see* in our mind's eye the characters and *feel* their struggles. Then, we need to *live* knowing this could actually be true.

Susan Clarkson Keller

Board Chair

The LAMB Institute

www.lambinstitute.org

4

Part One:

Ages 0 – 6

"Can a woman forget her nursing child, that she should have no compassion on the child of her womb? Even these may forget, yet I will not forget you." (Isaiah 49: 15)

"Hi my name is Tania, and in the following pages I want to share part of what has happened in my life. I know that in 1985 a girl who was thirteen gave birth to me, and then with a great disgust abandoned me when I was three months old since she was somebody who loved to party and lived a completely disordered life. She enjoyed going out and obviously I was a great obstacle and too much responsibility for her, so she decided not just to sell me but to also abandon me forever. Because of her mistake I began to suffer from since I was very little. I was sold to somebody who later gave me away to a woman (I don't know her name), but from there I arrived in the arms of my grandmother who made a great effort to take care of me with lots of mistakes. She was always talking bad about my mother saying mean things that bothered me a lot because I loved a fantasy, and everybody around me made it so that without even realizing it I began to hate her.   When we were alone my grandmother said to me, 'Tania do you know why nobody loves you? If you don't know I'll tell you: because you are the ugliest child that anybody has ever given birth to, you are like trash but not even the trash truck would pick you up, and that's why not even your own mother wants you. I wanted to cry, but I didn't want her to see me like that so I held in my pain by looking away.   'Tania, do you want to meet your mother?' And I was so happy and said 'yes yes yes please!' and she said that if I washed all the clothes and cleaned the house and kissed her feet, she would take me. 'Yes yes yes!' I said, and a month went by and I said are you going to take me to meet my mother because I was sure she would love me, and I wanted to be in her arms for at least one day, but that day never came. I insisted and the response was I already told you she doesn't want you because you're so ugly she doesn't want a stupid monkey. She hit me in the face very hard and the curious thing was that even though I was always treated badly I never let a tear go down my cheek."

Chapter One

The hospital nursery was quiet except for the murmur of a tiny radio and the frustrated beating of an overhead fan. All thirteen babies kept the silent vigil. Once visiting hours were over and the night staff present, there were no more feedings. Even the most pitiful, insistent crying was ignored. If the cause was hunger, no *pepes* were standing by, and if in pain the little patient would have to wait until morning, as a night requisition to the pharmacy required more energy than anyone was willing to expend, especially since the requisition was usually returned with a dull red *"Not In Supply"* stamped across the order.

"Thirteen," had been the ominous statement of Josefina, a stout day nurse. "One will be dead by morning. Hear me well. Nothing good ever came of *thirteen*."

At least eleven of the babies could look forward to the mothers' charge at dawn, armed with fresh bottles, diapers, and determination. The malnourished, HIV-positive mother of the miniscule bundle in the incubator had not survived delivery, and a healthy girl sleeping nearby had not been wanted. Her teenaged mother had disappeared three days earlier. Someone from Social Services would handle her discharge as soon as a space became available. The name 'Tania Maria Rivera Ramirez' was scrawled on a piece of masking tape at the foot of her bed.

Shadows from the full moon flickered on the faces of the infants as they dreamed. Windows were open to invite wandering breezes into the third floor *sala cuna* of Hospital San Antonio, which cradled its inhabitants with smudged walls, dirty floors, and stained sheets. The hospital had been built in the fifties with *gringo* aid money; the money that had continued to arrive each year for its maintenance and operation was mostly shuttled into private foreign accounts.   Government servants in Honduras were paid handsomely; they made sure of that. They had access to well-equipped private hospitals, and the poor were accustomed to shabbiness, were they not?   Despite the strikes, understaffing, and overcrowding, Hospital San Antonio remained open.   The poor needed a vestige of care, and the government was required to present "ongoing need" for the funding. Tonight peace prevailed in the hospital nursery, so much so that the nurses slept peacefully as Josefina's prophecy was fulfilled, and the incubator became the transparent coffin of its orphaned child. The fan beat aimlessly, and one overfed nurse's aide snored shamelessly as the innocent spirit was gathered to the bosom of the Almighty.   Shortly before dawn the nurses began to shuffle about, and before long the call was made to the morgue between long yawns and small talk.

"*Trece.* Josefina was right," remarked Ana, who was new on the ward and not yet accustomed to the frequent passing of children. "Poor thing, but she didn't have a mother anyway. It's almost too bad the other one didn't go, too. Heaven is a lot better than Social Services.   I wouldn't want my *dog* to end up in one of their homes."

An ancient woman named Isabel who had cleaned the hospital through several coups and natural disasters shook her head and lifted an index finger in the air.

"God knows what's best. If He left that other one behind, it's because He has something for her to do in this cursed world. And it's bad luck to wish death on anyone, even a motherless babe."

Ana paled, crossed herself, and pretended to be occupied with a cart of medications that had just arrived. She didn't know much about God, but everybody in Honduras knew something about death. Hadn't her own aunt just been killed at the gas station where she worked? A rich coffee farmer had come in with his bodyguard to buy a couple of beers when suddenly the glass went flying as a gunman riding shotgun on the back of a motorcycle opened fire with an AK-47. Both men inside the station were armed, but only the coffee heir was able to respond before succumbing to the hail of bullets. Ana's aunt was hit, and had died before the ambulance arrived. Only the bodyguard survived. And just before that a friend of her mother had been run over by a bus. Everyone she knew could tell numerous recent stories about death, and many of them were set right here in the hospital. The day before a little boy had been brought in with a fractured foot. Something went wrong with the anesthesia during surgery, and now the toddler was a paraplegic. Sometimes Ana felt embarrassed to tell people where she worked, but she needed the job and at least in the beginning had thought she could help people. Overwhelmed by the suffering around her, the lack of medicines and compassion, and the inadequacy of her training, she spent most of her shift sleeping alongside her coworkers. She prayed that her comment would not bring her bad luck. She'd had enough of that already.

The change in shift was announced by a shrill bell, and as Josefina received the news about the preemie with a satisfied look, eleven mothers rushed in to feed their little ones, who suddenly began to cry for the milk and love that were lost in the night. A few minutes later a *muchacha* sauntered in. Although she was painted and dressed like a woman, she couldn't have been more than thirteen years old.

"I've come to get my baby," she said brusquely. "Which one is it?"

"*Que verguenza!*" snapped Josefina. "You don't even know which baby is yours? Some mother! I pity the child born to such a one as you."

Seemingly unaffected by the tirade, the girl walked to the only unattended crib and picked up the quiet baby.

"Why doesn't she cry?" she asked flatly.

"Why should she? Has anybody been here to feed and hold her?" sneered Josefina. As she spoke, she swept her arm towards the other mothers, who directed a united disgusted face towards the *joven* who remained undaunted:

"What about you? Isn't that *your* job? Haven't you been taking care of her?"

Josefina marched over to *Cama Nueve* in righteous indignation. "It's *my* job to take care of *your* child?" she squealed. "This is a hospital, not Social Services. That baby is perfectly healthy and taking up a sick baby's bed. But since her *mother* hasn't had time to take her home, she's been waiting around for some social worker to come and check her out. Her *mother* obviously doesn't care two cents for her!"

"Well I'm taking her home right now," retorted the girl angrily. "You won't have to bother with her anymore." Then her bravado disappeared, and she murmured, "I had to get ready."

With those quiet words, she walked quickly from the nursery, her high heels clicking a telegraph message of fear and despair to which no one was willing to respond. Mother and

11

child were quickly forgotten as three newborns were rolled into the *sala cuna*.

The young mother, Santita, joined the line at the hospital check-out. She spoke to no one. When the baby fussed, she rocked her inexpertly. She didn't want to offer her swollen breast in front of so many strangers, although at least four women in her line of vision were doing that very thing. She knew that it was the most common sight in the world, but she was thirteen and proud, and could not accept the fact that she was the mother of a hungry baby. A boy suddenly appeared at her side.

"What are you doing here?" Santita demanded.

"Came to see the baby. *Our* baby. Let me see," the boy urged.

"For what? And what I am going to do with her? My father is mad and my mother just walks around crying. I don't want to be stuck at home changing dirty diapers, and you are a hateful mess! Go away!"

"I brought some money to pay the hospital. You could at least take it." He reached for the thin blanket to take a peek at the restless child. "Why don't you feed her? She's hungry."

"What do *you* know? Why don't *you* feed her? Did you bring milk? Do you think I'm going to open my shirt right here like some shameless old woman? I'm young and pretty, and I won't ruin my looks because of a greedy baby!"

"I'll buy her some milk with this money. You can't let her starve to death."

"Buy it then, and a bottle, too. If we're lucky she'll get sick and die. I hate her and you and the whole thing. I have to go home and face my father, and where will *you* be? Smoking pot and drinking beer with your friends without a care in the world!"

The boy trotted to an exit and as Santita took her turn at the cashier's window, reappeared with the purchases.

"Here," he said, thrusting a small bag at her. "Just remember that this isn't her fault. God wouldn't want us to wish her dead. If I had someplace to take her, I would, but you know how it is at my house. There is nothing there for a baby. At least your family can afford to keep her."

Santita gave him a hard shove and through tears cursed him soundly:

"*Vaya al Diablo,*" she hissed. "I hope you die, too, and quickly."

Hanging his head, the boy responded, "You don't know how many times I have wished that myself." In a sporadic movement of his right hand, he grabbed a corner of the blanket, pulled it aside and jerked his head forward to kiss the baby on the forehead.

"*Dios te cuida, chiquita.* Forgive us."

Santita clutched the baby tighter as the boy known simply as 'Lito' returned to the exit without looking back. She stuffed the receipt into the plastic bag he had given her and looked for a place to sit so that she could make a bottle for the baby who was now loudly lamenting her hunger and loss. Not that anyone cared; a hungry baby in Honduras was as common as a brown mouse in the corn crib. Hospital San Antonio was filled with

13

young and old who had never known a full belly.   Tania drank deeply.   Santita sighed. As a tiny hand wrapped around her finger, she tried to feel nothing for the child in her arms.   Since the moment she had discovered she was pregnant, she had been consumed with thoughts about how to rid herself of this problem.   Her mother's hysteria was nothing compared to her own desperation to be free again.   She could not, *would* not stay home nursing a baby! *Caramba!*   She knew better than to ask God what to do.   For quite some time she had not given Him the time of day, and her feelings about this child would surely not improve her status in His eyes.

As she mulled darkly, a light-skinned woman with a pasted smile sat beside her on the bench.

"Pretty baby."   The words were friendly enough, but the tone was hollow.   Santita felt a grey shadow joining with her own dark thoughts.

"Thank you," she responded without looking up.

"Where's your mother?" the woman asked.   "Has she left you taking care of your baby sister while she pays the bill?"

Santita knew that she should walk away.   Everything about this person spoke of doom and despair.

Instead she looked the *senora* square in the eyes and said, "The baby is mine." She sighed deeply as she spoke the words, conveying her deep unhappiness in having to make that confession.

"So sad," was the response, as pretended compassion crept over the face of the stranger.   "A baby needs love more than anything else. But you are very young. Perhaps God doesn't mean for this baby to be raised by you. You have your whole life ahead of you."

"Yes, exactly!" Santita burst out angrily. "Why should I give up my whole life for this baby? It's not as if her *father* is giving up anything! And my own father is ready to kill me! I wish I could make her disappear!"

These were cruel words, but they flowed from a frightened heart. While Santita lacked a mother's love for the baby, she also did not truly hate her. She hated *herself* for being so "common," and she wanted to study, party, be free. She knew that her parents' anxieties were simply an expression of what she already knew: that she was not ready to be a mother. And while she knew that the baby bore no blame, she felt the immense burden of the life in her arms as a wild desperation.

The nameless woman put her arm on Santita's shoulder.

"Perhaps I can help."

Santita trembled at the woman's touch, but an unholy hope took hold of her heart.

"How?" she asked, hardly breathing.

"I know someone who loves babies," was the reply. "And she would not expect you to give her up for nothing. You'll be able to buy some nice new clothes so that you can go out with your friends and forget this unpleasant experience."

"Who is this woman?" Santita asked. Receiving money for the baby was not something she had considered. But why not? If the *senora* loved babies and wanted to give Santita something in return, why shouldn't she accept?

"Just a friend. You won't need to know her name. My name is Maria, and I'll be happy to make the arrangements. There is one requirement, though. You'll have to nurse the baby for three months before giving her to me. My friend doesn't receive newborn babies; she likes them fat and pretty."

"Three months?" Santita's rising hope of unloading the bundle before leaving the hospital was interrupted by this unexpected prerequisite. But three months wasn't very long, and if she could look forward to money and freedom, all the better. Her mind raced with the new plan. She would tell her parents that a nice lady wanted to adopt the baby, but the legal documents would not be ready for a few months. That would calm their bitterness, and together they could anticipate a return to normal life.

She didn't look at Tania. Instead she stared straight ahead, focused on the "EXIT" sign directly in front of her and said, "Give me your phone number."

The well-prepared buyer pulled a small card from her pocket with handwritten contact information clearly visible.

"I'll be waiting to hear from you," she said, all business now.

Tania coughed nervously. "You will," she said. "You definitely will."

Chapter Two

Santita stirred her coffee, pushing her uncombed hair away from her mouth so she could drink. Why did babies have to be fed during the night, too? She had been tired and grumpy for weeks, and her only bright thought was the date circled on the calendar. She was almost there. She closed her eyes and imagined herself in new clothes at the disco, dancing and laughing with her friends, flirting with the boys. Yes, she would be back in circulation very soon. Her parents had believed the story about the woman who wanted to 'adopt' Tania, and although her mother seemed to feel real affection for the baby, she agreed that it was best for everyone. It was obvious that Santita wasn't ready for motherhood, and no one else in the family wanted to be responsible for her child, but they could not help noticing how beautiful she was. She was dark like Lito, and she had Santita's long lashes and fine, straight hair. Tania was a perfect baby. When friends and relatives saw her, they thought, "What a shame! Such a beautiful child, and born to an immature girl who doesn't love her!" When Santita looked at her, she thought, "I bet that woman doesn't get many babies as fat and pretty as this one!" She consciously rejected the affection that sometimes threatened to ruin her plans, and forced herself to focus on "life after Tania" when unwelcome, maternal feelings presented themselves.

The day before, she had carried the baby with her to the *pulperia*. As she approached the barred window to buy coffee and sweetbread, Lito suddenly appeared from nowhere. No doubt he had been waiting for her to come out of the house, and had followed her.

18

"*Puchika!* You scared me! What are you doing, keeping watch over your precious baby?!" Santita had not been able to forget the boy's words in the hospital, and she knew that he would be unhappy with her plan.

"People are saying that a woman is going to adopt our baby," he replied. "Who is she? Where does she live? How do you know she will take good care of her?"

"What difference does it make?" retorted Santita. "You've already said that you can't help with her. I don't want her. She'll be better off someplace else with somebody else, and there is nothing you can do about it."

"I talked with my grandmother," said Lito. "She says she'll take care of her. She doesn't want her grandchild to be raised by a stranger."

"Your *grandmother*? That old nag who lives down by the river in La Cantera? Never! Everybody will know that her raggedy girl is ours. We'll never get away from the wagging tongues. I don't want to see this baby again once she's gone, or know anything about her."

"How can you hate a *baby*? Your own baby? *Our* baby? You will live to regret what you're doing."

"What I regret is ever getting involved with you! How could I have gotten mixed up with such low-life! My mother has been right about one thing: Your family is garbage." Santita laughed. "In fact," she said, "Doesn't your grandmother make a living by going through the trash of families like mine? Maybe I'll leave her a bag of clothes once I have the new ones the *senora* has promised me."

"What *senora?* The one who's adopting the baby? She's *paying* you, isn't she?" Lito was astonished now and angry. "I knew you were mean, but I never expected you to sell the baby!" To Santita's astonishment, a tear rolled down Lito's cheek.

"What are you crying about? You can't possibly care about this baby! You haven't even had a good look at her, much less have something to cry about."

Obviously angered by this comment, Lito suddenly reached out and pulled the blanket away from Tania's face. He gasped. "She's *beautiful!*" he said softly. He reached out a finger to place in her pudgy hand.

Santita jerked the baby away. "Don't touch her! In three days she's leaving, whether you like it or not!"

"She's our own flesh and blood, Santita. You can't *sell* her. You can't trade a baby for *clothes.* What's wrong with you? Can't you see how beautiful she is? She has your eyes, Santita. Don't do it. Please don't do it. I'll take her to my grandmother. You won't have to take care of her, I promise. I'll never mention her again if that's the way you want it, but please don't sell her to a stranger!" By now Lito was sweating hard, and his face was very close to Santita's. He had never said so many words so strongly in his entire life, and pleading Tania's case was creating emotions he didn't know he had. "She's mine, too, and I won't let this happen! I won't!" He reached for the baby. He would take her and run.

"Noooooooooo!!!!!!!!" screamed Santita, so shrilly that a woman a block away ran to the door to see what was happening. "You will *never* tell me what I can and cannot do!" *Never!*" She held Tania in a death grip and glared at Lito through demonized eyes:

"I will do whatever I want!   Nobody can stop me! Not you, not anybody! You'll see! You'll *all* see!"

By now everyone within hearing had stopped to watch the two in their desperate quarrel.   Santita had become a holocaust of ire and spite.   Righteous lamentation had created a glowing aura in Lito's face.   It was the classic confrontation of the ages, and the world in front of a nondescript *pulperia* in an ordinary neighborhood stood still for an instant awaiting the resolution of this terrible moment.

But poor Lito wasn't strong enough to withstand Santita's fury, and with one last look at Tania, who had now joined the chorus of those who must protest as well as they can the suffering which has been thrust upon them, he fled.

Santita's heart began to race as she re-lived the encounter in her mind.   Lito had *cried*.   How could he care so much about the baby? She was the mother, and she had not shed one tear; in fact, she was looking forward to being herself again.   Was it normal to be so heartless? She had been raised in the church and wasn't completely without conscience. Still, she would never give Tania to Lito's ridiculous grandmother, Dona Marta.   People would know who she was, and she couldn't bear the thought of her own flesh and blood digging through garbage for clothes to wash and sell.   Better to sell her to a rich stranger and imagine the nice life she would have.   Didn't that woman say that the buyer loved babies? So what of her own infrequent nightmares and moments of doubt! She only had to take care of the baby for two more days, and then she would be free to do as she pleased. She would stay inside the house in case Lito attempted to take the

21

baby again.   Soon the deal would be finished and she could go shopping with her well-earned money.

Lito was no saint and he knew it, but he also knew that he could not let this happen. *His* baby, his little girl . . . what was her name?   Tania.   So beautiful, too.   How could he have loved someone who would sell their baby? And how could he get the baby before Santita closed the deal with this *senora*?   He was from a poor family.   Santita's parents had been furious when they discovered the *noviazgo*.   Their daughter was too good for a boy like him.   But Santita was strong-willed, and the more they stomped their feet, the more determined she was to be with Lito. Until the pregnancy.   They had used condoms, but obviously something went wrong, and from the moment that Santita discovered that she was pregnant, everything changed between them.   She was furious. Her first thought was an abortion.   They were free at the Planned Parenthood Center.   But a parent had to sign since she was only thirteen.   She wasn't ready yet to tell her mother and father.   While she debated, the baby grew, and by the time she made up her mind her mother had already figured out what was going on and refused to sign for an abortion.   "We are Catholic," she said.   "We don't believe in abortion."   End of discussion.

Santita prayed for a miscarriage, and asked her friends what she could eat or drink to cause one. Nothing worked. Then she thought of the *curandero*.   Surely his magic could get rid of this nuisance!   But she needed money.   Even the smallest treatment cost something.   She went to Lito first, but he was afraid of the *curandero*.   "Worse and worse," he had said.   "Now you're messing with the devil himself.   What's so bad about a baby? We'll think of something."

It was when Santita was desperately considering her dwindling options that her cousin from Catacamas came for a visit. Although Javier was the son of her mother's sister, he was not a favorite in their home. He was a *roquero*, dressed all in black, thin and bitter.

"I see you're having a baby," he commented as soon as they had a moment together.

"So?" responded Santita. She couldn't imagine why he cared. They hadn't spent time together since they were toddlers. When her uncle abandoned the family, her aunt had taken the two children to San Pedro Sula where she found work in a *maquila*. As a single mom, she was forced to leave them alone much of the time, and Javier started keeping company with a group of *roqueros*. By age fifteen, he was one of the leaders of the gang. He lived with them, had taken a "wife," and was involved in their activities. Not that anybody in her family knew exactly what the activities consisted of, nor did they want to know. To know was to be in danger. They were afraid of Javier and his *roquero* family.

"So I might be able to help you," he said grimly.

"How?" Santita wasn't sure she wanted help from this dark cousin.

"We have ways of ending pregnancies," he said.

"I don't have any money," Santita responded quickly. She couldn't begin to imagine how her cousin would perform an abortion. He hadn't finished fourth grade.

Javier smiled at the mention of money. "A different kind of payment would be fine," he said mysteriously. "Actually, we're not that interested in money."

"What would I have to do?" Santita desperately wanted to be rid of the baby. She could at least investigate this option.

"Meet me at the *cancha* at 11 p.m.," Javier said. "Sneak out. That shouldn't be too hard for *you*. Tomorrow I'm going back to San Pedro, so if you want my help, it will have to happen tonight." With that, he slid across the floor and into the early evening ambiguity of beginning and end.

Although Santita was trembling, she knew where she would be at 11 p.m. She began to plan her escape.

The neighborhood "15 de Junio" was one of the many sprawling *colonias* in Tegucigalpa that had been birthed as squatter settlements, *invasiones.* Santita's parents belonged to the group of two hundred families who had climbed the hillside, staked out lots, and put up makeshift shanties and even tents, prepared to withstand efforts to dislodge them. The hillside was owned by one of Honduras' richest families, so there would be little public sympathy for their case, should they decide to expel the settlers. Weeks went by as representatives of the *invasion* wrangled with the attorneys of the heirs. Each week brought more hope of staying. With hoes and pickaxes the pioneers marked out roads and lots, dreaming of the day when they would also have electricity and water. For now they either walked two kilometers to the river to bring the precious water in buckets to their homes, or they bought water from trucks that would come as far as the entrance to their neighborhood. For cooking they used tiny gas or wood stoves, and candles and flashlights served as lighting. It was imperative to have someone on each property

24

at all times, as the tenuous situation was an invitation to thieves who might at any moment supplant them, or more likely, take the few possessions they had. Night patrols were organized. They were essentially camping out on a hillside together, and the vulnerability was palpable.

Santita had not yet been born when her progenitors had made the decision to move to 15 de Junio. Her mom and dad had dreamed together of owning their own property, however humble it might be. They reckoned the known dangers and risks against the prospect of continuing to rent a *cuartito* in the neighborhood they had grown up in, and decided to take their chances. They were sick of the smelly sewers, incessant gossip and promiscuity of the *cuarteria*. An *invasion* would certainly have its own set of problems, but maybe they would be able to raise their family where there was fresh air and comeraderie. It had been their first experience of working together with friends and strangers, catholics and evangelicals, towards a common goal. At first it had been exhilarating, but as time went by and they toiled under the suffocating sun and endured long, frightful nights, they questioned their decision. Family members encouraged them to move back to "civilization." When they discovered that Santita's mother was pregnant, they returned to their original resolve. Their children would at least have a permanent home they could call their own. And as if a final divine seal had been stamped, word came from the rich family that the settlers would be allowed to stay and purchase their lots. Into this bittersweet state of affairs Santita was born with the assistance of a busy midwife who pronounced her *"sana y salva"* before returning to her own sloppily erected home.

Eventually Santita's family had exchanged their plastic tent for a one-room wooden shelter, and when her father got a job with the government, he built them a cinderblock home with a respectable latrine. Her mother set up a *pulperia,* and before long they were among the more prosperous families in the neighborhood: They consistently had food on the table, shoes on their feet, and a TV brought home proudly on credit. After a younger brother and sister were born, the family was declared complete, and the arduous business of daily bread and education kept everyone occupied almost without incident until the unwanted pregnancy. Santita's father had cursed loudly while her mother wept. The two younger children disappeared into another room and Santita remained darkly quiet, wondering how anybody could be more upset by this news than she was. "I don't want the baby," she had said. Her father stomped out and hadn't spoken a word to her since; her mother, obviously overwrought, simply said, "I'll take you to the clinic for vitamins."

One more pregnant teenager in the 15 de Junio didn't make much of a news splash. The neighbors gossiped for a few days, but most of them had started having children at a young age as well, so they soon moved on to other tales. Lito's mother was too timid to approach Santita's parents to talk about what would happen when the baby was born. His father had abandoned the five children and their mother when Lito, the youngest, was born, and they lived the frightening daily life of survival of the very poor. Lito sometimes went to school, but more often he was needed at home to help sell the tortillas that his mother and older sisters made in the wee hours of the morning. He had been working since he was five years old, and now at age fifteen, weary of the long days and low profits from the tortillas, sold marijuana instead. One day Santita and her friend Marjory had decided to "try *mota*," so they walked to Lito's corner giggling and acting as if they were already dizzy.

"We want some marijuana," Marjory said to Lito.

"How much?   Do you have money?"   Lito had asked, acting every bit the experienced businessman.

"We just want one smoke each," Santita had replied.   She didn't know anything about drug transactions, but didn't want to appear naïve to Lito.   She realized that she had not been paying attention when he had changed from a scrubby little boy into a *guapo* teenager.

"One smoke costs twenty lemps," the young trafficker replied. His heart was beating a heavy rhythm of lust as he talked with Santita, but he wasn't confident enough to let her know.

"*No problema.*"   Marjory reached into her shirt and pulled out some bills.   Lito placed the drug into her hands.

"Have fun," he said without smiling. The girls walked off without so much as a glance backwards.   Who could have known that a few weeks later Santita would be pregnant?

The heat of *verano*, a taste for drugs, and the passion of youth were the real parents of Baby Tania, and now Santita would secretly meet with Javier to see what could be done to rid herself of this frightful burden.

Chapter Three

Nobody played basketball on the 15 de Junio court. It had been constructed with USAID money, and was sorely needed as an alternative to street games, but within weeks of completion had been stripped of everything except the posts. One of the *pandillas* took it over, painted graffiti on the concrete walls, and assaulted anyone who came near without permission. Eventually they became bored with the game and moved on. Now the court remained empty most of the time. Occasionally children could be seen kicking a ball around during the day, but at night no one dared approach that area of the neighborhood. Bodies had been found there, and it was rumored that the *roqueros* held Satanic meetings when there was a full moon. Santita had heard the stories and had stayed away, but Javier's invitation girded her a bit. Her own cousin wouldn't hurt her, she reasoned. He and his friends would protect her. She would go. Whatever fear she felt would be worth ridding herself of the hated fruit in her womb.

Sneaking out, as her cousin had predicted, was no problem. The sun was not yet rising when her mother began preparing breakfast and school snacks in the small kitchen. Her father took his cold bath, grabbed a quick bite, and then started the long trip to work. The two younger siblings had to be at school by seven, and slept soundly until the last possible moment. By nine in the evenings, everyone was in bed, exhausted from the heat and activity of the day. Because Santita wasn't in school, she was more rested. She wasn't expected to do as much since she was pregnant, and she had never been inclined to do much anyway. She watched *novelas* much of the day, fussed at her brother and sister, and tried not to notice how hard her mother worked to keep the family provided with hot meals and clean clothes. Santita's dream was to marry someone who could take her out of this neighborhood, pay a maid to care for the house and their children, and give her a generous shopping allowance – yet another good reason to get rid of the creature who was disturbing her belly and her life. Santita slipped by her parents' room, and once outside the house took out the tiny flashlight she had stashed in her pocket, set her eyes and heart like flint, and started the treacherous walk to the *cancha*.

Loose gravel and potholes aside, the real danger of walking to the *cancha* late at night lay in possible encounters with thieves, drunks and *pandilleros* who would rob her first and then violently take and use her, very likely leaving her naked and dead in a ditch. Santita was well aware of the possibilities, but she had grown up here and knew which corners to avoid, how to keep her head down, and despite her recent weight gain, how to move quickly and quietly. Before long the *cancha* was in sight. Santita clicked off the flashlight, and now walked slower, listening for voices and watching for shadows that would belie the presence of others along the way. She reached her destination without incident and was relieved when Javier immediately stepped into the sliver of moonlight.

Santita, breathless from the exercise and peril, greeted her cousin happily.

"Thank God you're here!"

Javier's smile conveyed something other than happiness.

"Yes. Thank *God*. Come on."

"Where are we going?" Santita suddenly felt a sense of foreboding. Her heartbeat accelerated.

"Not far," replied Javier. "Follow me. And quickly."

His black clothing, dark hair and skin, and quick movement nearly caused him to disappear completely.   Startled, Santita called out, "Javier!"

"Shhhhhh!   Don't be stupid!" he said angrily.   He grabbed her arm brusquely and began to drag her towards the other end of the court.   Santita, truly frightened now, tried to pull free.

"Nobody made you come," growled Javier.   "Now that you're here, you're going to see it through."   The grip on Santita's arm tightened, as he stopped momentarily to fasten his eyes fastened on hers with blazing fury.

"See what through?" pleaded Santita, beginning to panic. Where was he taking her?   She felt certain now that she'd been wrong in assuming that her former playmate would never hurt her.   Every horrible story she'd heard about what *roqueros* reportedly did to their victims began to play through her mind, particularly an ominous comment made by a neighbor: "They *keep* the *head*."   Santita remembered laughing as a chill ran up her spine; she had felt that this neighbor was trying to frighten her, and doubted his words.   Javier's behavior was making the stories more credible by the moment.

"I changed my mind!" she cried. "Let me go!"   She was screaming now. Suddenly more hands were upon her, and a rag was stuffed inside her mouth.

"I thought you said she was coming willingly," an unknown voice whispered accusingly.

30

"What difference does it make now?" Javier rejoined. "Anyway, once we get her inside, she'll see that there is no turning back."

Rough hands picked up Santita, and she fought and kicked until the entire violent mass of captors and captive was swallowed by a ramshackle wooden house with shutters closed against the stifling heat and whirling dust.

Santita didn't realize until she was released from the human tumbleweed that she had closed her eyes tightly against what her heart perceived as deadly peril. She opened them now, and found herself in the company of about a dozen *roqueros*, one of whom was clearly in charge and who stared at her with contempt.

"Javier said that you wanted us to help you. Why are you kicking and screaming like a stuck pig?"

Santita was proud, young, selfish and ignorant. She could be mean-spirited and even cruel at times, and she had never let anyone look down on her. But the oppression in this house was suffocating, and everything in her was shouting, "Run! Hide! Get out of here!" There was a smell of sulphur and something else . . . Santita searched her memory until she found the odor: she had smelled it once when she had left her curling iron in her hair too long and it had begun to burn. She couldn't see a fire anywhere, but obviously something was being concocted on the premises. The house was one large room, it seemed, and it was filled with all sorts of glass jars, clay vases, boxes and old chairs. There was a long table in the center of the room with a knife laid carefully in the center. In one corner of the room Santita saw machetes and guns, and in another bottles of liquor and *guaro*. Someone was smoking weed, and this familiar fragrance mixed with the sulphur and burning hair created a nauseating kind of anesthetic. In an attempt to remain alert, Santita turned her eyes upwards and was met with the incontrovertible evidence of the truth of her neighbor's remark: human skulls hung from the rafters, witnessing to the hopelessness of her situation.

She stopped struggling. Tears began to roll down her face. She felt sure she was living her final moments.

"I . . . I thought Javier wanted to help me," she said pitifully. A couple of dark figures laughed flatly. Santita sought Javier's face, but the thick odor and her racing heart were slowing her movements and blurring her vision. As dizziness overcame the young victim, the black *roqueros* with their grim faces, the skulls hanging informally and ominously from the rafters, the flickering lights of candles and stubs, machetes and other primitive weapons, and dirty colored jars large and small wafted into her fading consciousness.

"Hail Mary, full of grace," she mumbled. "The Lord is with thee. Blessed art thou among women, and blessed is the fruit of thy womb, Jesus."

At the name of Jesus, someone let loose a bloodcurdling scream and the voice of authority shouted, "Shut up!" while slapping Santita hard on the mouth.

"Holy Mary, Mother of God." Santita was weeping now. She didn't know how the words were being formed in her mind, much less by her bleeding lips. "Holy Mary, Mother of God, pray for us sinners, now and at the hour of death . . . O my Jesus, forgive us our sins . . ."

A vile chant began which threatened to silence the prayer. Certainly the combined epithets of the roqueros easily drowned

Santita's mournful petition, but suddenly her head fell backwards and her eyes were met with a blazing light. She thought it was the old bulb she'd seen dangling among the skulls, but realized it was much too bright for that. The light seemed to warm her from the inside out, and as she felt its effect she also sensed that the light itself was pushing the prayer through her lips into the palpable darkness.

A brutal hand grabbed her hair, yanking her head forward, cursing God and calling upon the Father of the Unholy. A united bloodcurdling shriek completed the litany. But the light would not be silenced. Whether it was Santita's voice or not, the words leapt into the room with clarity and strength:

"Save us from the fires of Hell; lead all souls to Heaven, especially those most in need of Thy mercy . . ." Rough hands were upon her, but Santita was beyond conscious response. She could not remember afterwards if she was hauled, thrown, shoved, or carried. The warmth of the light remained with her during those final moments, although it would be many years before she recalled the sensation. When she finally lost consciousness, it was more a sinking into the light than a complete surrender to fear and darkness.

The drizzle of beer on her face and a pointed boot in her rib brought the teenager back from what was surely a foretaste of hell.

"Are you dead or alive?" a drunken slur inquired.

As images of Javier and the haunted house rushed into Santita's mind, an inner jubilant voice cried out, "Alive! Alive! I'm alive!" She opened her eyes and struggled to stand. The man with the pointed boot started to walk away, but Santita grabbed his pant leg.

"Where am I?" she gasped. She struggled to adjust her eyes to the clouded night.

Her savior kept walking, offering mysteriously, "Ask around. You aren't alone."

Santita could make out stones now, markers of past lives. The cemetery! Somehow she had ended up in the cemetery! As she attempted to sit, she realized that she had been placed in a shallow grave. Stiff and pregnant, she awkwardly jerked sideways, using one hand to push upwards and the other to reach for a bit of grass. The dirt was heavy and wet, and it was with great difficulty that she hauled herself upwards. Her hands unconsciously rounded her abdomen, seeking assurance that the baby was still there. Once she reached the grassy plateau, Santita lay back again to catch her breath. That she and her child were still alive was a miracle, and she inwardly breathed a word of thanks to God while panting and weeping. At that moment, the first rays of sun broke through the early morning cloud cover and struck the foolish girl at a point of reason. She would find her way home somehow, she thought. She had never been more aware of the depth of her own ignorance.

Chapter Four

Bruised and sore, and without money for transportation, it took Santita most of the morning to walk from the cemetery back to the 15 de Junio and then climb the long hill to her own home. She was too exhausted and overcome by the events of the night before to worry about her mother's reaction. She knew that she had had a very *very* close brush with death, and all she wanted now was a bath and her bed. Thankfully, the neighborhood children had gone to school and most of the mothers were occupied with household chores. Disheveled, pregnant, bruised and unsteady: all of this and more attracted little more than passing glances and comments in a place like "the 15". People had their own problems to deal with.

The knowledge that her survival of the encounter at the *cancha* was nothing short of a miracle had ended Santita's pressing thoughts about how to kill the baby. She would endure the pregnancy and let it come out, and then she would give it to someone. It would all be over in a few weeks, and then she could get on with her life. Her *life*! She had almost lost it by trusting Javier! And by almost being murdered herself, she had realized that she did not want to be a murderer. Her mother said that abortion was murder, and while the headstrong girl disagreed with her parents on almost every issue, she felt in her heart that her mother was right about this one thing. Before the confrontation with evil at the house of the *roqueros*, the idea of murder had not frightened her: it was her baby to do with as she pleased. She felt differently now – not exactly *religious* – but with a bright fear of coupling herself with people like Javier, who were in open league with the forces of darkness. No, she would no longer entertain the idea of killing the unborn child.   She would face the pain of childbirth stoically, and then she would free herself forever of the burden she carried.

This unspoken commitment carried Santita through the rest of the pregnancy, the horror of the delivery room, and the news that she had birthed a baby girl.   When she was approached in the hospital about giving the baby to a perfect stranger, she chose to see it as the answer to her prayers.   God had heard her promise, and now He was providing a home for the baby.   She had suffered enough because of her relationship with Lito.   She had paid the price, not him, and now a door was opening which would set her free.   She was   determined to walk through it without looking back.

After the fight with Santita at the pulperia, Lito returned to his house ashamed and guilt-stricken.   The brief glance into the baby's lively black eyes had been like a peek into goodness and happiness and beauty, and while he had known little of these things in his life, or perhaps *because* of the lack of contact with the lovely and the true, he felt desperately remorseful about his helplessness against Santita's will.   While he was sure that he could not allow her to trade their baby for money and clothes, he was just as sure that there was nothing he could do about it.   He had been left out of the equation, and everything he'd experienced in his young life had taught him that he was powerless against a higher social class, that unless he was willing to turn to violence, he must accept his inferior position and back away.

Lito's grandmother had always been a source of comfort to him, so he turned his steps towards La Cantera, the section of 'the 15' reserved for the poorest of the poor, addicts and thieves, collectors of trash of every kind, and an incubator for the worst gangs in the city. As Santita had pointed out with derision, Lito's grandmother collected used clothing from garbage bins in other sectors of the city. She washed out the clothes on a large smooth rock behind her shack, hung them to dry, and then sold them to people slightly better off than she was. Ironically, there had been a time when Santita's mother had bought clothes for her children from Dona Marta. It was honest work, Lito thought, much better than his own work as a marijuana dealer. Both his stepmother and grandmother had cursed him when they found out he was selling weed, but years of traipsing dusty streets selling tortillas for just enough money to make more tortillas and a pot of beans for supper had worn down his already weak principles. He would buy some meat for his anemic stepmother and arthritic grandmother. Why shouldn't they eat something besides beans and tortillas day in and out? He had always been easygoing and hardworking, but now a righteous anger was bubbling deep inside him. Although it wasn't satisfied by selling drugs, it could be anesthetized by the comforting presence of money in his pocket – money for food, electricity, water, shoes. He would never be rich, but when he walked home in the evening with a small bag of nourishment for his family, he *felt* rich. He just wished that his mother could prepare the evening meal without that look of resigned sadness that had moved in when she discovered he was a drug dealer.

The path that led to Dona Marta's house was a mixture of slippery, loose and sharp rock, but Lito skipped down it like a young goat. He'd run this path a thousand times and knew every stone. That orange-stained stone had taken a wedge out of a toe once, and that pointed one had caught his *chancleta* and sent him flying downhill headfirst into a broken nose. And over there on the left was the one that had cut open his knee as he ran uphill one day chasing his friend Walter.   And he mustn't forget the ripple of loose rocks at the final turn on which he bruised his tailbone so badly that he couldn't sit down at school for many days, forced to endure the brutal laughter of his classmates.   It had been a long time, though, since he'd fallen on this causeway; he'd mastered the small dangers of sticks and stones.

When he arrived at the mostly cardboard shack that belonged to his grandmother, Lito leaped the small fence and ran around to the back.

"Abuela! Abuela!" he called, although there was no place for her to be except in the one-room building or at the makeshift woodstove just outside the back door.   Most of her customers sought her at home, now that she was beginning to slow down due to rheumatoid arthritis.   In earlier years, she had gone out every day with huge bundles of clothes in a basket on her head, carefully balanced on a small cushion with the fingers of one hand.

"Ropa! Vendo ropa! Buena y barata!" She would pause outside the homes of regular customers and sometimes knock or ring the bell. If stopped on the street, she would look for a patch of shade, carefully lower the bulging sack, and begin to pull out pieces of clothing one by one, each neatly folded and sometimes even pressed with an old iron she heated on her woodstove.   She would cluck over her favorite blouses and skirts, seemingly mourning the moment of parting.   Her love for the clothing was contagious, and the buyer would begin to long for the item as if it were new and hanging on a department store rack.   Business had fallen off drastically now that she walked her route only once or twice each week, and she knew that she would be eating tortillas with salt and very little else if Lito didn't bring food.   She was also

aware that accepting his gifts made her a hypocrite, because she hated how he earned the money, but hunger could be desperately convincing, so she blessed the food and asked God to look after her grandson.

Dona Marta was lying on a mattress on the floor. The bed frame had rotted and been used for kindling long ago. The sacks of clothing piled almost to the ceiling gave the small space a musty smell that put off strangers, but seemed to the aching woman more like the breath of an old friend. These bags had kept her fed and clothed since she was a young woman. She had bought the first *fardo* with a loan from a microfinance program run by a nonprofit in the neighborhood. Every Saturday she proudly presented her payment at the dingy office until she had finally repaid the loan and also saved enough for a bigger, better *fardo*. That was her last loan; she managed her own business after that, always grateful for the help in getting started, but determined not to owe anyone anything again. She despised the heaviness of debt, and although she had never been able to improve her situation much, she felt lucky to have been able to provide for her children, albeit simply. The fact that they had left as soon as an opportunity came along had made her bitter and hard. Hadn't she worn herself out just to keep food on the table? She had done her best to keep them in school, and both had finished sixth grade. Now she didn't even know where one of them lived; they had walked out of La Cantera and never looked back. She hadn't seen Lito's mother in years.

"All I have are these old clothes," she would say, "But they don't need anything except a little space on the floor. I spent years raising ungrateful children. These clothes fed and educated them, and where are they now? Well, let them forget their poor mother! I hope they end up in hell or worse!"

Lito was surprised to find Marta lying down in the middle of the afternoon and said so.

"What are doing in bed, *abuela*? Don't you feel well?

"My bones are aching! I'll get up in a bit, but why don't you sit a minute with me and tell me what's going on in the world. I've hardly been beyond these four walls in days."

Lito sat on the least broken chair, dejected and silent.

"I heard about the baby," his grandmother offered. "Maybe it's for the best."

"You didn't hear that she's *selling* her," Lito mumbled. "Santita can't wait to go out in the new clothes she's getting for our baby."

Dona Marta struggled to sit up. "Where did you hear that?" she insisted. "It's probably just mean, idle gossip."

"No, *abuela*," the boy said. "Santita told me herself." A short smile appeared as he thought of the little face in the blanket. "She's beautiful. The baby, I mean. She's so beautiful. I told Santita not to do it. I tried to get my hands on the baby. But she says I don't have any say in the matter, that she's made up her mind and the baby is leaving tomorrow."

All signs of illness gone, the old woman was on her feet now.

"Did she say who she's selling the baby to?"

"No. People like that don't have names. Anyway, there's no way I could give Santita more than that woman is giving her.

Money is what she wants."   His voice dropped.   "I never thought she'd *sell* our baby.

Dona Marta's eyes had turned into restless fireflies.

"Tomorrow?   The meeting is tomorrow?"

"That's what she said."

"We'll see about that.   We'll just see about *that.*"

Chapter Five

Santita wanted to shout "Hallelujah!" The day had finally arrived. She looked at the little person next to her in bed and said aloud, "*Adios, Chiquita!* Today we are both starting a new life!"

She had talked her mother into buying a new dress for the baby so that the new mother would feel especially fortunate, and perhaps be even more generous in the exchange. Santita decided to wait an hour before calling the number she had carefully guarded these three months. A week before, she had dialed the number just to be sure and heard the same smooth voice on the other end: "Not to worry. Yes, we want the baby. Call me back in a week."

Tania began to fuss for her morning bottle, which her mother prepared with uncommon cheer. She hummed a favorite song and envisioned herself in the latest styles, dancing with her friends without a care in the world. "Tonight I'll be back in circulation," she murmured to herself. "I'm putting this nightmare behind me for *good*."

Just then the phone rang, and without greetings her 'friend' ordered, "We'll meet you at 10:00 by the Francisco Morazan monument in the park. Don't be late. Don't bring anybody except the baby. Don't do anything to attract attention, or the deal is off." Before Santita could say anything in return, the call ended.

In conversations with her mother and others, Santita had presented the adoptive mother as "very nice. She loves babies, but can't have any of her own. She'll spoil Tania rotten!" After this brusque call and its brutal businesslike tone, the girl felt a tiny crumb of conscience surfacing: *What if the woman wasn't good to the baby? What if she was sending her own baby to a life of suffering?*

These thoughts dissolved almost as soon as they appeared. The woman on the phone wasn't going to be taking care of Tania. She was just the go-between. No doubt the real adoptive mother was waiting anxiously right now at her house, eager to hold the baby and show her off. That's why they wanted her to get to the park in the morning! The mother couldn't wait any longer for her little girl.

Santita quickly prepared bath water for Tania and herself. She wouldn't be late. In fact, she would leave as soon as they were ready. This was a meeting she was determined not to miss. As she was buttoning Tania's frilly dress, her mother came in. She had obviously been crying.

"I don't know about this, Santita," she said weakly. "After all, she's our own flesh and blood. I've never thought well of women who give their babies away. We might regret this later on."

"Oh, mother! You've got to be kidding! We've been talking about this for three months. They've already called, and we're practically out the door. And anyway, it isn't your decision. She's *my* baby, and I'm not changing my mind now!" She pushed past her mother and practically ran from the house. *Nobody* would stop her now.

The buses stopped very near their house, and to Santita's relief one was approaching. She tried to appear calm and composed to her neighbors at the bus stop, but her heart was racing. She found it difficult to focus her eyes and thoughts, concentrating on getting a seat and forgetting her mother's grief. Since she was carrying a baby, she climbed on first and sat down quickly. It never occurred to her to take note of the other passengers. If she had, she probably would not have worried herself about the old woman in the back whose face was partially covered by a worn shawl. She had only seen Dona Marta on a few occasions, and had never been interested in remembering her face.

It was a busy Saturday morning, and the park was filled with buyers and sellers. Santita had been here many times. She jumped off the bus confidently, the baby snuggled against her bosom where she had stuffed a bit of money and her cell phone. She knew it wasn't yet ten o'clock, so she decided to enjoy being out in public and walk around a bit. Her circular ramble inevitably brought her to the entrance to the cathedral where a variety of beggars kept vigil.

"Are you baptizing your baby today?" croaked an unfamiliar voice.

Santita turned quickly to see who had spoken. To her surprise, one of the old women on the stairs of the cathedral had reached up to touch Tania's trailing blanket, and to her shock, she realized the woman was blind.

"All life is from God and must be dedicated to Him," the woman continued. "Go inside and join the baptismal line."

"H-how did you know I had a baby?" Santita stammered. She was trembling now, and wanted the woman to let go of the blanket.

46

"All life is from God, and those who know God testify to its sanctity." These remarkable words from the mouth of the ugly, scarred *anciana* jolted the young girl in a place so deep within her that she had just now become aware of its existence.

"I'm not her mother," Santita heard herself saying. "I mean, she isn't my baby."

"All life is from God, and He entrusts it to whom He will," the horrible voice proclaimed. "The baby came from Him and belongs to Him. You are the one who will decide her fate."

Santita was ready to run now. How did this old crone know that the baby was a girl? Why was she saying these strange things? What did it mean? She jerked the blanket out of the wrinkled clamp and ran towards the statue of Francisco Morazan, praying that the delay at God's house had not cost her the freedom she idolized

Suddenly, the voice on the phone registered in her head: "Don't attract attention or the deal is off." Santita braked, caught her breath, and made certain no one was staring at her and Tania before continuing. She felt that the old woman was still hanging onto the pink blanket, staring at her through cataracts, bringing accusation after accusation. The weight slowed her feet, and a coldness crept into her bones. An insistent voice was replaying the words in her mind: "All life is from God . . . All life is from God . . . All life is from God," and worst of all, "*You* are the one who will decide her fate!"

"*No!*" Santita shouted. "It isn't my fault!"

"Of course it isn't, my dear." And an arm circled her shoulder, leading her away from the park and her dilemma. Leading her towards the consequences of her hasty decision.

The arm directed the dazed girl towards the taxi stand, and she was aggressively helped inside, still shaking from the encounter with the blind beggar. Tania was extracted from her embrace, pronounced "very nice," and after an undetermined amount of time, the taxi stopped and Santita was helped out. She was left on the corner of a busy street in Comayaguela holding a large plastic bag with one hand and her pounding heart with the other.

Dona Marta had had little trouble following the young mother on this final journey with the unwanted baby. She witnessed the encounter at the cathedral with a hard heart. She couldn't hear what the beggarwoman was saying to Santita, and she didn't care. For most of her sixty-two years she had stayed as far away from church and God as possible. When Santita broke free and ran, Dona Marta struggled to keep up with her, but soon realized that she was headed towards the statue, so she joined a small group of tourists walking quickly in that direction. She knew that whoever was waiting for the girl would be on the look-out for intruders. She must be very careful. Sure enough, as Santita reached the horse and rider, a woman came alongside her pretending to offer a loving embrace.

"*Vibora!*" Dona Marta exclaimed under her breath. She had seen this woman before, and was absolutely certain now that Tania was not being carried to a loving home. When the woman and her prey got into the taxi, Marta quickly slipped into the one next in line and asked the driver to follow closely.

"Don't let them out of your sight," she said. "It's a matter of life and death."

The first taxi weaved through the busy downtown traffic, crossed the bridge into Comayaguela, and not surprisingly to

Dona Marta, moved towards one of the large redlight districts. At a busy corner, a door opened on the taxi and Santita was basically shoved onto the sidewalk.   The teenager looked traumatized, as if she could barely stand, but Marta's mission was not with Santita.

"Keep going!" she urged. "We can't let them get away!"

Both taxis struggled up a steep, narrow alley and then onto a wider, unpaved street.   The taxi carrying Tania stopped, and the woman and baby emerged purposefully.   When it became evident that they had been followed, the go-between was furious.   Quickly paying the driver, she confronted Dona Marta.

"What are *you* doing here?" she shouted. Her anger attracted the attention of some of the people hanging around nearby.   Free entertainment was always welcome in this part of town.

"That's my great-grandbaby," Marta responded fearlessly. "I've come to take her home with me where she belongs."

"You have no right to this baby!" was the bitter reprisal. "Her mother doesn't want her, and we made a deal. You can't do anything now."

"I can report you to the police," said Marta.   "I know your name and where you live.   I saw you bring the baby up to this godforsaken area of town with my own eyes, and I saw you give Santita a bag of goods in return for the baby. Now give her to me or you will find yourself in jail!"

The woman laughed, but a crowd was gathering and she had clearly lost some of her bravado.   She directed her gaze upwards into the window of one of the nearby buildings and appeared to be receiving instructions.   Suddenly she spat on the sidewalk and shoved Tania at the indignant grandmother.

"A curse on this baby and a curse on *you*!   The devil take you both!"

Dona Marta crossed herself and held the baby tightly, as if to shield her from the *maldiccion*.   She had asked the taxi driver to wait, so without a word she slid quickly back inside and shut the door.

"Leave this place quickly!" she ordered.   "*Rapido!*" The driver didn't need more encouragement.   He rarely accepted fares to this section of town.   With a squeal and a spray of dust, they began the journey back to la Cantera.   Tania cried for a bottle and Marta sighed with relief.   She had faced the enemy and won.   She pulled back the blanket to get her first look at her great-granddaughter.

As the taxi pulled away from the street known as "*Callejon Perdido,*" the woman in the window accepted her defeat – for now.   She could wait.   Her eyes swept the cribs and playpens in the large room set aside for the babies.   Each one represented a large profit, and she was a greedy soul. She had a buyer for Tania and didn't want to report the loss, but she could call her "birthing house" in La Esperanza to see if any of the women kept there for that purpose had produced a girl recently.   If so, she could satisfy her current buyer.   She might get another chance to go after Tania.   A deal was a deal.

Santita was in a stupor as she stood on the street corner clutching the bag.   She was in the wrong part of town to be all alone with a load of merchandise, but her mind was a blur of accusing voices, demonic faces and a stone horse which reared up to trample her.   Just as she was opening her mouth to scream, a city bus stopped less than two feet in front of her and she heard the familiar call, "*Los Proceres! San Jose de la Vega! 15 de Junio!*" Like a zombie she climbed in and found a seat somewhere in the middle.   The familiarity of the bus, its movements and smells, began to clear her mind and when the busboy came by for her fare, she was ready.   As she reached for the small purse hidden in her bosom, she held the big soft bag against her stomach.   It was a poor substitute for the warm, wriggling bundle she had just exchanged.   As she placed the lempiras into the hand of the chanting boy, something broke within her and she wretched violently into the aisle of the old bus in a futile attempt to purge herself of the self-inflicted nightmare.   The passengers seated nearby cried out with dismay as they tried to avoid the putrid spray: "*Caramba! Ay, Dios! Grosero!* "   No one cared that the girl was in a death throe of pain, and not a hand reached out to comfort her.   Each one sought to avoid contamination while uttering anathemas and broadcasting disgust. Some opted to exit at the next stop and take another bus, and the rest attempted to look the other way.   Santita was utterly alone in her confusion and misery, and as the vehicle screeched to a stop near her home she stumbled out through the vomit and shame, leaving the hated prize on the seat, a coarse monument to selfishness and stupidity.

A few blocks away an old woman carefully and skillfully maneuevered the long stairs into the part of La Cantera known as "*El Hoyo,*" possessively holding baby Tania and greeting neighbors along the way.

"What do you have there, Marta?" called out her friend Anita, who was washing dishes in the *pila*.

Marta paused to pull the blanket back from Tania's face. Anita gasped.

"Where in the world did you get *that*?" she asked.

"She's my own flesh and blood," Marta responded. "Lito's baby with that girl in 'the 15.' She's mine now, all mine."

"She's a beauty," commented Anita, but she looked doubtful. "Don't you think you're a little old to be raising a baby?"

Marta nodded. "Yes," she said. "Much too old. But she was falling into the wrong hands, and I'm not so old yet that I can look the other way while my own flesh and blood is sent to the devil."

Anita's eyes filled with tears. "So many of our children have become nothing more than merchandise," she said softly. "I've wondered about what we can do. It seems like a giant monster that grows stronger and fatter every year on our little ones. You did well, my friend, and if you need a hand, you can call on me."

"*Gracias*," the now exhausted savior returned with a smile. "I need to make a bottle. Little Tania is hungry." She struggled for a moment with the rusty lock on her gate before disappearing into the nondescript shack which would now hold two inhabitants instead of one.

Chapter Six

Santita stumbled into her house, walked straight through to the back and began to wretch so violently that her mother came running from the kitchen where she was cleaning up the lunch dishes. Even when nothing more came up, Santita wretched and then wretched some more. Then she began to weep huge heaving sobs until she sank to her knees and hands in her own vomit.

"What happened?" her mother was pleading. "Tell me what happened!"

What *had* happened? Santita was no longer certain of anything. Did she really hear that old woman say that *she* would decide Tania's fate, that God had entrusted *her* with that huge responsibility? Did she really give her own baby to a complete stranger? How did she get home? She couldn't remember. She had a big bag. Where was it?

"Santita! Santita!" She heard a familiar voice saying her name. How could she answer? How could she ever speak again after what she had just done?

Her mother was trying to help her up now. "Come on. Let's go to the *pila* and get you cleaned up, and then you can tell me everything that happened. Santita let her lead her to the small cistern, and then clean her up as if she were a little girl again.

"Do you want something to drink? Some water? I made lunch. Are you hungry?"

Santita moaned. Tears ran down her face.

"Oh dear," was all the distraught woman could think to say. She couldn't imagine what had happened to cause such a transformation in her daughter. She had seemed so happy in the morning, so glad to be taking the baby to her adoptive family. What had gone wrong?

"Did the family like Tania?" she ventured.

At the mention of the baby, Santita doubled over again as if she had been punched soundly in the abdomen. She groaned with pain and would have fallen again if her mother had not caught her arm. She led her to her room and helped her lie on her bed. Walking quickly to the bathroom, she moistened a washcloth which she placed tenderly on Santita's forehead. Probably she was reacting to the loss of the baby, she thought. Although she had anticipated feeling liberated once Tania was gone, she was now responding as any mother would at the loss of a child.

"Don't cry, dear," she soothed. "They'll take good care of Tania. She's such a beautiful little girl, and they waited three long months to get her. They are probably showing her off to everybody they know."

Santita closed her eyes and trembled from head to foot. Her mother pulled a sheet over her, thinking she might be feverish and chilled. As the sheet reached her middle, Santita grabbed it and pulled it over her head like a shroud. Taking this to mean that she wanted to be alone, the mother stood slowly and walked quietly from the room, closing the door on the inert, pallid body of her oldest daughter.

For the rest of the day the concerned mother went quietly about her daily responsibilities, and when Santita did not emerge from her room all afternoon, she decided to let her rest. It might take her awhile to recover from the loss of the baby. In a way she was relieved by Santita's reaction, as she had sometimes felt embarrassed by her daughter's enthusiasm about giving little Tania away. Santita was young, but many girls in their neighborhood had babies that age, and they loved to dress them up and show them off. Women were nurturers by nature, she thought, and she had found her own daughter's aloofness toward the baby strange and uncomfortable.

Toward early evening with the smell of beans and tortillas wafting through the house, Santita's father returned from work. Although he had been sweating in the hot sun all day on a road job, he had also been thinking about the baby and imagining the delight of the adoptive family upon receiving such a lovely little girl. He knew that his wife wanted to keep her first grandchild, but since Santita was intent upon giving her up, he had supported the decision, especially since the father was Lito. He did not want a boy like that hanging around their house. Drug dealers kept very dangerous company, and if washing their hands of Lito meant washing their hands of the child as well, then so be it. With all of these thoughts crowding his mind, he entered the kitchen, dropped his lunch pail on the table and wasted no time in asking the questions he'd asked himself silently all day:

"How did the adoptive family like the baby? How did it go? Where's Santita? Is she happy?"

"She's in her room," his wife replied without changing position. Making tortillas required a certain rhythm of rolling, patting, pressing and then laying them carefully on the skillet.

While four cooked, she was rolling and pressing the next four, intermittently reaching across to the pan to touch her fingers to the hot ones, causing them to puff and breathe.

"She came home very upset, sick to her stomach. She went straight to bed."

Surprised by this information, the father walked to his daughter's bedroom and rapped on the door.

"Santita. Santita, I'm coming in." He opened the door. With the window closed and no lamps lit, the room was musty, warm and shadowy. He stepped inside.

"Santita. How are you feeling? Your mother says you have an upset stomach."

The body on the bed remained still.

"Can I get you something? Do you want to tell us what happened today? We want to know how things went with the baby."

The word 'baby' seemed to trigger a response. A moan rose upward from the bedcovers, and Santita moved slightly.

"How about some water? Your mother is making supper. Do you think you can eat something?"

The lack of response from Santita troubled him. She had seemed so eager and optimistic in the morning. He had not come into his daughter's room much since she had gotten older. As with most teenagers, she would come home and shut her door to the family. He felt like an intruder, but his anxiety pressed him forward. He took a few steps toward the bed.

"Tell me about the people who have Tania," he said. "What are they like? I bet they weren't expecting such a beautiful baby." He tried to lighten the air in the room with a little cheerfulness. "I guess you're glad you won't have to get up in the middle of the night anymore to give her a *pepe*." He had arrived at the bed now and switched on the lamp next to Santita's head. Her eyes were open, but she didn't turn towards her father. As he leaned in to look at her, the smell of urine struck him full in the face. Surely she hadn't wet the bed, he thought, and yet he knew she had. Her eyes were red from crying, and her hair was tangled with sweat. She was still wearing the dress she'd put on in the morning for her big day with Tania, and it reeked of stale vomit. The ominous odors and unseeing eyes joltingly answered the insistent questions in his heart, and instead of touching Santita tenderly to comfort her, he backed quickly out of the room and walked quickly towards the kitchen.

His wife had finished her work at the stove and was putting the food on the table.

"Call the children," she suggested as he entered. "Supper's ready."

"Santita looks terrible," he responded. "She didn't say anything. I think she wet the bed, and she is still wearing the clothes with the vomit."

They looked at one another for a moment. Neither knew what to do. They had no experience in giving away children, and since Santita had been making her own decisions for quite some time now, they felt insecure in their concern.

"I'll go check on her," the mother finally said. "You get the other children and have your supper before it gets cold."

She pulled off her apron and walked away decisively. Her husband obediently and with a sense of relief went to look for the two younger siblings.

From the kitchen to Santita's room was only a matter of a few steps, so the good woman hardly had time to think about what she should do. As she opened the door to the bedroom and recognized the smells described by her husband, motherly instincts took over, and she knew that the first order of business was restoring cleanliness and order.

"OK, *mi amor*," she announced. "We're going to change these sheets, and we're going to change *you*! A nice bath and some clean bedsheets will make you feel like a new person."

A new person. A new person. The phrase bounced around in Santita's confused consciousness. If only it were that simple.

Chapter Seven

At four years of age, Tania had rarely been out of La Cantera.   Her Mami Marta often left for several hours at a time to search for clothes and sell them, but she didn't take Tania with her.   She usually left her with their neighbor, Anita, or sometimes with Lito.   Anita was brusque, but she made sure the thin toddler got enough to eat, and she always bathed her and checked her hair for *piojos*.   Her own mother had hated lice, so she had inherited a certain neurosis that stemmed from never being able to get rid of them once they found their way into her little house.

"I don't want you infesting my *casita*!" she would bark. "I have enough trouble without having to boil my sheets and clothes and everything else!   I don't know what Marta was thinking when she brought you home!   Little children always end up with lice!" And then after her tirade, she would go to her tiny gas burner and fry Tania an egg which was inevitably followed by some small treat, a packet of cookies or a box of juice, obviously purchased in anticipation of her visit.   Aside from these infrequent gifts, Tania lived almost exclusively on beans, rice and tortillas.   Lito stopped by every now and then with an offering for the household: powdered milk, bananas, rice, a *bonbon*.

"She's too skinny!" he always remonstrated.   "Can't you fatten her up?"

"With what?" the old woman retorted.   "A banana and three days' worth of powdered milk when you feel like bringing something?   I barely keep us alive on what the clothes bring in. You disappear for days on end and then come around fussing at me about your child? I know where your money goes – for drugs!

How could you be so stupid? You'll never have any kind of life now, much less be able to do something for this creature."

"Come here," he'd call to Tania, ignoring his abuela's complaints. "Come here and eat this bonbon." He'd peel the paper off and stick it into Tania's smile. She liked his visits because of the sweets and his tenderness towards her. Her Mami Marta was grumpy whether Lito came by or not; it was her nature and the little girl often went weeks without so much as a hug or a pat on the head. Her irritable caretaker loved to remind her how she had saved her "from certain death or worse," always adding that her mother hated her and practically threw her in the garbage, and that she had an irresponsible father who had asked her to take Tania in and then left her with all the responsibility. Once when Tania asked to be taken to meet her mother, Marta gave her all sorts of tasks to do to 'win' this special treat. But in the end, as the child protested that she had done everything that had been asked, Marta had flown into a rage:

"Do you know why your own mother didn't want you? Because she said you are the ugliest child that has ever been born! She said she'd rather die than have a stupid monkey like you!" This tirade was followed by a hard slap in the face. Pale and shaken, but without a tear in her eye, Tania had retreated to her bed.

Tania was too young to fit these pieces together. Still, she understood that Mami Marta was the only person in the world who was willing to take care of her. She both feared and clung to the old woman, but naturally there was an emptiness where a mother's love should have been. This emptiness was becoming the defining characteristic of her life.

61

On this particular day, Mami Marta was leaving Tania en La Cantera so that she could try to sell some freshly scrubbed clothes. At certain times of the year there was so little water, it was even more difficult to get "garbage clothes" clean enough to sell. The dry season lasted a full six months, and by the end of the fourth month the city was rationing water in every neighborhood, but especially in poor areas like La Cantera where people paid a pittance for utilities. Most of the houses didn't have plumbing, so twice each week the inhabitants would carry barrels and buckets up to the last house at the top of the descending stairs into the Hole. This house had been designated as the water source for La Cantera, and several spigots had been installed for that purpose. During the precious hours of water flow, hoses were connected to the spigots, and someone from each household stood in line to fill whatever receptacles were available to them. Fights often broke out over places in line and sizes of the receptacles. Old women and single moms with babies were sent to the front, and since Marta qualified on both counts, she rudely insisted on being first every time. Now that Tania was older, however, she was encountering resistance from the neighbors. The day before had been a water day, and Marta had marched up the hill with her old plastic barrel.

"Let me by!" she had barked when she reached the long line. "Move! I'm going to the front of the line!"

"*Perra!*" breathed a younger woman who had run out of patience for Dona Marta. Get in line like the rest of us, *viejita*! You aren't crippled yet, and that baby you're raising is old enough now to help carry your barrel."

Marta was incensed by the epithet, and wasn't about to go back to standing patiently in line. She had done that for more than forty years. Somebody else could do it now. She spat at the feet of the angry woman and gave her a smile which said something like, "Go to hell. I'd like to see you make me get in line." The other woman suddenly laughed and said, "Let her go first! She's so bitter that all of her children ran off as soon as they could, and all she has left is a narco grandson and his bastard daughter! Go ahead, old woman – you *deserve* it!" A strong show of approval increased Marta's rage, but she had gotten her way and she marched to the front as if she had just been crowned monarch. Tania trailed along behind her, oblivious to the usual remarks: "Pity. She's a beautiful child. Too bad she fell to that old witch." "She'll have her going through the garbage with her as soon as she's a little bigger." "That old bag will never put the poor thing in school." "They say her mother's rich. No wonder she dumped that sorry grandson and the girl. What if she turns out stupid like him?" In La Cantera there were no secrets and no mercy.

Lito was coming to watch Tania today while Dona Marta went to work. Tania hoped he'd take her to the river to play. Even at this extremely brittle time of year, the river offered a trickle of water, fetid and filled with trash. The children waded in nonetheless, eager for a respite from their tiny homes and the terrible heat. A few trucks continued to mine the river's sand, the business that had given the neighborhood its name. Filling one dumptruck with sand took most of a hot day, and the shovelers were given fifty lempiras for the grueling work. Dona Marta had been a shoveler when she was young, but the backbreaking nature of the job, hard pregnancies and poor nutrition had closed that door of employment, so she had turned to finding and selling cast-off clothes. It was not uncommon for a sand laborer to pass

63

out from dehydration before the day was over, and of course this meant forfeiture of salary for that day.   Since the houses in La Cantera had no access to potable water, and the river water was contaminated, the only safe drinking water was either bought in bags and bottles, or boiled at home.   The cost was prohibitive for many people, so they   suffered the effects of constant dehydration or ran the risk of drinking water from the river.   The children's tummies were filled with parasites from the unclean water and food they ingested every day of their lives.   It was not uncommon for young children to die from diarrhea; by the time they were taken to the crowded and understaffed public hospital, it was too late to rehydrate them.   Their defenses had been broken by poor nutrition since before birth, and they had no strength to recover.   Education wasn't the problem: international organizations and mission agencies sent people around regularly to preach on the importance of boiling water before drinking it, but they didn't leave behind the wood that was necessary to boil the water, and they couldn't know the desperate logic of choosing an egg over a piece of *lena*.   Among the poor, table grace is like throwing a 'hail Mary' up to heaven: "Lord, may this food fall well in our stomachs."   Oh, for the grace to live another day, perhaps without a headache, stomach ache or the wracking ache of malnourished bones!

Lito arrived with a small bag of goodies for Tania.   Now that he was a drug user himself, he profited little from his work as a trafficker, so his gifts were small and few.   Still, Tania was delighted and grabbed the minuscule bag of colored marshmallow bits as if it were circus candy.

"Let's go to the river!" she begged, grabbing her father's hand.

"Ay, *que huco!*" he said, turning up his nose. "How can you stand the smell down there?"

"I want to put my feet in the water," she pleaded. *"Please, please, papi!"*

The sun (and everything else) gave Lito a headache these days, but lying down on the shabby bed in Marta and Tania's house was out of the question, so he let the little girl lead him down down down the steep stairs until the steps were rocks, and then they were carefully avoiding garbage and human waste in an attempt to reach the trickle that was the river. Several children were already there, all of them known by Tania, and she called out to them.

"We're coming, too! Look, my papi is here! He brought me candy!"

Most of Tania's playmates were also being raised by single mothers and grandmothers, so Tania's situation was hardly out of the ordinary. It was unusual, though, to see a child with her father playing in the river, and several of the children ran nearer to get a closer look at Lito.

"Are you Tania's papi?" one little boy asked dubiously.

"Of course he is!" Tania remarked indignantly. "I just said he was, didn't I?"

"Don't you think we look alike?" Lito teased.

A slightly older girl made a big show of studying Lito's face carefully and then studying Tania's.

"Maybe a little," she concluded. "Anyway, I don't even know who my papi is, so who cares. We'll let you play with us if you don't do anything weird."

"What do you mean by that?" Lito asked. He was feeling nauseated from the smell of the contaminated river, and wasn't really in the mood to play.

"Some of the men come down here looking for us, but they want us to take off our clothes and let them touch us," the girl said. "Or they want us to touch *them*. We try to run and hide when we see them coming. I hope those aren't the kinds of games you like to play."

"No," he said. "I don't really feel like playing anything, but what you're talking about isn't a game, and you shouldn't let those men touch you. Ugh, the smell down here makes me sick to my stomach."

"It goes away after awhile," a very dark-skinned boy assured him. "You have to put your feet in, and then you can't smell it anymore." His earnest instruction made Lito smile.

"Lucky me," he said half-heartedly. "I'm wearing flip-flops, so I can definitely put my feet in the water."

"Vamos!" Tania cried, pulling him towards what was basically an open sewer this time of year. She seemed to be seeing a huge waterpark instead, and her excitement was contagious.

"OK, OK," her father answered. "Let's go have some fun in the river." He let the little girl lead him to her favorite spot and tried not to think about what he was stepping into, but just as

Tania started splashing around, the earnest, dark-haired boy squatted and emptied both barrels. He smiled at Lito.

"Whew, now I feel better! We don't have a bathroom at my house, and my mom won't let me go on the steps. She says I'm too old for that. So I have to come all the way down here. Anyway she slipped on some once and almost broke her neck. Don't worry – it'll run down the other way, not by you." He yanked his shorts high and ran off. Lito raised his eyebrows, but the rest of the children ignored the entire performance. They were looking for interesting rocks, splashing one another, and sharing news.

"My mom got a job," offered a small child with wild, uncombed hair. "She's working in somebody's house."

"Who's taking care of you and your brother?" Tania asked.

"Nobody. Mami leaves the food cooked, and I watch my brother. She wanted to leave us locked inside the house all day, but it's so hot! We're not supposed to be in the river."

"What time does she come home?"

"In the nighttime. My little brother is sometimes asleep when she gets home. She's always dead tired and just eats and goes to bed. Then she has to leave really early to get breakfast ready for the family she works for."

"I bet she makes a lot of money," Tania offered hopefully. "My Mami Marta doesn't make very much selling clothes."

"Mami says she has to spend a lot of her pay for the bus back and forth so she can be with us at night. Her *patrones* won't give her bus money. They said she should find somebody to take care of us so she can live with them. They even said why doesn't she put us in an orphanage! I think they must be mean people."

By now several hours had passed since a hit, and Lito's thoughts turned towards drugs. He had to figure out where to get some money. He was dead broke, and nobody would give him anything on credit anymore.

"Come on, kid," he said to Tania. "We have to go back to the house."

"No, papi!" Tania protested. "It's too hot up there and there's nothing to do! Please let's stay longer!"

"I said let's go," her father replied. He held out a trembling hand and pulled her brusquely towards the stairs. "It stinks like hell down here, and I need something."

Tania knew better than to argue with him. Besides being bigger and stronger, he was erratic, and she had seen that even her grandmother couldn't reason with him at times. They walked quickly up the long stone stairway, finally reaching Dona Marta's house, and Lito opened the small lock with difficulty, as his hands were shaking noticeably.

"What's wrong?" Tania asked. "Why are you shaking? Are you sick?"

"Shut up!" was the reply. "Wait outside!"

The little girl didn't know why she wasn't allowed into her own home, but her father seemed angry about something, so she sat quietly on the step until he came out. He was carrying an old feed bag which was weighted down with something.

"Come on!" he barked. "Hurry up!"

Tania wanted to asked what was in the bag, but she was truly frightened by now.

"Can I stay with Anita?" she inquired.

"Shut up, I said!"

"Please, Papi.   I don't want to go with you. Anita will watch me."

Lito was sweating heavily now, and letting go of Tania's hand, gave her a shove.   Tania understood this to be his permission to stay behind, and she ran quickly to Anita's door.

"Tia Anita!   Tia Anita!   *Abre la puerta*!"   Lito didn't wait to see if the door opened, but walked quickly up the remainder of the stairs and disappeared from sight.   In a few moments, the door cracked and the familiar face peered out.

"What are you doing?   I thought your father was coming today."

"He had to go," was all the girl thought to say.   "I didn't want to go with him."

There was no need to say more.   Anita was aware of Lito's activities, and although she had not planned to keep Tania, she would not have wanted her to accompany her young father on his drug errands.

"Well, come in then and quickly! Every thief in La Cantera will be in here while we're standing in the doorway!"   She put a hand behind the child's head and pulled her inside, noticing that she wore the smell of the river.   She would lay aside her sewing and give the girl a bath and something to eat.   Although she considered her own life to be one of hardship, she couldn't help wondering again how such a pretty child could have had so much bad luck already. God had a lot of explaining to do.

Chapter Eight

Marta had visited almost all of her regular clients, but had only sold a few pieces of clothing. Hot, hungry and thirsty, she began to curse her parents, children, and grandchildren.

"*Maldito todos!*" she declared out loud. "I could lie down right here and die, and not a soul would care! A curse on the day I was born! A curse on God Himself!" She lowered the basket of clothes perched on her head and sat on a stone.

"*Buenos dias.*" It was a cheerful voice, heavily accented. Marta looked up into the midday glare of the sun.

"*Buenas tardes,*" she responded glumly. Three *gringas* and a nicely-dressed young Honduran girl stood smiling before her. One of the women said something in English.

"She wants to invite you to a special event," the teenager explained. "It's for women in this neighborhood who would like to learn how to sew with a machine. Afterwards we'll learn how to sell what we've made so that the women can start their own businesses."

"I already have a business," Marta remarked drily. "It's in this basket."

"Can we take a look?" the girl asked.

"Sure. Maybe you'd like to buy something," was the sarcastic answer, certain that they would take one look at the pathetic contents of the basket and keep walking.

An animated conversation was going on among the ladies as they passed around the basket rags. Marta had no idea what they were saying, but nobody had ever responded to her clothing with such enthusiasm.

"Excuse me." The translator addressed the tired woman with respect and kindness. "These women want to know if they can buy everything in your basket. They would like for you to be free tomorrow to come to the sewing class."

Everything in the basket! Marta could hardly believe what she was hearing. Instead of going home to an empty cupboard and a hungry little girl, she would be able to cook something special. She wasn't eager to go to a sewing class, but she could decide about that later. She wasn't one to miss an opportunity for making money. She began to calculate how much the clothes were worth – plus a bit extra since the buyers were *gringas*.

"*Doscientas lempiras*," she said, waiting for the usual negotiations.

"Are you sure that's all?" the girl asked instead. "We want to be sure that you are able to come tomorrow." The three northamerican women smiled at Marta as if she were a very special friend indeed. All of this kindness was making her uncomfortable.

"Two hundred is plenty," she grumbled. She wished she'd asked for more, but she was wilting under these sunny faces and wanted to get home.

One of the women took two bills and an invitation out of her bag, placed them in Marta's hand, and said something in English.

"She says God bless you, and she hopes to see you tomorrow." At this, the old woman's mouth curled. *Christians!* She should have known! And she had just cursed God! Well, what did she care? What had God ever done for her? She would be happy to spend this Christian money on food for herself and Tania.

"*Gracias,*" she managed with a tight smile. "See you tomorrow."

The ladies moved on with their purchase, and Marta carried the empty basket under her arm. Neither party looked back. If they had, Marta would have seen them giving away the clothes as they walked, and the missionaries would have seen a brief, heated confrontation between the street vender and a young man who was in a very big hurry.

"Where are you going? Where's Tania? What have you done with her, you dog?" Marta was genuinely concerned about her granddaughter's whereabouts. She could see that Lito was out of his mind.

"Get out of my way, old woman!"

"Old woman?! You don't even recognize your own grandmother?!" Marta had the young man by the middle of his shirt, which had been her favorite place to grab him as a little boy when he was misbehaving. This time, though, he didn't back down.

"Get your hands off me, you old witch!" he drooled. "If you don't get out of my way, I'll wring your ugly neck and throw you in the river." He was stumbling, and his eyes were showing more white than brown. Marta realized that he truly didn't know or care who she was.   She released her grip on his shirt and stepped aside.

"*Basura,*" she said under her breath and spat on the ground. "You're nothing but a piece of trash now, and I wash my hands of you."   But Lito was already well on his way to wherever he could get a hit, and he didn't hear these parting words – not that he would have cared.   His mind was on only one thing now, and he would do whatever was necessary to get it.

Dona Marta's mind was on only one thing, too: Tania. Where had he left her? She was traveling light, now that she had no clothes to carry, and she walked quickly towards La Cantera. There had been many days when she'd wished she hadn't taken on the responsibility of a baby. She was a hard woman who had never learned how to give or receive affection, but Tania was hers.   One day she would need somebody to take care of her, and her own children were no longer around. Now Lito was a lost cause, too.   Tania was her best hope at this point. She started down the winding stairs in La Cantera, and stopped in front of Anita's house. She was about to knock when she heard Tania's voice.   Breathing a sigh of relief, she decided to run to the pulperia before picking her up. They would celebrate her big sale with *arroz con pollo.* The child loved chicken. They would eat well, sleep early, and she'd decide about the Christians *manana.*

Drugs were strange masters. Lito didn't recognize his own grandmother, but he knew exactly how to get to the door that would calm his desperation.   He knocked loudly, scraping his knuckles, and was answered by a cool voice.

"What do you want?"

"Open up! Hurry!"

"Go away! We don't have anything for you!"

Lito kicked the door, cursing.

"No *dinero*, no nothing!" the voice responded. "Get out of here or you know what we'll do!"

Lito's subconscious told him that he would never get anything empty-handed. He was too far in debt for that. He had to find some money quickly to stop the pounding in his head and the uncontrollable shaking and sweating.

He walked quickly down the street into the whirling dust of the dry season, his desperation a bottled cyclone, threatening to explode. The few people in his path hurried cautiously by. Lito turned the corner and collided with a young couple holding hands and laughing. The husband, dressed in office clothes, had been at home having lunch with his wife, and she was walking him part way back to his job.

"*Estupidos! Torpes!*" Lito spat out as he attempted to regain his balance. The man had his arm protectively in front of his wife, who was now trembling. Drug addicts were all too common in their neighborhood, and they could be dangerous.

"*Perdon*," responded the youthful husband. "Sorry we ran into you. *Ven, mi amor*." He pulled the hand of his frightened wife, and they tried to slip by Lito, but the way was blocked.

"Wait! Give me your cell phone! Hurry up!" White foam was spraying from Lito's mouth, and his eyes were on fire. Husband and wife looked at one another, sharing a silent conversation. Both had grown up in this neighborhood, and had known hunger and fear from an early age. Fernando, the office worker, was completing a practicum with one of the non-profits. He had felt lucky to find something so near his house, and felt good to be participating in a small way with work that was helping people get ahead. He was an accountant with the microfinance section of the organization, having struggled for years to get through school. He and his wife, Yesenia, led a small prayer group in their home. They had only been married for a year, and had just left their newborn baby girl with Yesenia's mother.

"*Si!*" answered Fernando nervously, as he reached inside his jacket for the phone, letting go of his wife's hand, eager to have this encounter behind them. But the hand reaching inside the jacket triggered an association in Lito's muddled mind: that's where pistols were hidden. This guy was going to shoot him! Suddenly a knife appeared in Lito's left hand. Yesenia saw the metal and screamed, but it was too late for Fernando to react. The knife had been used before, and despite his crazed state, Lito pushed through shirt and flesh into the heart of Fernando. He fell to the ground with only moments to live. Yesenia was hysterical now, and would have jumped between Lito and her dying husband except that a strong arm grabbed her from behind and pulled her out of harm's way. Lito quickly searched the body, taking wallet and phone, and ran off towards the only relief he knew. As the drug addict disappeared, people who had been watching from behind closed windows and doors came out to help pick up the pieces of what they had felt helpless to prevent.

A few hours later, the news of the young accountant's death reached La Cantera. The killer, as usual, was not identified. Dona Marta had no way of knowing that it was her grandson. She, Anita and Tania sat down to the unexpected gift of chicken and rice while talking and laughing about the silly gringas who had paid two hundred lempiras for a basketful of rags. Dona Marta was fairly certain that a Christian sewing class was the last place in the world she wanted to be.

Not far away, a small *velorio* was being held. Fernando, whose life a few hours earlier had held such promise, was laid out in a simple pine coffin, his graduation photo placed at the head of the box. Those who loved him wept. Others shook their heads, lamenting the violence which terrorized their daily lives. They had no place to go and no way to defend themselves. Fernando and Yesenia's brothers and sisters from church were preparing a small service. The pastor opened his worn Bible and searched for a word of hope.

Chapter Nine

Santita tightened her pony tail and picked up her pace. She couldn't be late for class again. Her parents would be humiliated if she were sent home after all they did to get her here. Anyway, she liked Siguatepeque; it was cleaner and quieter than Tegucigalpa. The people were open and friendly, and she enjoyed her classmates in the nursing school. She had always found it difficult to stay on a schedule, but the nursing instructors were very strict, and this time she was sure she would not be forgiven. It wasn't a long walk from the dormitory to the academic building, and as she hurried down the walk Santita was relieved to see the other students outside, talking. Apparently she wasn't late after all.

"Santita! Over here!" An outgoing, chunky girl who looked a bit like a toasted marshmallow in her white nurse's uniform was waving to her cheerfully.

"*Hola* Juanita!" Santita responded. "I'm so glad I'm not late!"

"You *are* late," her friend responded, laughing, "But the teachers are in a meeting, so they haven't rung the bell yet. You got lucky."

"For once!" exclaimed Santita. "Getting into this school was the first great thing that ever happened to me, and I'm terrified of getting expelled. My parents would kill me!"

"What are you talking about?" Juanita smiled. "We just got here! The teachers are always strict at the beginning. After all the paperwork and interviews to get in here, they aren't going to kick you out for getting to class late!"

At that moment, the bell rang loudly, conversations ended, and the white wave of students flowed into the building.

The day always began with a devotional, and Santita invariably found it difficult to concentrate on what was being read or shared. Her mind wandered off to Tegucigalpa, to her house with her parents and siblings, and sometimes to that crucible of time four years earlier which had nearly derailed her. The day she gave her baby away, she went to bed and didn't get up for two weeks. Her mother patiently fed and bathed her, talking nonstop about everyday things. Her dad looked in on her each evening when he came home from work, acting as if all was well. One day her head cleared enough to get into the shower, and the water seemed to work some kind of miracle, restoring her will to live and giving her just enough energy for that day. And then the next. Something was broken deep down inside, but it was this hidden grief that gave her the courage and maturity she needed to move on. She got back into school, finished ninth grade without incident, never speaking again of Tania or the nightmares, which visited less frequently but never disappeared entirely. During her final year of *ciclo comun* when she and her classmates were considering which route they would take for their final three years of high school, her mother came home with a flyer about the nursing program in Siguatepeque. It was a long shot, but she decided to apply. Her mother encouraged her to pray the rosary more frequently, and went herself to extra masses so that God would hear their prayers. When they received the news that Santita had been accepted, the entire family rejoiced. Her mother cried, and her dad looked bigger somehow. They all went to church together that night and offered special gifts of thanksgiving. It seemed like a miracle, and maybe it was. Santita felt as if God was saying that He had forgiven her for the drugs, pregnancy, and even her decision to sell her baby. At the church that night with her family she bathed in God's forgiveness, truly thankful for this unbelievable opportunity to learn skills which would enable her to help others, and make a living at the same time.

Of course Santita knew that Tania was with Dona Marta. She had no idea how she got there as she had never spoken to Lito again after that day at the pulperia, and she also didn't know if Tania was better off in La Cantera than she would have been with that other woman. She tried not to think about her baby's feelings, health, or future. She didn't know how to deal with the lurking shadow of depression which threatened to pull her down again into inertia, so she just kept going with her daily activities. Her mother seemed to know when she was sliding, and she would think of an outing they could take together, or give her a little pep talk. One time she sent her on a youth retreat with their church. Santita couldn't remember much about that weekend; it seemed impossible for her to focus on the presentations or get involved in discussions. She couldn't take her eyes off the huge *Cristo crucificado* on the wall behind the altar. 'Had He really done that for *her*?' was the question that had played over and over in her mind. Despite what was being said to the contrary, she was quite sure He hadn't. He had seen what she'd done, and although He could forgive many things, He had to have a special place in His heart for little babies, and a particular dislike for mothers who didn't love their own. She remembered weeping at the final mass, someone praying for her, hands on her head. When she got home all she could say was that it had been fine. Her mother seemed disappointed.

The nursing school in Siguatepeque was run by *evangelicos*, which was one reason Santita had been sure she wouldn't be accepted, but she wasn't the only Catholic student, and there was a Mormon, too, and a Jehovah's Witness.   There was even an Episcopalian, whatever *that* was! Juanita went to some kind of church that forbade women to wear pants, but apparently her friend wasn't very devout because she just laughed and said, "It's dumb, I know, and this Saturday I'm going to the *mercado* to buy some jeans.   My mom will never know, and don't you dare tell her!"   The daily school devotional was basically a reading from the Bible and then somebody talked about it afterwards.   Although the students themselves sometimes got into doctrinal discussions, the school administrators, pastors and teachers avoided the points which divided them and focused on the historical Christian message of redemption in Jesus Christ.   Santita had never been to any kind of church except Catholic, and she thought she would hear and see things which would offend her religion, but so far she had only experienced a few moments of surprise.   Her mother had packed her rosary, which she had rarely used at home, and she left it tucked inside her suitcase.   When the students were invited into the chapel the first time, she was startled to enter a large room that looked like an auditorium: no cross, altar, statues, or candles.   In large letters behind the podium was written, *"The beginning of wisdom is the fear of God." (Proverbs 1: 7)*. Santita had grown up in the church but knew very little about the Bible. When she saw the verse, that secret pain inside gave a little cry. Because of her experience with Lito and Tania, she more than feared God; she was terrified of Him. She didn't see how that terror could lead to wisdom, but the Bible was true, wasn't it? She realized that when it came to God she had more questions than answers.   Maybe she would learn more than nursing at this school.

"Santita!   Wake up!   We're going to class now!"   Her friend Juanita was shaking her soundly.   "What's wrong – didn't you get any sleep last night?   Are you homesick or something?"

"Sorry," was the mumbled response.   How could always-smiling-Juanita possibly understand?   She felt an urge to genuflect before leaving her desk, and then found the thought amusing.   "Let's go, Juanita," she announced.   She had better keep marching, or she might just be tempted to hide herself away in a convent, walking barefoot in the pine straw and passing long hours staring at Madonna and child.

True to her word, Juanita came banging on Santita's door early Saturday morning, clamoring to go to the market.

"I can't go by myself!" she insisted.   "What if there are *ladrones* like in Tegucigalpa and they try to steal my money.   You have to be my lookout!"   And then peals of laughter: "Some lookout! You can't even stay awake half the time!   Oh, come on – God, send your angels!"   And more peals of laughter.

The Siguatepeque market wasn't as big as the markets in the capital city, but Santita and Juanita felt right at home as they squeezed between stalls, avoided shouting vendors, and kept their eyes open for pickpockets.   Santita could hardly believe that Juanita had never in her life worn a pair of jeans, and was delighted to be able to help her friend with something that was easy and familiar, but that seemed as mysterious to Juanita as Proverbs was to her.

"I want a blue pair and a black pair," Juanita said decisively.   "I've been planning this day for *years*."

"What size do you wear?" Santita asked, approaching a stall with an experienced eye for quality.

"How should I know?" was the reply. "My mom made my skirts and didn't let me wear anything else."

"I can't believe that!" was Santita's incredulous response. "How could you live for seventeen years without pants?!" And she had thought that her own parents were strict! She couldn't wait to thank her mother for not making her wear homemade skirts her entire life.

Juanita was searching the stacks of jeans, pulling out one and then another that obviously would not fit her short, ample body. Santita knew that it was time to roll up her sleeves and take charge. She spoke to the stall owner.

"We need jeans for my friend. She doesn't know what size she wears. Could you find a few for her to try on?" Although Santita had always avoided trying on clothes in the market, she knew there was no way around it today. The saleswoman, eager for a sale, loaded them down with six pairs of jeans and pointed toward a ragged curtain behind the stall. Juanita was undeterred; she looked as if she were leading a military charge with all odds in her favor.

"Oh, Santita! Come on! Come on! I can't *wait* to see what pants feel like!" She slipped behind the curtain, sort of, and Santita tried to keep her covered while she yanked off the hated skirt and started pulling on pants. There was a good bit of grunting and bumping into the curtain and Santita before the shout of victory finally came.

"They fit! They fit! This must be my size! Glory hallelujah God is good all the time!" Juanita burst from behind the curtain dancing joyfully. The pants were too long, but she had tucked her blouse into a snug fit at the waist.

Santita, hysterical herself, held up her phone to take a picture.

"Noooooooooo! No photos!! What if my mother sees!" Juanita shrieked. The girls fell against a table, attracting the attention of other shoppers and a serious gaze from the stall owner.

"Come on, Juanita," said Santita, pulling on her *amiga*. "Get your shoes and let's pay and get out of here." They bought two pairs of the forbidden jeans and two equally sinful knit shirts, satisfying the vendor, and filling Juanita with unspeakable joy. Pushing their way through the corridors, they found the street again and arm in arm headed in the general direction of the nursing school.

"We're not going back already, are we?" protested Juanita.

"Haven't you transgressed enough for one day?" giggled Santita.

"We have to at least get a *baleada* or an *enchilada*. I never go to the market without eating something." Juanita was looking in all directions as the shopping now moved into her area of expertise. "Come on, there's a good place." She steered Santita toward a tiny *comedor* with a short line of customers and two wooden tables. Holding tightly to their bags, purses and one another, they moved towards the enticing smell of beans and tortillas.

"Te invito," said the happy sinner, smiling at Santita. "I want to celebrate, and I especially want to thank you for helping me find my first jeans." Turning to the cook, she placed their order: "Two baleadas with eggs and plenty of cream," she said. "And two Cokes." Santita knew that Juanita's family did not have a lot of money, and that her friend had probably just spent her entire first month's allowance, but she didn't want to spoil the spirit of the moment.

"Thank you," she said graciously. "I'm honored to be with you on such an important day. If we don't do anything worse this year than buy jeans and drink Cokes for breakfast, I think we'll be just fine." She thought to herself that she had not felt this good in about four long years.

Chapter Ten

The day after killing Fernando, Lito woke up under a bridge. He wasn't alone. A couple of people were heating beans over small fires. Others still slept. A baby whimpered in the arms of a thin girl who absent-mindedly opened her shirt to put the baby to her tiny breast. The sun was already hot and schoolchildren scuffled by, kicking up the endless dust, fighting and playing, oblivious to the little world under the bridge. Theirs, too, was a life of survival, and they had some idea of the fine line between their tenuous existence and that of the bridge people.

Lito didn't sit up right away. While he remained stretched out on the ground his head throbbed painfully, but he knew from experience that the simple act of raising himself to a sitting position would probably provoke retching and dizziness. He was simultaneously hungry and nauseated; his filth had penetrated his soul, and he knew without remembering the details that he had taken another innocent life. He felt for his knife with its sticky indictment. Who had it been this time? And for what – already the trembling had begun again, the insistent clamoring for more drugs. How had he come to this? He wasn't such a bad person, was he? He had simply wanted to put food on the table, wear shoes instead of *chancletas*, buy a drink for his girlfriend. Was that so terrible? But of course that was back when he was the master of the drugs. Now that they were in charge, he was a thief and murderer, sleeping on the ground and cleaning his knife in the river.

"Hey there. Can I help you get up?" Lito felt a hand on his arm and jerked away. He wanted to jump up with knife in hand, but struggled just to open his eyes.

"Go away!" he growled. "I don't have anything."

"I don't want anything," the voice replied. "I'd like to help you if you'll let me."

"I need money," Lito slurred. "Gimme some money for food."

"I can take you to a place where you can fill your belly."

Lito pried one eye open and tried to focus on the face of the stranger. He saw a smile, a scar, an earring and a knit cap. The man was on one knee. He took out a rag, sprayed it with a water bottle, and gently washed Lito's face. Now both eyes were open, and Lito struggled to push himself away from this strange kindness.

"What are you doing!" he remonstrated. "Don't touch me!"

"OK, OK," the stranger responded. "Do you want some breakfast? I know where there's hot food, bath water and clean clothes."

"Do I know you?" Lito asked, more awake now.

"You are my brother," was the unexpected response. "We share the same father: God in heaven. He wants you to come home."

Lito's mind was muddled, but he knew this man was not his brother – and what was he saying about God? Just yesterday he had killed somebody, and he didn't even remember who! God loved good people, not scum like him. He vaguely remembered that someone had just called him *basura*. Was God collecting garbage today? A bitter smile appeared at the thought.

"Ah, so you think that's funny!" The scar danced as the stranger laughed. "Come on," he urged. "The tortillas will get cold, and nobody likes cold tortillas!" A muscular arm circled Lito and raised him to his feet. With his head swimming and throbbing, the young assassin allowed himself to be led like a child down the street. What difference did it make? He had no money and no place to lay his head. He was soon to learn of a certain Nazarene with a similar story of poverty and homelessness. His "brother," Amos, could hardly wait to talk to this lost lamb about the unconditional love of his Shepherd. But first they would share a meal and wash off the stench of the street. Amos, too, had woken up under bridges and knew firsthand of the tyranny of drugs. He was still amazed that his former hunger to steal and kill had been converted into a drive to go out and bring in those who were 'beyond hope.' He talked softly to Lito as they walked towards a shabby place called the "Lighthouse," never taking his hand from his shoulder, silently asking God to welcome home yet another prodigal son.

The Lighthouse looked just like any other house in the neighborhood from the outside. There was no sign over the door and no other indication whatsoever that some eighty people were living here, making what would be for some of them a final attempt to get off the street. The door was locked, but when Amos rang the bell a young woman appeared almost immediately.

"Amos! You're just in time for breakfast! Who's your friend?"

"He isn't my friend. He's my brother – although I haven't learned his name yet. We'll get some coffee into him and see if that clears his head a little. What's for breakfast?"

"Oatmeal, of course.   When have we ever had anything else for breakfast?"

Amos and Lito slipped in, the cheerful girl locked behind them, and all three climbed the narrow stairwell into the smell of sweat, oatmeal and strong Honduran coffee.   Apparently everybody knew Amos, and as they called his name, grabbed his hand and slapped him on the back, he answered with his trademark greeting: "Hey, Carlos, Cristo te ama!" "Hey, Pancha, Cristo te ama!" "Hey, Felipe, Cristo te ama!" Music was blaring, so people shouted to make themselves heard.   All of this incredibly chaotic noise only made Lito's head hurt more.   He put his hands over his ears and fell into a ragged chair as far away from the speakers as he could get.   Why couldn't everybody just be *quiet*?"

"Hey man," called Amos. "Come get some oatmeal."

Lito's stomach was growling, but not for oatmeal.   The thought of putting something soft and milky into his mouth made him nauseous.   He lowered his head to his knees and ignored Amos' invitation.   Undeterred, the unlikely saint approached Lito with a bowl of breakfast, went down on one knee again and held a spoonful of oatmeal to the killer's mouth.   The hot smell provoked an immediate, violent reaction and an explosive load of vomit hit Amos' face like a thrown pie.

"Aarrrhhhhh!!!" responded a toothless, scruffy old man nearby. "*Dios mio!* Somebody get a rag!"

The odor of the vomit was like the stench of the river in La Cantera, and people moved away quickly.   Except Amos who began to laugh.   He didn't even try to wipe the vomit from his hair and face.   His laughter was so deep and genuine that others in the room began to laugh, too.   Pretty soon everyone except Lito was laughing.   The girl who had opened the door came running with a towel.

"What's so funny?" she asked, and of course she began to laugh, too. It was impossible not to join the chorus.

"This awful puke," Amos blurted out, still laughing.   "It reminds me of what I've left behind.   I'm so happy not to be puking anymore like this poor brother. I could have been dead a thousand times, and I'm so happy I'm not."   He lay back on the floor and spread out his arms.   The vomit lay on him like a ragged ski mask.   He stopped laughing, but his smile was bigger than the combined laughter of everyone in the room.   All eyes were on Amos now, and not a few were filled with tears.

"I'm so happy," he whispered. "Thank you, Father."

Chapter Eleven

Tania was with Anita who was making a small pot of *arroz con leche*. Marta was spending another day with the Christians. "Why not?" she had snorted. "They give us lunch." Promising Anita that she would bring her something from the workshop, she shuffled off, looking small and vulnerable without her giant clothes basket. Once inside Anita's gate, Tania had immediately requested her favorite dish.

"I don't have any raisins," her friend had protested.

"*No importa*," Tania pleaded. "You make the best *arroz con leche* of anybody!"

"*Vaya*," responded the plump woman, smiling. "You don't have to lie. I'll make it." Tania clapped happily and asked to turn on the radio.

"Let's listen to *ranchera*," she said. As a familiar band crooned, Tania held a carrot to her mouth and sang into the "microphone," doing twirls around the tiny outdoor kitchen.

"Be careful!" Anita warned as Tania nearly careened into the pot of rice.

"When is it going to be done? I'm hungry!" The thin child put both arms around Anita's hips and gave her a pitiful, pleading look.

"I can't make the rice cook any faster. Why don't you watch cartoons for a few minutes?" Tania jammed the carrot into Anita's apron pocket and ran to the television.

"Did you know I'll be old enough to go to kindergarten next year?" she yelled as she flipped the channels on the old set. "Mami Marta is going to make me a uniform. She's learning how to sew with the Christians. She says maybe she won't have to sell old clothes anymore. Maybe she's going to make uniforms and sell them with the other women at the workshop."

Anita appeared in the doorway smiling cynically. "So your Mami Marta is going into partnership with the Christians, is she?"

"She says they don't make her pray out loud or anything and they give them lunch and let them take home the stuff they make. And if they learn how to sew right they can be part of a group that's going to make uniforms for school and sell them. Mami Marta says sewing is better than walking all day in the sun and dust. She says maybe she can teach me one day, but I want to go to kindergarten first so I can learn how to read. I'm going to read the newspaper to Mami Marta and maybe get a job in the mall or teach school myself. I'm almost five and you can start kindergarten when you're five you know." With this final comment Tania found the channel she wanted and plopped on the sofa. Anita shook her head and returned to the *arroz con leche.* That Marta! What a hypocrite! She just hoped those Christians knew what they were getting into. She scooped out a small bowl of rice for her little charge and set it aside to cool for a few minutes. Although she liked to act as if it were an imposition to keep Tania so much, she enjoyed the company. She missed having someone to cook for and the little girl was appreciative of every bite. She had to admit that she sometimes felt jealous of Marta, and that she also didn't consider her worthy of Tania's affections. Oh, well. Today Tania was with her. Hurrah for the Christians! They would keep Marta busy while she and Tania kept one another company. She filled another small bowl and carried the steaming rice and milk into the house. Cartoons, "a poor man's breakfast," and the chatter of an innocent child: Anita decided to sit down and enjoy the moment, leaving the wash and the housecleaning for later.

"Mmmmm!" remarked Tania enthusiastically. "See! I was right! You *do* make the best *arroz con leche*!"

"Everybody in Honduras knows how to make it," was Anita's grumpy response, but she enjoyed the compliment. "One day I'll teach you how to make it, too, and then you won't have to beg me for it every time you visit."

"Mami Marta says I'm too little to cook. She says I'll burn the house down. One day when she went to the pulperia she was gone a long time and I got hungry so I tried to cook an egg. But when I cracked it the insides went all over and the shells, too. Hardly anything was in the pan. I was afraid of what Mami Marta would say so I cleaned it up and threw it away. Other girls my age cook, though. Mercedes makes food for her brother and her, and she's my same age."

"Your Mami Marta is right. It's dangerous for little girls to cook."

"Mercedes' mom works a lot. She leaves food for Mercedes and Gabrielito most of the time, but sometimes she's too tired to cook. Mercedes knows how to cook eggs, and she can heat up beans and rice. Her mom used to leave money for tortillas, but when the tortilla lady found out that Mercedes and Gabrielito are alone all day every day, she called somebody and they came to Mercedes' house and asked her a bunch of questions. They said that they couldn't be by themselves and that they would have to go to social services. They left a note for Mercedes' mom."

"What did Mercedes' mom do about the note?" Anita asked. She, too, had been a single mom. Hard decisions had to be made every day. Worry was a constant state of mind. No money, no support. She felt sorry for Mercedes' mother, Claudia, who worked very hard and loved her children but had no family nearby to help.

"She cried," Tania replied softly. "And she stopped leaving money for tortillas and told Mercedes and Gabrielito not to go outside anymore and not to answer the door if somebody knocked."

"How do you know all of this?" Anita inquired.

"Mercedes told me at the river. They can't stand being inside the house all day. They go out the back, crawl through the boards and play in the river. They make sure they're back home when their mother gets there."

Anita sighed. It all sounded so familiar. What child wouldn't risk punishment and the dangers of the river in order to avoid being taken away by strangers? The Social Services people would never go down to the river. She was relieved that Marta left Tania with her. She had little to offer the child, but she was sure that Claudia would consider herself rich if she had one adult in her life who could care for her children while she worked. More often than not the people who offered to watch these children ended up exploiting them. She had heard of a woman in another neighborhood who was caring for three girls Tania's age in her home while their mothers worked, but in addition to making them clean for her, she offered them to men in exchange for food or small sums of money.   When it all came to light, the woman was sent to jail for a few weeks.   Nobody bothered to look for the men who had raped the girls.   Who cared about three poor children in a city filled with violence and corruption? Who had cared about *her*?

"Tia Anita! Tia Anita! What's wrong?" Tania was shaking her arm and looking into her distracted eyes.

"Nothing, child," she murmured.   "Let's turn off this TV and take the corn to the *molinero*.   You can help me make some tortillas for lunch."   Tania jumped up happily, silenced the television, and grabbed Anita's hand.   Together they found the container of soaking corn by the *pila* where Anita stopped to wash her hands and take off her apron.   The grinder was only a few blocks away, but the tired woman welcomed the short walk with her little friend.   Perhaps the change of scenery would chase the dark memories from her mind.   The opportunity to provide for Tania what had not been provided for her encouraged her heart, but the shadows in her mind always seemed to be nearby, ready to intrude on her brief moments of happiness.

"Tia Anita! Watch me!"   Tania was hopping on one foot from step to step.   "Can you see me?" she called.   "Watch!" While Anita trudged up the troublesome cement stairway, Tania skipped and laughed and chattered, obviously delighted with the day and her companion.

"Can you do it, Tia Anita?"   The challenge was issued from Tania's position, which was ten or twelve steps higher than hers.

"No, I can't," the woman puffed. "Nor do I want to try."

"It's easy!" Tania laughed. "Come on – you just lift up one foot like this, and then you jump very hard on the other one. If you want, I'll hold your hand."

"How about if I hold *your* hand?" a familiar voice rejoined. Suddenly Lito was beside Tania, reaching for the hand extended towards Anita.

"Papi," she said uneasily. "What are you doing here?"

"Coming to get you," he replied a little too quickly. "I'm taking you on an outing. Give me your hand."

The appearance of Lito had quickened Anita's step, and as the unexpected visitor reached out for Tania's hand, he found it already enveloped in the older woman's protective grasp.

"Marta didn't say anything about you coming by," she challenged.

"I don't need her permission. Tania is my daughter. I can take her anytime I want to." The slurred words and redness of the eyes belied Lito's precarious condition and heightened Anita's motherly protection.

"I'm going with Tia Anita," Tania offered, moving slowly behind Anita in a defensive position.

"You're going with *me!*" Lito's voice was raised in anger, and he lifted a hand as if he would strike the girl.

Anita planted herself squarely between the two. The encounter had occurred opportunely directly in front of the pulperia of Anita's friend Jasmin, who was watching with concern from behind the window.

"Tania, go inside the pulperia," Anita said loudly so that Jasmin could unlock the door for the little girl, who instantly obeyed and in the blink of an eye was safely enclosed.

"Come back here!" growled Lito. "Come out, you little monkey! I don't have time for stupid games!" Anita and Jasmin's eyes met; Lito would have to get past both of them if he insisted on taking Tania. Once again Anita placed her short solid body between the father and daughter. She folded her arms and glared.

"You aren't taking that child anywhere! Now go away before you get into trouble! And may the good Lord cover us with His wings!"

At the invocation of God, Lito shuddered. He felt hunted. In his confused state he looked around to see if that man named Amos was nearby. His mind blurred into a simple prayer: "Father, take my little brother into Your loving arms. Rescue him like you did me." Didn't Amos already rescue him? Maybe he should start running. Sweat was pouring down his face and into his eyes.

Anita took advantage of Lito's hesitation and ran inside Jasmin's pulperia. Jasmin dropped the heavy wooden window cover, locked the door, and all three scooted into her living quarters behind the store. Tania, trembling, crawled into Anita's lap.

Lito lingered between reality and hallucination. He couldn't remember where he was or why he was there. Both hands went to his throbbing head. He tried to focus on something, anything. Drugs. Yes. That's what he needed. Then what was he doing here in La Cantera in front of a closed pulperia? Was he going to buy something? He reached into his pockets and found no money. He cursed. As he turned to go up the steps, he tripped on a rock and fell hard on one knee. More cursing. Eventually he climbed to the top and reached the line of people waiting for water.

"Gimme some water!" he slurred. The women and children in line moved away from him.

"I said gimme some water!" The man running the pump picked up a wooden bucket and slammed Lito on the left side of his head, cutting his ear, and knocking him to the ground.

"Get out of here, you bum!" A group of older boys began to kick the dazed addict. Women and girls threw stones. "Go away! You stink!" Somehow Lito crawled off on all fours like a dog, followed by the cruel children taunting and hurting him. When he reached the road, he pulled himself into a patch of shade and lay down defeated. He didn't move for a very long time.

At the pulperia the women waited a few minutes and then carefully cracked the shutter of the store window.

"Is he gone?" Tania whispered.

"Yes, child," said Anita. "Thank you, Jasmin. You saved us."

"Glad to help," replied Jasmin. "I wasn't making any money today anyway. At least this pulperia was good for something!" The small group laughed halfheartedly. It had been a close call. Neither woman needed imagination to guess why Lito was intent upon taking Tania. It was common practice in their neighborhood to trade sex for drugs, and many men preferred children.

"I don't ever want to see him again!" Tania suddenly announced. "I don't care if he is my father! I hate him!" Bursting into tears, she shoved her face into Anita's skirt.

"Hush, child," Anita responded, gently stroking the little girl's smooth hair. "He's gone now and he isn't going to hurt you. We've seen to that!"

"Let's have a Pepsi." Jasmin declared. "Pepsi always calms my nerves." Without waiting for an answer she took a large Pepsi out of the cooler, opened it and served three glasses. The freezing liquid bit into their frazzled emotions, clearing their heads and drying Tania's tears.

It would be three years before Tania saw her father again.

Part Two:

Ages 7 - 8

"The sacrifices of God are a broken spirit; a broken and contrite heart, O God, you will not despise." (Psalm 51: 17)

"When I was seven years old I liked school and my doll and my friend Anita. I still dreamed about my mother, but she didn't love me because she didn't come for me. My grandmother told me to forget about her because she never wanted me, and I knew that was true because I prayed and prayed to God to make her come but she never came, and my father abused me with his mouth and his hands.   He came to my house and carried me to his house and abused me. I loved him but I was afraid of him. I didn't understand things and that what he was doing to me was bad. I was innocent. I always went to school. I liked to study and made good grades. I only made bad grades in mathematics, and I felt proud because I made good grades, but afterwards I didn't want to go to school because everybody talked about their mom and dad and that bothered me.   It made me jealous to see my classmates with their moms and dads, and their parents were proud to see their

children. When there were programs and family events, I felt very bad because I didn't have a mom or dad. I felt that I was the poorest of all and that I didn't have anything. My classmates made fun of me because sometimes my clothes didn't fit. My father had problems. He came to my grandmother's house when I was seven years old to take me with him. He abused me, but I did it because I was little. I think my grandmother knew, but since he was like her son she didn't do anything. Nobody did anything.

Chapter Twelve

Graduation day!   Santita and Juana and their classmates could hardly believe the three years of study were finished and that they would soon be working real jobs full-time, receiving a salary, beginning their adult lives.   Santita's family had come to Siguatepeque for the ceremony and celebration, and everything seemed perfect.   Santita wasn't an honor graduate, but she had done well, earning the respect and friendship of her teachers and classmates.   She had also learned a great deal about God and the Bible and while she didn't consider herself an *evangelica*, she knew that some of her beliefs now were different from those of her family.   The students had participated in a weekend retreat each year, and these outings always left Santita thoughtful and changed.   It was on the final retreat during her senior year that she finally allowed herself to deal with her feelings about Tania.

She had tried to forget.   She had tried to move on.   She had told herself over and over again that the child was better off without her.   She was with family, wasn't she?

And yet the shadow of darkness remained.   She had abandoned her baby. She had been very young and foolish, and she didn't know God in the same way she did now, but that didn't change the fact that she had handed her baby to a complete stranger and walked away.

After three years of devotionals, worship services and retreats, her heart was open to hearing God on the matter.   Not that she wasn't fearful, but she knew that she needed peace.   So on the final retreat she asked the chaplain for a moment of his time.   They went apart and she blurted out the entire incident.

By the end her face was covered with mucous and tears, but instead of receiving the remonstrance that she was sure she deserved she felt a hand resting gently on her shoulder and a handkerchief pressed against her face.

"First of all, Santita, I want to remind you that God loves you unconditionally." The chaplain paused for a moment. "That doesn't mean He approves of what you did, but He has never stopped loving you. He sees how much you have suffered because of your decision about your baby, and He knows how sorry you are. He forgives you, Santita. Now you must forgive yourself."

"How? How can God forgive me? How can I forgive myself?" All of the anguish of the years was finally coming out. While Santita couldn't understand unconditional love and forgiveness, she hungered for it. She wanted to be rid of the dark shadow of guilt forever.

"God can forgive you because God is Love," the chaplain replied with a smile. "He died on the Cross of Calvary so that we can be forgiven of all our sins."

"I'm sure *you* never did anything like I did with Tania," Santita protested.

The chaplain smiled and there was a sadness in his face. "I wouldn't be so sure about that, my child. The enemy wants each one of us to think that we are alone in our sin, that we have done the worst imaginable thing, and that nobody and especially God will ever forgive us. But the truth is that many of us have done truly terrible things, and even worse than that, we *are* terrible. We wish evil on others, and we turn our back on the people who love us. I, too, have needed God's forgiveness, and I am still filled with thankfulness for the day I realized that He had truly forgiven me. I want you to experience that thankfulness and peace, too."

"But how?" the young girl asked. "I want to, but I don't know how."

"Would you be willing to pray with me?" the chaplain asked. "I could say the prayer, and you could repeat it after me."

"OK, sure," was the weak but hopeful response.

"Let's hold hands and close our eyes. We'll have a moment of silence first, and each of us will invite the Holy Spirit to be present in our prayer. Then I'll pray in phrases, and you can repeat them after me."

"Lord Jesus, thank you for Your unconditional love. Thank you for dying on the Cross so that my sins can be forgiven. I want to ask You to forgive me today for all of my sins, but there is one in particular for which I need a special touch from You. Forgive me, Lord, for abandoning my baby girl. Forgive me for being selfish and foolish. I am so sorry. Give me the peace that passes understanding so that I can hear Your voice and know what I am to do now. I'm your child and I invite You to be Lord of my life so that from now on I can live in Your perfect will. In Jesus' Name. Amen."

They prayed slowly, stopped frequently so that Santita could weep some more and then continue with her confession. At the end of the prayer, the chaplain took out a small bottle and asked the broken girl if he could anoint her with oil as a way of sealing the moment of reconciliation with God:

"Santita, I anoint you with this oil in the Name of the Father, Son and Holy Spirit. You are sealed as God's own forever.

You have been forgiven of all your sins and are now free to love and serve the Lord with all your heart, soul, mind and strength. Amen."

A long, heartfelt hug concluded the session. Santita not only felt like a new person; she now knew what she had to do about her baby girl.

That had been two weeks before graduation, and although she had spoken to no one on the subject since then, she had thought of little else. Tania would be almost seven years old by now. She was probably in first grade or even second! All of Santita's reasons for distancing herself from the child had vanished during that short life-changing prayer, and as soon as graduation was over she would look for her child. It might be too late to take her home, but she would be a responsible mother and do all she could to support and encourage the little girl. And wasn't seven an important number in the Bible? Didn't they learn that it was the number of perfect fulfillment? Seven days of creation, seven hikes around the city of Jericho, seven churches of Revelation, and seventy times seven when trying to forgive. She couldn't help but feel hopeful.

And so it was that her graduation from nursing school, which had been the focus of her life for three years, faded into the background as she looked ahead to her reunion with the child she'd left behind. Her parents and siblings, teacher and friends saw her smiling face and assumed she was proud and happy to be graduating as a nurse. She was, but she had also been set free to plan and dream; the shadow was gone and now there was only the light of hope. Santita could hardly wait to get back to Tegucigalpa.

Chapter Thirteen

Lito had started coming around to the house again. The first time, a couple of months earlier, Tania had not immediately recognized him. Marta was surprised and irritated. Almost three years had passed since the day he had tried to snatch Tania, but her anger had not cooled.

"What do you want?" she asked. "Where have you been?"

"*Hola, abuela,*" was the disarmingly familiar reply. "I've been living in another neighborhood trying to get my life together. I'm not doing drugs anymore. I got a job working with a mechanic. I wanted to see you and Tania."

He did look cleaned up and different. His eyes still carried a hint of that strange fire, but he had brought a heavy bag of groceries and they had no food in the house, so Dona Marta opened the door and let him in.

"*Gracias, abuela.*" He placed the food on the small table and turned towards Tania. "*Hola chiquita,*" he said smiling. "I want to say I'm sorry and I hope you'll give your *papi* another chance." Tania looked at her grandmother for instructions, but Mami Marta was also unsure of the young man's intentions, so Tania took a seat as far away as possible, never taking her eyes off Lito.

Lito's face darkened for a moment, but he quickly put the smile back on and began to take things out of the grocery bag.

"No candy and bananas this time!" he announced. "I brought beefsteak and potatoes, milk, cream, sweetbread and mangos." As he spread out the feast, Tania's mouth began to water and her grandmother's face visibly softened.

"Well!" she said. "Finally you're good for something! I'll light a fire and we'll soon sit down to a grand meal!"

Llto turned his attention to Tania again. "I have a small present for you, *hija*. I know it's your birthday on Saturday, so I thought I'd get you something a little early." Lito reached into a worn backpack and pulled out a wrinkled gift. "Here, take it. I hope you like it."

Tania couldn't resist a present. They had been few and far between in her life. She approached Lito cautiously, reached out for the gift, murmured a quick thank you and retreated to the chair in the corner.

"Go ahead, open it," her father urged. "It was the prettiest one in the market."

Tania quickly tore off the paper and found herself holding the doll of her dreams. She touched the long black hair and then the moving eyelids. The dress was pink satin and she wore matching shoes and lacy white socks. Tania's hands were like those of a blind child as she caressed every part of the doll.

"Do you like it?" Lito asked eagerly. Tania could only nod. She held the doll close to her chest and slipped behind the curtain to the bed where she slept with her grandmother. She felt this moment was too private to share. She had never before had a dream come true, and she wanted to be alone with the precious doll. She took her customary place against the wall, crossed her legs and stared at the plastic treasure.

"What shall I call you?" she asked out loud after awhile. "You need a name. Let's see. I like Maria Jose or Isabela. But no. Since you are all dressed in pink, I'll call you Rosa, my beautiful Rosita. We'll be best friends and I'll tell you all my secrets. This is where we sleep. Would you like to meet Doggie?" She picked up a stained and ragged stuffed animal. "Doggie, this is Rosa. She's living here now with us."

As Tania escaped into the world of little girls and dolls, Marta and Lito questioned one another on the other side of the sheet which divided the room.

"How have you been, *abuela*?" started Lito. "I'm sorry for what happened before. The drugs took over my life. I know there's no excuse for the things I did, but I want to try to make it up to you."

"We've gotten along," the older woman replied. "Tania's in school now. Second grade. She's bright and makes good grades. You scared her to death that day you tried to carry her off."

Lito hung his head. "I don't even remember much about that day," he confessed. "Thank God nothing happened. I was a fool."

"Where are you living? Who are you living with?" Marta was warming up to the conversation now, feeling her old affection for the boy.

"En Las Brisas. There's a rehab center for addicts. A guy named Amos found me under the bridge and took me there. I ran off the first couple of times, but then I stayed and got clean. One of the other guys got me a job helping his brother, a mechanic. I'm learning how to fix cars." While talking, Lito moved towards the curtain and peeked behind it.

"She's really grown, hasn't she?" Lito remarked. "She looks a lot like Santita. Always has."

"People admire Tania's looks," the grandmother replied drily. "Sometimes it's a curse instead of a blessing to have good looks. What about you? Do you have a woman?"

"Sort of," was the evasive response. Lito had not dropped his hand from the old sheet; Tania hadn't seen him, and he continued to watch her play with the new toy.

"I'm not ready to take on the responsibility of a family just yet. Now that I'm off drugs and working, I want to help you and Tania. I know it sounds stupid after all that's happened, but that's why I started selling drugs in the first place, to help my family. They don't pay me much at the shop, but I'm still living at the rehab place so I don't have many expenses. I saved up some money to come here today and say I'm sorry."

Dona Marta had never been a sentimental woman, and she listened to Lito's speech with her usual skepticism. Her eyes had not strayed from the food she was cooking over the fire as the boy had rambled through his short attempt to receive his grandmother's forgiveness.

"I guess you can come around," she said flatly. "We could use some help. It might take awhile to get Tania to trust you again."

"I know. I really screwed up. I don't even know why I'm still alive." Lito's voice sounded so strange as he finished this statement that Marta looked up from her cooking. She noticed that Lito's hand on the curtain was trembling.

"Are you all right?" she asked. "Your hands are shaking."

"Yeah," he said weakly and sat down. "The drugs did something to me. Something permanent, I guess. I have these things called flashbacks, and sometimes I get shaky and weak. I don't know if I'll ever be normal again."

Marta's mind went to the son of a neighbor who was in a wheelchair and whose mind was gone. He had overdosed. Many times she had thought he'd be better off dead. Well, at least Lito wasn't as bad as that. He was working. Maybe he'd be all right with time.

"Supper's ready!" She would focus on the moment. There was no reason to be morbid. "Tania! Supper!" But the little girl was already halfway to the table. She was hungry and didn't have to be asked twice.

"Where's your doll?" Lito asked.

"You mean Rosa? She fell asleep. She isn't hungry."

"Good!" Marta joined in. "More for us!"

After that visit, Lito came regularly on Thursdays, his day off from the shop. He always brought food and sometimes a little gift for Tania who started looking forward to his visits. Marta was glad for the help, of course. At one point she had given up on Lito, and he still wasn't able to do much for them, but as time went by she started taking advantage of his visit to run errands or visit neighbors. It would be good for Tania and Lito to have some time together, she reasoned, and she deserved a little time for herself.   He only came over for a few hours each week; it was only fair that he share in the parenting.

Tania didn't mind when Marta left them alone the first couple of times. Lito was more patient with her. He joined in her games and talked with her. Sometimes they walked down to the river or to Jasmin's pulperia, stopping by to say hello to Anita. Lito had asked their forgiveness, too, and although they were cautious of him, they saw that Tania enjoyed his company. Both knew how hard Marta could be, and it was nice to see Lito and Tania walking hand in hand. Within a short time, the young man had gained everyone's confidence, especially the little girl's, so much so that Tania invited him to her next school program.

"It's a talent show," she said. "I'm going to dance with some girls in my class."

"Really?" her father asked.   "I didn't know you could dance."

"They taught us a dance," she chattered on, "And we have a special dress, too."

Lito and Tania were sitting on the front step of Marta's house eating *charramuscas*. They had been to Jasmin's pulperia. It was a hot day and the frozen fruit tasted delicious.

"Is your dress here?" Lito inquired.   "Can I see it?"

"Sure!"   Tania was delighted to show off the pretty red sequined dress. She ran inside the house and quickly brought it out.

"I bet you look beautiful in that!" Lito remarked enthusiastically. "Why don't you put it on and I'll take a picture

115

with my cell phone."   Tania rarely received this kind of attention and was thrilled that her father was so interested in the dress and her program.

"OK!" she said.   "I'll be right back."   She dashed behind the curtain into the little bedroom and began to take off her shirt.

"Let me help you with that."   Lito's voice startled her. She hadn't noticed that he had followed her into the house. Since he was already lifting the shirt over her head, she didn't protest.

"Now for these," he said, reaching for her shorts.

"I can do it," the little girl said, putting her hands on the waistband.   Even Mami Marta didn't help her get undressed anymore.

"I want to help you," her father insisted.   "I'm your father, aren't I?   Fathers are supposed to help their daughters.   I wasn't here to help you for a long time, so now I want to make up for it."

Tania accepted the explanation.   She had always wanted a mother and father like other children in her school.   Maybe some of her classmates still let their parents help them undress.   She took her hands away from the waistband and let her father remove her shorts.   Now she was naked except for her underpants, and she reached for the dress.

"Wait a minute," Lito said quickly.   He had a strange look in his eye, and his hands were trembling.   "I haven't seen you like this since you were a baby."   He put both hands on her waist and pulled her to him, running his hands up and down her back.   "My baby, my baby," he said.   His mouth was on her neck.   Tania had no idea what was going on or what to do.

116

"I'm going to put on the dress," she said. "Remember, you wanted to see me in the dress." But Lito didn't seem to be hearing her. Suddenly one hand went inside her panties, and she gasped and tried to pull back.

"My baby, my baby, my baby," he kept repeating. His eyes were closed now and both hands were groping, reaching between her legs.

"No!" Tania said loudly. "No! I don't like that!" She began to fight him, but he just grabbed her tighter.

She screamed. Lito's eyes opened but he didn't seem to see her. Her panties were down to her knees. She tried to pull them back up. Lito seemed frozen. As Tania struggled to cover herself, her father struggled to return to consciousness.

"What?" he murmured. "What's this? What's happening?" He sat on the old bed behind him and put his face in his hands.

Tania quickly pulled on her clothes, all thought of the red dress behind her. As soon as her shirt was over her head, she ran from the house and nearly knocked over her Mami Marta who was coming in the door.

"Where are you going?" the grandmother asked sternly. "Where's Lito?"

"Back there," the child panted. "He's back there." She pointed to the sleeping area.

"Is he asleep?" the woman asked. "Did he fall asleep and leave you alone?"

"No. He isn't asleep." Tania had tears in her eyes and was obviously agitated. Marta looked towards the curtain, not certain she wanted to ask any more questions.

"Why don't you go to Anita's for a little while?" she said. "She made *tamalitos de frijoles*." Food was the last thing on the little girl's mind, but she tore out of the house as if she were starving. Marta walked slowly behind the sheet and found LIto with his head in his hands rocking back and forth.

"What happened? What's the matter with you?" Lito began to moan softly, and then he began to cry.

"Stop it!" the old woman commanded. She despised displays of emotion, especially tears from grown men. "Pull yourself together! What happened?" She walked over to the weeping man and grabbed his shirt. "Get out of here!" She didn't know what else to say or do. All she knew is that she did not want a pathetic person in her house. She had enough problems. "Get out, I say! Hurry up!"

Lito rose slowly and shuffled out the door. He was without a doubt the worst person he had ever known.

Chapter Fourteen

Santita's younger sister had moved into her room while she was in Siguatepeque, but her parents had bought another bed so that they could share. Karlita was a pretty thirteen-year-old, very much like Santita at that age. She liked boys and music and anyplace but home. Santita wanted to warn her of certain dangers, but she knew that Karlita would never listen. She had been the same way. All she could do was pray and try to be a better role model this time around. She began to concentrate on two things: getting a job and reuniting with Tania. She felt that she should find a job first so that when she went to see her little girl she could tell the grandmother that she was in a position to help. She knew that she would not be well-received after so many years, but the woman was poor and perhaps would welcome financial help. She would help with Tania's schooling, maybe even put her in a Christian school next year if she found a decent job. The public schools were chaotic and dangerous. Teachers were on strike about a third of the year, and gangs, drug dealers and prostitutes did business at the gates of the schools, even the primary grades. She didn't like to think of Tania walking back and forth to the primary school nearest La Cantera, although she hoped that the grandmother or maybe Lito walked with her. She had heard nothing about Lito in all these years, but had hoped for Tania's sake that he had left the drug scene behind.

She had prepared her resume at the nursing school as a final assignment, so with her documents in hand Santita began to visit clinics and hospitals. Unemployment was high in Honduras, but there was a need for trained nurses. The graduates had been encouraged to look for positions in San Pedro Sula where the pay was better, but Santita didn't consider that option because of Tania.   She believed that God would help her find a good job now that she was willing to take responsibility for her mistakes and try to be a mother to her only child.   She left a copy of her resume in about fifteen places, carefully taking notes on each one so that if they called, she would be able to remember the details of each location.   Returning to the hospital where she had given birth to Tania was painful.   Was she really that awful, selfish teenager who had insulted the staff and negotiated with a baby broker?   Lito had tried to stop her – Lito the drug dealer.   Despite everything, even her attempts to abort, Tania had been born.   God had intervened.   As Tania walked through down the fetid hallways of the public hospital, she tried to imagine herself working there.   Would she eventually turn into one of the bitter nurses she'd encountered in the nursery?   It must be discouraging to work in a hospital filled with stained sheets, peeling walls, and desperately poor patients.   More often than not there was no medicine in the pharmacy, inadequate equipment in the intensive care units, and insufficient personnel. Sometimes employees went many weeks without being paid, and then more weeks on strike.   And yet Santita knew that these were the places where God's love was most needed.   She hoped she would be willing to accept the challenge if this was where her job opportunity appeared.

One day she received a call from a private clinic inviting her for an interview.   The woman on the phone was curt and unfriendly, but Santita responded enthusiastically.

"Thursday at 10? I'll be there! Thank you very much!"

She could hardly sleep Wednesday night, so she spent a lot of time in prayer, asking the Lord to open a door of employment for her. "I just want to serve You, Lord, and take care of my baby," she said over and over. "I'll work wherever You want. Just show me clearly. You know how hard it is for me to hear Your voice."

Her family members wished her luck and her mother promised to go to the church to light a candle for her. While everyone had noticed that Santita's faith had taken on a different form at the nursing school, no one discouraged her, and Santita often continued to accompany her mother to the Catholic masses. "Thanks, mom," she said, truly grateful. She knew that God heard her mother's prayers; didn't the Bible say that people looked at the outside of a person, but God looks at the heart? Santita's mother had a faithful, believing heart. "Light two candles if you want!" she said nervously, trying to be optimistic and cheerful.

"I'll visit Mary, Jesus and James," her mother said. "Three is a holy number." And she gave Santita a squeeze and pinched her cheek as if she were a toddler again. "Hold up your head and let them know how special you are!"

Once she was on the bus Santita allowed this brief encounter to repeat itself in her mind, and tears came to her eyes. She knew that God was showing her the reality of love and forgiveness through her own mother, and she prayed she would be able to pass it on one day to Tania.

The clinic was on a busy street heading into downtown Tegucigalpa, so Santita had no trouble locating it. She was a little early, but decided to go inside and take a look. There were a few people in the waiting area, including the inevitable crying baby. The anxiety that pervades hospital and clinic waiting rooms was evident here as well. Serious, impatient faces. The baby's mother was constantly placing her hand on his forehead and encouraging him in whispers to be calm. Soon they would be with the doctor and all would be well. Behind a small window sat a noncommittal receptionist. Yes, the doctor was in. He was very busy. Please sit down. He would get to each one as soon as possible.

Santita approached the window. She had sent her curriculum here with a friend, so this was her first visit. The receptionist apparently saw her from the corner of her eye.

"Write your name on the list and have a seat. The doctor will be with you as soon as possible."

"I'm not a patient," Santita responded. "I have an interview for a nursing position."

The stony woman put down her magazine and stared Santita full in the face.

"Young and pretty," she stated flatly. "And right on time. I'll tell the doctor you're here. No doubt he'll see *you* right away." She returned as quickly as she had predicted and motioned to Santita to enter the clinic area.

"His office is the last door on the right. Dr. Humberto Pineda. Good luck." She seemed to want to say something else, but lowered her head instead and walked quickly back to her office. Santita knocked lightly on the door.

"Come in, come in!" a resonant cheerful voice called. The young girl opened timidly and stepped into a typical office with desk, sofa and file cabinet.

"Sit down," encouraged the doctor, a young man with large black glasses and a charismatic smile. "Don't be nervous. I'm looking at your application, and I think we're going to be good friends. I enjoy hiring nurses right out of school, fresh and enthusiastic. I don't like those tired, fat grumpy women." At this he screwed up his face in a way that made Santita laugh. He laughed along with her.

"There, that's it. Relax. Why did you decide to become a nurse?"

"My parents suggested it at first because of the school in Siguatepeque. But I like it. I like helping people feel better. I'm hoping to study more at the medical school here in Tegucigalpa. But for now I know I need experience."

"Exactly!" affirmed the friendly doctor. "You need experience, and in a clinic like mine we see all kinds of cases. Right now there are several patients in the waiting area. Maybe you'd like to see them with me, and we'll both decide later about the job?" With those words he jumped from his chair and walked briskly around the desk. Santita didn't have time to say yes or no. Well, why not? Now seemed as good a time as any .

"In the room across the hall there's a nurse's uniform. You need to put that on – and be quick about it. I'll tell Mirna to send someone back. We'll be in the clinic." The doctor seemed less relaxed now. There was an edge to his voice.

"Yes, sir," Santita responded. "I'll be right there." As Dr. Pineda walked towards the receptionist, she stepped into a storeroom and dressing area. Three uniforms were hanging on a rack next to a small mirror. Santita checked the sizes and was surprised to discover that they were all her size! Was this a sign

124

from God? The nursing school chaplain had said that they should look for Him in the little things. As she thought about this, she wriggled out of her "interview outfit," a gift from her mother ("You'll need something new and professional for your job interviews"), and then slipped into the uniform. Glancing into the mirror, she saw her uncertainty staring back and all she could think of was the Lord's Prayer, taught to her by her mother as a little girl. *"Padre Nuestro, que estas en el cielo, sanctificado sea tu nombre . . ."* As she trotted towards the clinic, the familiar words calmed her soul and reminded her that she belonged to God and so did each one of the patients – oh, and Dr. Pineda, too. God bless Dr. Pineda.   By the time she reached the examination room, she was ready to get to work.

Dr. Pineda was putting on gloves from a box on the side table and indicated to Santita that she should do the same.

"You look different," he remarked. "Not so scared."

"I said a little prayer while I was changing," she replied with a smile. "God reminded me that He is in control."

"Oh. God. I see." Dr. Pineda also smiled, but it was a short, wry version. "Are you a Christian then?"

"Yes, sir," was the unashamed response. "The school in Siguatepeque is run by *evangelicos*, and I learned a lot there about the Bible and what it means to be a child of God."   As Santita spoke, the woman and baby entered the clinic. The infant was still crying, and the mother still shushing.

"Miss Martinez, take the baby's temperature," Dr. Pineda instructed Santita. Turning to the mother he added, "Put the baby on the table, please, and tell me what has been going on with him."   The mother was obviously relieved to share her concern about her child and poured out the story of his fever, loss of appetite and incessant lamentation. As the doctor examined the child, Santita observed that he was practiced and thorough, and yet despite the friendliness in his office, he seemed more robotic now, uninterested in the people around him and focused on the procedure rather than the patient.

"We'll need some lab work," he informed the mother. "In the meantime we'll give him something for pain and to slow the diarrhea." He wrote the indications on a slip of paper which he gave to Santita. "Miss Martinez will inject the baby. When you have the lab results, bring him back." He gave the lab order to the anxious woman and left the room.

"Is he going to be all right?" The dark circles under the woman's eyes spoke of a sleepless night. The doctor had said nothing to encourage her.

"I think so," Santita replied, patting her arm. "He probably just has a stomach virus. Once you get the lab work done, we'll know exactly what kind of medicine he needs. In the meantime, the shot will help him sleep. He's in God's hands, you know."

At the mention of God, the mother's eyes brightened a little.

"I've been praying so hard," she said. "He's my first baby. He cries and cries and I don't know what to do." A sob caught in her throat, and then she began to weep. "I've been so afraid and worried."

"Could I pray for the baby?" Santita asked. She could hardly believe she was saying that! When had she ever prayed for anyone except herself?

"Oh, would you? I don't know how to pray properly, but I believe in God and I know He can heal my little boy."

While Santita was praying a short, simple prayer for the baby, Dr. Pineda walked by the door. He just shook his head and kept going. Doctors healed sick babies. Medicine healed sick babies. Prayer was just so much superstition, but if it made ignorant people feel better, so be it. He didn't need God. He was smart, young and had a plan for his life. He didn't need an invisible superpower taking credit for everything he'd done for himself. He would have to teach that pretty little nurse a few things about real life in the real world.

Chapter Fifteen

Although Tania had always had an ache in her heart where a mother's love should have been, the pain intensified when she started school. Many mothers walked their children back and forth to school, packed them a lunch, and gave them a kiss good-bye at the gate. Mami Marta simply woke Tania each morning and fussed at her until she was out the door. She often went to school without breakfast, and if there were no cold tortillas from the day before, she went hungry all morning. Sometimes the government provided a cup of milk for each student, which she gobbled greedily as milk was a rare treat at her house. School was dismissed at midday to make room for the afternoon students, and most of the children hurried home to a hot lunch. Most days Mami Marta left something for Tania on the little stove if she went out. Other days there was nothing, and Tania would knock on Anita's door. She was never turned away, but it still wasn't as if Anita had been thinking of her all morning, looking forward to having her little girl home from school for lunch.

Tania often joined a group of children from La Cantera who also did not have a parent to accompany them to school. They were an unruly bunch and their appearance caused people to shake their heads as they strolled by. Unkempt, uncombed hair, dirty faces, wrinkled clothes, shoes without socks – their appearance advertised the absent mother. Tania tried to be neat and clean for school, but there wasn't always water at her house to wash her uniform or her hair, and Mami Marta would only buy her one uniform for the entire school year, so if she got dirty she had to wash it as soon as she got home so that it would be dry for the following day. The blue skirt hid dirt well, but the white shirt got more and more stained as the weeks went by. "Can't your mother buy you another shirt?" said her teacher one day, shaking her head and pointing out each stain in Tania's shirt. The little girl just shook her head and looked down. Her *mother* -- where was her mother anyway? Mami Marta said she hadn't wanted her:

"And who *would* want you? Your mother said you were an ugly little monkey, and she was right! You're a stupid nobody! Now stop asking about that person who didn't care about you! Who has been taking care of you since you were a little baby? Me! Shut up and go play!"

She had asked Lito, too, about her mother but he was also discouraging:

"She didn't want you, OK? She's selfish and mean and only cares about herself. She isn't thinking about *you,* so stop thinking about *her!*"

Alone with Rosita, Tania poured out her heart: "Did my own mother really call me an ugly monkey, Rosita? I've never heard a mother say that to her own little baby girl! I know I'm not pretty like you, but maybe my mother never saw me. Maybe I was born in the hospital and then somebody stole me. She never got to see me. Maybe Mami Marta stole me! Do you think my mommy has been looking for me all this time? I'd give anything to see her."

In her dreams, sleeping and waking, Tania's reunion with her mother was always a fairytale. They ran into one another's arms and didn't let go. They held on for hours, crying tears of joy. Her mother sometimes whispered sweet things in her ear: "Oh, my baby! My sweet girl! I've missed you so much! I'm so sorry

I haven't been there to love you!"   And Tania would answer forgivingly, "It's all right, Mami. I knew all along that you wanted to be with me, that you didn't throw me away. I love you so much!"

Tania would act out this reunion with Rosita. Sometimes she would be the mother and sometimes the child.   She never got tired of the dream and gave it hundreds of variations, all happy and filled with reconciliation and happiness. It became an obsession, and she often got called down in school for daydreaming.   The slightest sadness would send her fleeing to this secret refuge, and her imaginary mother would make everything right.   While the anesthetic quality was temporary, it was played over so many times each day that she began to spend more time in her fantasy world than in the real one. But who was there to notice? Her grandmother had never given Tania more care than the absolute minimum, and as she grew and became more independent, she received less and less attention.   There were no flesh-and-blood hugs for Tania, no lips to kiss her tears away, no kind words to soothe the ache in her lonely heart. Before she had started school, she hadn't been confronted so often with her loss, but as she sat at school events with the other children whose parents were absent, she watched the family groups around her and wept inside.   Why?   Why couldn't she have a real family who loved her?

One day, shortly after the incident with Lito, she began a new prayer: "God, please make me an orphan. My mother gave me away. My father is bad. My grandmother doesn't love me. If I were all alone then maybe somebody would take me home, somebody nice who doesn't think I'm ugly. Please, God. I want to be an orphan."

Not far away, a young woman was dreaming of a day not so far in the future when she would be reunited with the daughter she had condemned to this horrible hopelessness. Once she had a job she would look for little Tania. She would take her into her arms and beg forgiveness. She would tell her that Jesus had forgiven her, and that she was a new person. By God's grace they would start again. Her precious daughter would receive her love with open arms and they would live happily ever after.

Chapter Sixteen

Amos was on his way to the auto shop to see Lito. During the early morning service at the safehouse, he had asked the Lord to show him what was keeping Lito from giving himself fully to God. He was off drugs and working, and people congratulated him for getting off the street, but Amos knew that the change was superficial, and that unless the young mechanic allowed the Holy Spirit into the deeper places of his heart and soul, he could fall even further than he had before.

"Father, help me to see deep inside Lito's heart with Your eyes," he prayed as he walked. "Give Lito the courage to give you *everything*, to let You love him into wholeness and holiness." He was close to his destination now, humming one of his favorite praise songs and smiling with faith and hope, when two men appeared from nowhere and blocked his way.

"What are you smiling about, *paisano*?" The one who spoke had tattoos from his chin to his waist. He was wearing a mesh shirt that revealed the unconditional tattooed commitment to his gang. His jeans hung low, and Amos was certain he carried a pistol in the back waistband. The other boy, for they were both about sixteen, said nothing. In his left hand was a *chiva*, and from the way he fondled it there was no doubt that he was capable of accurate, lethal stabs.

"*Hola, hermanos,*" Amos replied. "*Bendiciones.*"

"Save your blessings, Christian," the talker snarled. "We'll take your phone and your wallet, and hurry up."

"Of course, my brothers." Amos fished an old worn-out phone from a front pocket and his billfold from the back. It was equally ancient. The silent partner reached for them, and then passed both to the leader.

"You call *this* a phone?" he said angrily. "Does it still work? There had better be some cash in the wallet or you'll be at St. Peter's gate!"

"The Bible says that we are not to lay up treasures on earth where they can be stolen," Amos said, smiling. "Jesus wants to be our treasure. He wants to be *your* treasure."

Just then nine lempiras floated from the wallet onto the road.

"The Bible says that we are to give to anyone who asks, so I'm thankful to be able to give you my phone and my wallet."

"The Bible says! The Bible says! Who cares what the Bible says!" The boy was furious, and he suddenly pulled the pistol from his back waistband and pointed it at Amos. "What does the Bible says about *that?!*"

"Blessed are the peacemakers," responded Amos, closing his eyes, "For they shall be called the children of God. Love your enemies, bless them that curse you, do good to them that hate you, and pray for them that despitefully use you and persecute you. Lord, I do pray for these young brothers. They need to know your love. . . "

"Shut up or I'll kill you!" The pistol was very close to Amos' forehead now. Suddenly the quiet boy spoke up.

"Let's get out of here, Jacko. We can hit on somebody else. Come on!" He tugged on the mesh shirt nervously, his face pale and frightened.

Amos dropped to his knees, moved by the fervency of his prayer: "Lord Jesus, have mercy on their souls. Reveal Yourself to them so that they can know Your love . . . " He weeping now, his heart broken by the darkness in the souls of the two boys.

"Look at him – crying like a baby! He's scared to death! The pistol was dancing around Amos' head now. "Pow pow!" shouted the boy. "You're dead! You hear me? You're dead!!" He made a sound like laughter, grotesque and beastly.

"God so loved the world that He gave His only Son, Jesus Christ, so that whoever believes in Him will not die but instead have eternal life. Thank you for the gift of eternal life, Father. I want these boys to be in heaven with me one day. . ."

"Yeah, he's scared, so let's go! He's got nothing. Come on!"

The *pistolero* threw the phone and billfold at Amos' knees and spat upon his bowed head.

"While you're praying, *cristianito*, tell your God this: tell Him that Jacko *hates* Him. I hate Him! Tell Him *that!*" Amos, lost in communion with Holy Spirit, said nothing as the thieves disappeared. A dirty little boy who had been watching the encounter from behind a parked car darted in and snatched the nine lempira.

"Forgive these lost lambs, Lord. They don't know what they're doing. Love them into Your kingdom. . ." Amos continued praying until an impatient truck approached with the horn blaring.   He rose slowly from the ground and moved to the edge of the road, wiping the tears and grime from his eyes with the tail of his shirt.

Chapter Seventeen

Santita was hired at the clinic, and although the salary was low she started work right away. Once she had more experience she could look for something better, but for now she was living at home with few expenses, and she was eager to find Tania. Although the clinic wasn't run by a church or mission, Santita found many opportunities to share the love of Christ. Praying for the baby that first afternoon had conquered a fear inside of her, and now she often asked patients if they would like for her to pray with them. The mother of the baby had even come by to let her know that her little one had recovered: *"Thank you for praying. I know that helped."* They had embraced, blessing one another in God's name.

"Dios le bendiga."

"Si, Dios le bendiga." Santita had not seen the woman again, but often thought of her. "Lord Jesus, thank you for showing me how much it blesses people to receive prayer, and that you don't have to be a pastor or a missionary to pray for people. It's true what they taught us in Siguatepeque: health professionals who know Christ can help people heal physically *and* spiritually!"

The only negative aspect of working at the clinic was having to deal with the proud doctor. Santita realized almost immediately that his intentions towards her were less than honorable. He was always inviting her to come into his office, which she consistently declined. One day when the waiting room was empty he invited her to walk with him to a nearby coffee shop.

"Let's go get some coffee. My treat."

"Thank you, but I need to work in the medicine closet. I want to put some labels on the shelves."

"That can wait," he said impatiently. "I'm your boss and I want you to go with me."

Santita sighed. In nursing school she had taken an ethics class. Sexual harassment had been one of the topics. Some of the students had not believed that it was worth discussing; surely they would be safe at work! The young women in the program were accustomed to the *machismo* in their culture, but one of their reasons for studying was a desire to gain respect. They looked forward to the comeraderie of fellow health professionals.

"Don't be naïve," their ethics professor had admonished them. "Many male doctors consider it part of the nurse's job description to be available to them sexually. Some of them are coercive, threatening to have you fired if you don't comply. Sadly, many of the most educated men in our country persist in seeing women only as objects of pleasure. Be very very careful."

Dr. Pineda was obviously one of these men. During her first days at work he flirted casually with Santita, undoubtedly assuming that she would quickly succumb to his charms. When he found her resistant, he began to take advantage of moments here and there to touch her, usually by placing his hand on her shoulder. One day as she was alone in the treatment room preparing to nebulize a small girl, she heard the door close behind her and suddenly two strong arms were around her, reaching for her breasts. She struggled to break free, the syringe waving wildly.

"Come on," the doctor whispered. "You know you want to be with me. Give me a kiss." He bit her on the neck and she shrieked loudly.

"Shut up!" he ordered angrily. He started to unzip her dress, and as Santita fought back, the uncapped syringe made contact with the doctor's thigh.

"Ow!" he grunted, freeing Santita, and as he looked down to examine the damage, she pushed by him and out the door, running into the office of the receptionist who simply smirked at the shaken girl.

"He doesn't waste time with his young, pretty nurses," she commented, studying her nails. "Did you think he hired you because of your nursing skills?"

Since that day only a week before, Santita had prayed every morning for the grace to avoid the predator's overtures. She had not even received one paycheck yet. How would she ever be reunited with Tania if she lost her first job?

"You go ahead," she replied as Dr. Pineda insisted that she join him for a cup of coffee. "I don't drink coffee anyway. I have things to do here."

The doctor reddened a little. He moved very close to Santita and his voice took a dangerous tone.

"Look, you little bitch," he hissed. "This is my private clinic and I decide who stays and who goes. I can replace you in an hour. If you don't do what I say I'll throw you out on the street and make sure you never get another job in this city. Then you'll be praying for *yourself*, won't you? You *need* this job. You can think about that while I'm gone because if you don't do exactly what I say when I say it, I'll find somebody who will."

As soon as he out the door, Santita slipped into the medicine closet and closed the door, trembling and tearful.

"Lord, I need Your help," she whispered. "I *do* need this job. Didn't I promise to find my little girl? Isn't that what You want? If I lose this job I may not find another one. Please show me what to do!" Her hands were over her face now, the tears flowing freely. She didn't hear the door open and was startled when a hand rested on her arm.

"Get out of here," a familiar voice urged gently. It was the receptionist, and she too was crying. "He's a snake, and he won't give up. Once he gets what he wants, he'll toss you aside like an old shoe. Believe me, I *know*."

"But I need the job," Santita protested. "He hasn't even paid me yet. He says he'll make sure I never work anywhere else." She had grabbed the older woman's hand, and both women allowed the tears to flow freely.

"I'll write you a letter of recommendation," the receptionist said quickly. "And I'll stamp it with his signature. I don't know if he'll pay you for the days you've worked, but I'll make the check and see if he'll sign it. You need to get out of here *now*. The doctor always gets what he wants, one way or another. I'm not a Christian like you are, and I found a living hell when I came to work in this place. Now *go!*" With that, she shoved Santita's purse into her arms and urged her towards the back door.

Santita paused just long enough to give the woman a short embrace.

"*Gracias,*" she murmured. "I asked the Lord to tell me what to do, and I believe He is speaking to me through you. Thank you. Goodbye." With that, she fled into the alley behind the clinic, turning her steps towards the nearest bus stop, blinking tears into the oppressive heat of the day. Glancing back, she saw Dr. Pineda exiting the coffee shop, cup in hand. The determination in his step confirmed to Santita that she had gotten away just in time. With a silent word of thanksgiving, she boarded a waiting bus. She had prayed and God had answered. As she once again faced unemployment and uncertainty, the only words which came to her mind were, "Lord, have mercy. Christ, have mercy. Lord, have mercy."

Chapter Eighteen

Marta had not asked Tania again about her strange behavior that day with Lito, mostly because she suspected the truth. In her experience, women were obligated at times to do whatever a man wanted. She had learned this lesson herself at a young age when she was left alone with an older cousin. She would do what she could to keep Lito away from Tania, but she had to think about their basic needs as well, and they couldn't afford to lose the food and money Lito brought to their home each week. She blamed Lito's behavior on the drugs and alcohol he had consumed. Maybe he would get better, and then he would look for a woman his age. In the meantime she doubted he would hurt Tania. He had seemed remorseful that day, so perhaps he wouldn't touch her again. Comforted by this line of reasoning, she opened the door with a smile the following Thursday, and even gave her grandson a one-armed hug.

"You look well, *hijo*! How is your job going?"

"They don't pay me enough, but there are plenty of cars to fix. Anyway, what else can I do? Everybody is looking for jobs. At least I have work."

"That's the right attitude! Thank God for a steady job!"

"Where's Tania?" Lito asked, looking around the empty house.

"She's at Anita's house. She ran over there a little while ago."

Lito frowned. "She knows I come on Thursdays."

"Yes, and she knows this is Thursday. I don't know why she insisted on going to Anita's. I thought *you* might know." Marta had taken the bag from Lito's arms and was taking out the ingredients to make a beef stew.

"What do you mean?" Lito responded. There was an edge to his voice and he looked away. "How would I know?"

"It seemed as if you had some sort of misunderstanding the last time you were here," Marta said calmly. "You both seemed upset, and Tania hasn't spoken of you all week."

"Shut up, old woman! What kind of problem would I have with my own daughter? It was nothing! She asked me for some money and I wouldn't give it to her. That was it. She ran out and didn't come back. If she wants to keep pouting about that, then let her. I gave her a present, didn't I? That should have been enough."

"All right, all right," Marta rejoined. "You don't have to go on and on about it. She's just a little girl, only seven years old. You're her father, and you don't have to give her everything she asks for. Calm down."

But Lito was pacing now, and sweat was forming on his forehead.

"I don't know why I even come over here," he panted. "I come every single week, and I buy you food and presents with the little bit of money they pay me. But you don't appreciate it! No, you don't appreciate it! You don't care about *me* – you just want the stuff I bring! Well, I don't have to keep bringing it! And if Tania isn't here to see me, then I'm not coming anymore!"

143

This last statement alarmed Marta, who had grown accustomed to the good meals on Thursdays. Who did Tania think she was, refusing to see her own father? If she drove Lito away, there would be no more brown bags filled with goodies.

"I'll go call her," she said quickly, taking off her apron. "I'm sure she wants to see you and has lost track of the time. She and Anita get in front of the television and forget about everything else. Now just have a seat, and I'll go find Tania." She handed Lito a glass of Coke and hurried out the door.

Anita and Tania were sitting in front of the television watching cartoons. Tania had not forgotten about her father's visit, and although she had not mentioned what had happened to anyone, she was terrified now of being left alone with Lito. What if Mami Marta took off again? No, she would spend the day at Anita's house. Mami Marta and Lito could have a visit, and they wouldn't have to share the food with her. Anita, glad for the company, welcomed her inside and made some eggs and tortillas. Then they both settled onto an ancient sofa on the family room side of the curtain that separated the one-room house into two spaces. Before long, while laughing heartily at the nonsense on the screen, they heard a familiar voice and sharp banging on the gate.

"Anita! Tania! Open up! Hurry!"

"*Dios mio!*" exclaimed Anita, wiping tears from her eyes. "Why is she being so dramatic? You'd think she was having a baby or something!" At this extraordinary thought, the unlikely friends burst into laughter again.

"Or maybe the President dropped in for a visit!" Tania offered, enjoying the moment. "Or maybe the latrine turned over!" She fell back on the sofa, overcome by her own humor.

"Anita!! Tania!!" The hammering was more insistent and the voice angrier.

"Come on," Anita urged, grabbing Tania's hand. "We'd better go see what's gotten your grandmother so excited."

"You go," Tania answered, the smile instantly gone from her face. "I'm staying here."

"Have it your way," said Anita, noting the strange look in Tania's eyes. "But if it's the latrine, I'm too old to lift it." Her attempt to bring the smile back to Tania's face failed, and she turned towards the gate with a hard determination.

"Anita! I know you're in there! Hurry up! I don't have all day!" Marta was getting angry now and feeling ignored.

"All right, all right!" Anita called back. "I'm coming! Stop your pounding and screaming!" She reached the door quickly and drew back the latch. As soon as the squeak ended, Marta burst in.

She pushed past Anita and into the house. Tania appeared to be transfixed by the television, so much so that she did not even turn her head when her grandmother entered the room shouting.

"What's the matter with you?" Marta grabbed her arm. "I said let's go! Now come on!"

"I want to stay here with Anita," the child replied softly. "I want to watch cartoons."

"You can watch them at home with your father," the older woman urged. "He wants to see you."

"I don't want to see him," Tania answered without turning her head. "I don't ever want to see him again." This statement was made with such conviction that Anita knew instantly why Tania had come to her house that morning.

"*Dios Santo en los cielos!*" she said with indignation. "Did he touch you? Marta, did you let that delinquent touch Tania? He's never been any good!"

"Shut up, Anita!" Marta responded angrily. "You don't know anything! He hasn't done anything! Has he, Tania? He's your father, that's all, and he wants to see you. And he says if you don't come and see him, he won't bring you anything ever again. No more food or presents!"

"I don't care. I don't want anything from him. I hate him."

Anita was furious now, and she turned to face her neighbor. "You know good and well that Tania wouldn't be acting this way for nothing! Something happened with Lito, and she doesn't have to see him anymore if she doesn't want to."

"What do you know, old woman?" Marta was also fuming now. She was outnumbered and in the wrong, but she would still have her way. "Lito brings us food and money every week. Who else does that? And Tania is his daughter. He has a right to see her!"

"See her, yes. Touch her, no. You should be thinking of Tania."

"I *am* thinking of Tania. I can't make enough money to take care of us. We need Lito's help. I'll make sure nothing happens. I won't leave her alone with him. But she has to come with me and that's that. Come on, Tania!"

Tania was moved by Anita's defense on her behalf, remembering the day they had hidden in the pulperia. No one else ever defended her. She looked at this kind friend for guidance. As Anita's eyes met hers, the anger turned to resignation. She understood only too well Marta's fears, and she also know that there was probably not a woman in La Cantera who had not been abused by a man.

"All right," she said. "But don't leave her alone with him for even a moment! If you have to go somewhere, send her back to me."

"Do I really have to go?" Tania pleaded. "I don't want him as my father."

"Yes, you really have to come," Marta insisted, taking her by the hand. "And you have to come right now. I hope he hasn't left already. And he *is* your father, the only one you'll ever have. He provides for you. That's more than your mother has ever done!"

"I hate my mother, too!" Tania was crying hard now. "I hate both of them! I wish they were both dead!"

Anita crossed herself and put an arm on Tania's shoulder.

"Don't say things like that, child," she remonstrated gently. "We mustn't wish people dead. God will be offended."

"What do I care?" Tania blubbered. "Where is God anyway? He's never around for *me*! I hate Him, too!" She buried her face in Anita's apron and stretched her small arms as far as they would go around her broad hips.

The child's desperation and sincerity touched a deep chord in Anita. Despite the crosses in her home, the masses and prayers, she had wondered more than once herself where God was. And she certainly understood Tania's fears. Her own stepfather had terrorized her for years, and then she had run into the arms of a violent alcoholic. The children they had borne rarely communicated with her, so bereft of love had been their home. Even now, with this precious baby holding onto her for dear life, all she could do was pat her on the head and say, "*Esta bien, mi amor.* Go with your grandmother." She knew that Tania was very likely being taken to humiliation and desolation, but she felt a weary helplessness.

Marta pried the weeping girl from Anita's hips and dragged her out the gate and down the street to their house. She felt little more than a sense of urgency; compassion had been shouldered out by suffering and disappointment as the years had gone by. Survival. It was her responsibility to make sure they both lived through each day, and she had felt it a mercy to let Tania know from a tender age that suffering was their reality. She was convinced that she had saved her granddaughter from a more severe life, but she could not spare her the daily humiliations of the poor woman of the barrio. She sighed deeply as she pushed on the door to their home, grimly resigned to surrender Tania to Lito.

Chapter Nineteen

Santita had not lost touch with her friend Juanita after graduation. They talked on the phone and occasionally met at the mall or in the market. At their first reunion Juanita had jubilantly announced that her mother had changed churches:

"She found my jeans, and I was scared to death!" she said laughing. "But then she confessed that she had gotten tired of the rules too, and was going to a more progressive church. Now we shop for pants *together*!" And she gave Santita one of her signature bear hugs. Santita couldn't say that she'd never met a Christian who knew how to love; Juanita was the most loving person she had ever known besides her own mother. The day she walked away from her first job, she called this trusted friend.

"Can you meet me?" Apparently her attempt at a cheerful voice failed.

"What's wrong, Santita? What happened?" asked Juanita with real concern.

"I'll tell you when I see you. Can you meet me somewhere? The mall?"

"Of course! I haven't even started looking for work yet. My mom said that work could wait, that she's missed me so much she wants me all to herself for awhile. Can you imagine?"

"Maybe your mom should talk to my mom. It looks as if my mom is going to have me all to herself for awhile, too." At this, her voice broke and the tears came.

"Ah, I take it your job didn't work out after all," Juanita said sadly. "Well, don't hang your head! God has something better for you, that's all. I'll see you in front of the coffee shop in one hour!"

Santita got off the bus in Las Brisas and walked slowly up the stairs to the mall. Juanita would probably be late. She lived way out in El Carrizal, so a one-hour trip was characteristically optimistic. Why couldn't she have Juanita's glass-half-full attitude? Nothing seemed to get that girl down. It would be good to spend a couple of hours with her sunny friend. But then what? She had been so hopeful that she would be able to see Tania soon, but she didn't dare appear empty-handed. She was indebted to Dona Marta for ensuring that her little girl hadn't fallen into the hands of people completely unknown to her. Tania could have been lost to her forever. At the same time she had heard that Marta was a hard woman, and she could hardly blame her for the low opinion she undoubtedly had of Tania's birthmother. For years she had shared that opinion. Now that she had received God's forgiveness, she was hopeful of making things right, but this setback in employment was a bitter disappointment. Holding her child was an insistent hunger now, and she resented every moment they spent apart. If only she could let Tania know how she felt!

"Hola, guapa!" The sudden hug and greeting startled Santita and she shuddered.

"Sorry! I didn't mean to scare you!" Juanita laughed. She was always laughing. "I bet you thought I was going to be late! I forgot to tell you that I was at the supermarket in Las Torres with my mom when you called. They have chicken wings on sale today, so we rushed over to get some. Only my mom would ride buses across the city to get chicken wings!   Anyway, here I am, so let's go get some coffee and hear the bad news."   She grabbed Santita's arm possessively and pulled her towards the coffee shop.   Practically no one else was there, so they were soon seated at a table with coffees and *chilenas*.

"So what happened?" Juanita said through a full, sugary mouth.   "Did the doc hit on you?"

At this bull's eye guess, Santita's eyes watered.

"You didn't let him do anything, did you?   Please tell me you didn't, because if he touched you, I'm going over there right now with my umbrella to give him a poke where he most deserves it!"   This visual image brought a peal of laughter from both girls.

"Oh, Juanita!   You have a gift for cheering me up!   I knew you'd get me laughing. No, he didn't do anything. He wanted to, and I almost let it happen, but the secretary practically pushed me out the back door.   I think God used her to save me from a terrible experience."

"Thank the Lord!" Juanita exclaimed.   She hadn't imagined that the threat had been so deadly.   "They told us about those guys in school, remember?   I guess we all hoped it was an exaggeration, but it looks like it's the norm not the exception. I'm so glad you got away!"

"Me, too.   But I'm so disappointed about Tania.   I'm dying to see her.   I can't hope to win her back without a job.   I've been dreaming about her almost every night.   I have this sense that she needs me right now more than ever!"

"Well, just go over there and tell that old woman you want to see her. You are her mother, you know.   You have rights."

"Not really. I never even registered her as my daughter. Those awful people told me not to. I don't have any legal rights, and without money I feel sure the grandmother will never let me near Tania." Santita sighed deeply. She often felt the depth of the consequences of that hasty decision so many years before.

"Don't give up!" Juanita encouraged. "Hey, I have an idea! Dona Marta doesn't know me. I could go to her neighborhood and just see what I can find out about Tania."

Santita brightened. "But how?" she worried. "Nobody is going to open their door to a complete stranger. You'll stick out like a sore thumb over there. You know how it is in the barrio: anybody new is suspicious. You could even be in danger. No, you'd better not try it."

"Let's think about it for a minute," Juanita responded. "I could pretend to be lost. Or somebody from the government, maybe from Social Services."

"Worse and worse," responded Santita. "Everybody *hates* Social Services. They won't tell you anything!"

"Hey, I know!" Juanita announced. "I'll pretend to be with an NGO looking for children for a scholarship program. I'll take somebody with me. Maybe my brother will go. We'll act like we're looking for deserving kids for school stipends! *Everybody* will talk to us!"

"Do you really think it will work?" Santita asked hopefully. "You aren't afraid? What if they asked questions you can't answer? If they find out you're faking, they could kill you!"

"Then I guess I'd better wear my tennies so I can sprint for safety!" This visual image was even funnier than the last. Juanita hadn't sprinted since she was in kindergarten, if ever.

"All right. All right," Santita acceded. "I confess that I'm dying for some information about Tania. I wish I could go myself, but I know I can't. Juanita, I don't know how to thank you for doing this."

"I've always wanted to be a detective," Juanita smiled. "And my brother owes me a few favors. He won't want to go, but he will. Anyway, we'll get it done as quickly as possible and get out of there. That place has a bad reputation. I want to help you get your little girl to a safer place." Her dimples disappeared with this last sentence. She was clearly sympathetic to the plight of an innocent child in a barrio like La Cantera. "And the sooner the better," she added, sipping her coffee. "The sooner the better."

The following Saturday morning, Juanita and her brother Julio got off the bus at the soccer field in Flor del Campo. Buses didn't run through La Cantera, so they would walk the rest of the way. As in all of the poor innercity neighborhoods in Tegucigalpa, the roads were unpaved, dusty and filled with trash. El Carrizal was no different, so the siblings were accustomed to the dingy billiard halls and careworn faces that greeted them as they began their short journey to Tania's neighborhood. Julio was grumpy. He could think of several places he'd rather be and said so.

"Oh be quiet!" Juanita remonstrated. "We're doing a good deed. God wants His children to help other people. We might be able to rescue Santita's little girl from a terrible life."

"What if her life isn't terrible?" Julio asked resentfully. "Maybe her grandmother spoils her rotten. Maybe she *likes* her life. And anyway, how are we going to find her? This is a big neighborhood, you know."

"We'll find her," his sister assured him. "La Cantera is smaller than Flor, and anyway we know her name and how old she is. Besides, God will help us." Never dismayed by circumstances that would wilt others, Juanita strode purposefully down the main drag. She was on a mission, and her brother's irritability just made her more determined. She sincerely loved Santita, and she did not share Julio's optimism about Tania's life with her grandmother. She prayed silently that the Lord would help them find this lamb who had strayed far from the mother who carried her in her heart. Jesus was the good shepherd, right? He would lead them to Tania.

"Well, which way do we go now?" They had reached an intersection, and all three choices looked basically the same.

"La Cantera is by the river," Juanita replied. "Which way looks like it leads towards the river?"

"Straight ahead," said Julio. "I can smell it, and the road dips down, too." Just then a little girl with a basket of tortillas on her head walked towards them on the road.

"Which way is La Cantera?" Juanita asked her cheerfully.

Saying nothing, the skinny child looked back the way she had come.

"Thanks!" said Juanita. "You're pretty smart, Julito!" She grabbed his hand and dragged him towards the dip in the road. For the first time that morning, he laughed.

"Do you really think we should be holding hands?" he teased. "We're supposed to be professional NGO workers, remember?"

"Oh, dear!" Juanita exclaimed. "You're right! I never was good at playacting!" When she tried to put on a serious expression, Julio doubled over.

"My sister, the social worker!" he cried. "I haven't seen you look that serious since the time I ate all your ciruelas."

Now Juanita was laughing, too.

"OK, OK," she said. "Now stop! We have to do this right. If we mess it up, we won't get another chance. Everybody will know we're faking. Let's stop at that pulperia and see if we can get some information."

"All right," Julio agreed. "But you do the talking. I just came along for appearances."

"*De acuerdo*," Juanita responded, all business now. "You just nod your head and open your notebook and write something in it every now and then."

By now they had reached a once brightly painted store. Posters advertising soft drinks and snacks decorated the outer wall. Written above the barred window were the words, "*Pulperia Dios es Bueno*." No one was in sight inside, so Juanita clinked a coin on the bars.

"*Hola!*" she called loudly.

"*Ya voy!*" was the brusque response, and within moments a wrinkled woman appeared drying her hands on a rag.

"What do you want?" she demanded, as if Joseph and Mary were pleading for a room. It hardly seemed the correct attitude of someone in need of making a sale. The two young people knew that as strangers, they were being warned. No doubt there was a pistol in the rice bin.

"Good morning!" Juanita responded cheerfully. These women were the best sources of information in the neighborhood. The store owner looked old and bitter. All the better. They were in need of some unbridled gossip.

"First of all we're dying of thirst in this heat. My bro-, I mean my co-worker and and I would like two Cokes." Julio smiled. Maybe this wasn't going to be such a bad morning after all.

"We would also appreciate some information, but maybe you're new here and don't know anybody," Juanita added as the woman poured their Cokes into plastic bags.

"Are you kidding?" the woman scoffed. "I was one of the first squatters in this cursed place! Been here for thirty years. I know *everybody*. But that doesn't mean I'm giving out any information." She looked Juanita square in the eye.

"Of course we wouldn't expect you to tell us anything personal," Juanita said hurriedly. "We're not with Social Services or the police or anything. We work for a private NGO." The next part Juanita had practiced at home after reading something similar on a webpage.

"We are dedicated to the empowerment of women. Our organization was founded as a response to the widespread oppression of women in the world. We believe that the best way to make women free and independent is through education. Our

157

target populations are the girls and women who live in neighborhoods such as this one. In fact, my co-worker and I are investigating the possibility of opening a scholarship program in La Cantera. My name is Juanita and this is my co-worker, Julio."

As the phony social worker played her part, Julio guzzled down his Coke and the store owner visibly changed her expression.

"Well!" she said. "It's about time somebody did something for women! We bear the children, keep the house, cook the food and please the men – and for what? They march off and leave us for a younger version."

"Exactly!" Juanita agreed heartily. "We recognize the sacrifices made by poor women. We have seen your suffering and have developed programs to improve your quality of life."

"You're not with a church, are you?" the woman suddenly asked. "Because the churches are only interested in getting you inside so they can take your money. And if they do have food or something to give away, you have to take off your makeup and put on a long skirt to get it." She said this last part with a sly smile. She had probably played the game a few times herself.

"Oh, no," Juanita assured her. "Our agency isn't affiliated with any religious organizations or churches. We believe in the power within each person. If we can help young girls and women find their inner power, anything is possible." Julio raised his eyebrows; he hadn't heard the speech and was impressed with his sister's ability to speak emphatically about ideas she certainly didn't believe. He hadn't known her to be much of an actress before, but she was winning the Golden Globe today.

158

"So, what kind of information do you need?" A little cheer went up in Juanita's heart. If this gossip opened up, they could be looking at Tania very soon.

"The first program we're interested in starting here is a scholarship program for young girls who are in kindergarten through second grade. We believe in getting an early start so that even children understand that they have unlimited potential. Would you happen to know any little girls that age?"

"This neighborhood is full of children," the informer said with a tinge of disgust. "They're *everywhere*. You'd think nobody around here knew about birth control. Every few months somebody comes around to talk about safe sex and give out condoms, but it doesn't do any good. Children keep having children. A woman who can't take care of one baby has three more. And then they come around here begging for credit. It isn't *my* fault they can't control themselves."

"Of course not." Juanita put on a sympathetic face. "You can't be expected to take care of every child in the neighborhood. You have your own family to think of." Julio turned sideways so that he couldn't be seen rolling his eyes. It was a good thing Juanita was the spokesperson. He would have lost patience with this dreary hag a long time ago.

"Kindergarten to second grade, you say? That would be about five to seven or eight years old, I guess. A lot of children that age don't even go to school. Their parents can't put them in. The people who live over there by that light pole have two girls about that age."

"Great!" Juanita exclaimed. "Julio, could you make a note of that? Can you think of any others?" She leaned in towards her new friend as if there were no one else in the world.

"Hmmm . . . let me think. I don't really know their ages. Seems like they all grow up overnight. There's a little girl in that blue house up there." She pointed to a tiny block home further into La Cantera. "And I think Dona Marta's granddaughter is about that age. Now *she* could use some support! Marta is meaner than a snake. She has the girl in school. I've seen her in a uniform. But she's a sad little thing, and no wonder. Her mother tossed her aside when she was born and her drug addict father dumped her off with old Marta."

Juanita's heart was beating so hard she could hardly breathe. Julio had set his coke bag on the small shelf and pretended to be writing every word.

"She sounds like just the kind of girl we want to help," Juanita remarked with emotion. "Where does she live exactly?"

"You go past that blue house and down the stairs. Be careful. People who don't know how to walk them sometimes fall. Go down about halfway to the river. It's one of the worst shacks. It's on the left and there's a little sign about clothes for sale. Marta sells used clothes."

"Let's see, that's four girls." Juanita wanted to rush headlong down the stairs to find Tania. "Where would you recommend that we start? Is one of the girls more in need than the others?"

"Definitely the one that Marta has," the woman was quick to reply. "Anything you could do for that poor creature would be a mercy." She leaned in close and whispered, "They say her own father abuses her, if you can imagine." Juanita shuddered.

"It's just like you were saying," the crone added. "Women are *nothing* in places like this. Less than nothing. Use us and throw us away. But I do feel sorry for such a pitiful little thing as that one--Tania, I think she's called. At least most of us had a mother who did what she could for us. Not her. She was just a baby when Marta got her. Said the mother didn't want her. Tried to *sell* her." The gossip was on a roll now and couldn't get the dirt out fast enough. "Who knows where she'd be . . .not that she's done much better with Marta."

Juanita felt an overpowering urge to defend Santita, to shout how young she had been – and that she had changed. She wasn't the same selfish teenager who had handed her baby to a complete stranger seven years ago. But she quieted the voice of loyalty and played the confidante instead.

"How terrible!" she clucked. "Women like that shouldn't have children."

"She wasn't a woman exactly," was the rejoiner. "She was practically a child herself. Got mixed up with Marta's grandson. He deals drugs. They say the drugs messed up his head and that's why he goes after the little girl. Sounds like an excuse to me! They ought to lock him up and throw away the key."

Juanita was ready to get away from this conversation now, but didn't want to seem overly eager to break it off.

"I'm so glad we stopped here to talk with you. You have been so helpful! I think we'll see if Dona Marta is at home. We have to interview at least three people today and make a report

161

to our supervisor on Monday.   Thank you so much for getting us off to a good start."

"No problem."   The woman smiled at them in a friendly manner.   "And if you ever have any programs or anything for an *anciana* like me, I'd be grateful. You seem like good people, and if I don't have to accept Christ again I might participate."

Juanita laughed at the little joke. "We'll let you know.   As I said, we're just investigating at this point.   If our organization decides to open some work in La Cantera, you will be the first to know."

"*Adios.*"   The woman and the rag melted from view as quickly as they had appeared. Juanita and Julio looked at one another with a determined unity of purpose.   They both knew they had to get Tania out of La Cantera and into Santita's arms.

Chapter Twenty

Amos had gotten Lito the job at the mechanic shop. He knew the owner and had asked him to take on Lito.

"Do you know how to fix a car?" the greasy mechanic had asked. His head was under a hood, and his overalls testified to long hours with dirty vehicles.

"I can fix a flat and change oil," Lito had replied hopefully.

"Dios mio," had been the instant response. "A *woman* can do that much!"

"Come on, Chico," Amos had urged. "You're always complaining about how you can't get everything done. You need help. Give the boy a chance."

Chico straightened up and took a long look at Lito.

"I don't want any drugs around here," he said to both men. "And I don't want *mareros* hanging around. I don't want any trouble."

"He's at the safehouse," Amos assured him. "He's off drugs and alcohol. He's not in a gang. He's a good kid trying to make a fresh start."

Lito looked down. He didn't deserve a compliment from Amos. He had fought him at every turn.

"That true?" Chico asked, looking straight at Lito now. "'Cause I don't want any of your old friends hanging around my shop."

"I don't have any friends," Lito said softly. That much was true anyway. He still knew people in the drug trade, but he knew they weren't his friends.

"I need a job. I'll work hard. I'll do anything you say." His hands were in his pockets and his eyes were on the ground. He waited to hear the inevitable no.

"All right then," Chico said instead. "You can start by cleaning up that car over there. We just finished with it. Give it a good washing inside and out. The owner will be by this afternoon to pick it up. When you finish that, you can find the broom and sweep up around here. Any tools or parts, anything like that, you can put over there on that shelf."

Amos was smiling. He slapped Chico on the shoulder. "Hey, thanks," he said. "God bless you!"

"Don't start in on me with your Jesus stuff," Chico grumbled. "We'll see how he works out and then decide if he can stay. What's your name anyway, kid?"

"Lito. And thanks."

"We'll see if you stay on or not. Work hard, mind your own business, get along with the other guys, and maybe we'll keep you. To start with you'll just be doing the stuff that nobody else has time to do. Not real mechanical work. If we have a chance we'll teach you. In the meantime, just do as you're told."

"Yes, sir," Lito had responded quickly and gratefully. "Any kind of work is fine with me."

"That's the right attitude," said Chico. "Now get started on that car."

As Lito hurried towards his first assignment, Amos put a hand on Chico's shoulder.

"Lord, thank you for Chico's generous heart. Thank you that he gave Lito a job. Bless this shop, dear Father, and bless your son Chico. Amen."

"Get out of here," Chico ordered as soon as the prayer was over. Amos smiled and ambled over to where Lito was searching for a rag to wash the car. The hand falling squarely on the top of his head startled Lito, but before he could scoot out from under, it clamped hard and Amos' voice boomed.

"Lito is your son, Father. Thank you for giving him this opportunity. Give him a heart of service. Amen!" As he withdrew his arm, he reached for a large sponge just above the head of the new employee. "Here!" he said, tossing it to Lito. "Now get to work, and don't stop until the boss says so."

"Hey, thanks," was the uncomfortable reply. "I don't know why you help me so much. All I've ever done is give you a hard time."

Amos was already walking towards the street. "Just thank God!" he called back.

"And if you ever need your car washed, let me know!" Lito joked. It was his first attempt at being humorous in a long time, and the short laugh which followed was better than a shot of penicillin.

"Yeah, right! I just don't know which one of my cars to bring in first!" As the eyes of the good Samaritan locked with the eyes of the angry sinner, a tiny ray of hope shot into Lito's heart.

He scrubbed the filthy auto as if he were scraping bitter years from his broken life.

Don Chico worked himself hard and expected his employees to do the same. That first day they toiled until seven, and just as they were cleaning up, a Toyota Hilux drove onto the lot. The driver rolled down the window and honked the horn. One of the mechanics outside of driver's view spat on the ground and cursed.

"Why doesn't he just whistle at us like dogs? I don't know why Don Chico puts up with him."

"Who is he?" Lito asked. The late-model truck looked out of place on the lot. Chico specialized in getting tired vehicles back on the road, and the small space was full of dented cars and trucks, most of which had been here before.

"Don Claudio." The words were dripping with open disgust. "Thinks he's the *jefe maximo* of the whole neighborhood. He runs the lumberyard and he's a slimy crook." This mechanic, Paco, had worked with Don Chico since he was a boy and thought of the older man as a second father. Years earlier he had been on his way to participate in a robbery when the gruff shop owner had grabbed his arm and pulled him into the shop.

"I've been watching you take to the street more and more," Don Chico had said, staring him straight in the eyes. "I know your daddy drinks and your mama works late, but that doesn't mean you have to turn into *basura* like those boys you're hanging out with."

Paco had hung his head in shame. He had only planned to be a lookout, but the strong honest hand gripping his arm had reminded him that stealing was dirty and wrong. The hardworking neighbor had probably never stolen anything in his life. He wasn't a churchgoer, but everybody respected him. Respect. That was something Paco longed for. The son of a drunk was lower than a good dog. At eleven he was too old to cry, but he recalled a tear trying to force itself out of one eye.

"You stay here in the shop," Don Chico had commanded. "Go get that broom and start sweeping. There's coffee and bread in the office when you're done. Go on! Hurry up!"

And Paco had never left. Twelve years later he was one of the best mechanics in the shop, and he was fiercely loyal to the man who had undoubtedly saved him from prison or death.

Don Chico had approached the truck and was talking with Don Claudio who obviously had no intention of getting out. After a few moments Don Chico looked around for Paco.

"Go get the toolkit," he instructed in a tired voice. "We're going up to the lumberyard to fix one of the trucks."

"I knew it," Paco mumbled angrily, but he called back, "I'll go, sir. I can fix it. I'll take the new guy with me. You go on home to supper."

Lito had been looking forward to home and supper himself, but he warmed to the idea of being chosen.

"Yeah," he chimed in. "I'll go with Paco. *No hay cuidado.*"

Don Chico nodded, said something to the lumberyard manager, and shuffled back into the office. The Hilux backed quickly off the lot, spraying dust everywhere as a final message of superiority.

"Come on," Paco said. "He couldn't even give us a ride. I'll get the tools and we'll go on the moto."

With Lito precariously clutching a heavy bag of wrenches and screwdrivers with one hand and Paco's right shoulder with the other, the two young men bounced and skidded the several blocks of dirt roads to the lumberyard. The Hilux was already there, parked next to a long flatbed truck loaded with cut wood. Don Claudio saw them wheel in and motioned furiously.

"Hurry up!" he barked. "This truck has to leave tonight and it won't crank. I'll have Chico's head for sending a couple of boys to fix it if you don't get it running!"

Lito looked at Paco, expecting a rebuttal, but his friend knew how to control his tongue.

"Yes, sir," he said simply. "We'll do our best." He grabbed the tool bag from Lito's shoulder and walked with determination towards the open hood of the flatbed. Lito noticed that the tires on the old truck were almost completely bald.

"How far does this thing have to go?" he asked Paco once they were alone with the engine.

"All the way to Choluteca," was the answer. "They ship the wood out from there."

"On *those* tires?" Lito sputtered. "They're shinier than a baby's behind!"

"You mean Don Claudio's head, right?" Paco laughed. "Why do you think he wears that hat? The old *pelon*! I'd give anything to take him down a peg or two. He treats Don Chico like a servant boy."

All the time he was talking, Paco's hands were moving here and there around the engine of the old flatbed. Although a lightbulb had already been hung from the hood, the young mechanic used a tiny flashlight to get a closer look.

"Go crank the engine," he instructed Lito without looking up. "I want to hear what it sounds like."

Lito jumped down and ran around to the driver's door which had been left open. He pulled himself into the worn seat and checked to be sure the truck was in neutral, then turned the key. A tick-tacking sound was the only response. Lito turned the key back to the off position. The cab smelled like sweat, oil and greasy enchiladas. A girlie magazine had been left on the passenger seat, and the floorboard was covered with junk food wrappers and empty soda cans. Lito reached to open the dashboard, but closed it again quickly when he saw the revolver inside. Highway bandits were common in Honduras; he presumed the gun was for self-protection. His mind went suddenly to the confrontation with a nicely dressed young man with a tense face. Images ran together: a hand reaching inside a jacket, a woman's scream, the coolness of a knife, the feel of a cell phone, dust in his mouth, blood on his hand.

"Lito! Hey! Lito!" A rough hand was gripping his arm, shaking him hard.

"What's wrong with you? Did you take something?" Paco's angry face was inches from his left ear into which these questions had been hissed.

"No, no." Lito struggled to return to the present. "Of course not. I just . . . I was just daydreaming or something. Remembering. . . I don't know."

"I need you to go back to the shop," Paco said abruptly. He obviously wasn't interested in Lito's memories. "The starter's bad, so go ask Don Chico if we've got something to put on this antique. And hurry up. You know how to drive a moto, right?"

"Yeah, sure," Lito said foggily. "I'll get going. The starter. Be right back."

Paco had already returned to his place under the hood, extracting the starter and shaking his head. One of his brothers had died from an overdose. He knew all about flashbacks. Maybe he shouldn't have let him take the motorcycle. Maybe he should have gone himself. He shouldn't let the old *peludo* make him so anxious. Why doesn't he go home? He glanced across the yard at the light in the old man's office. Don Chico had told him once that he and Don Claudio had played soccer together as boys. They grew up on the same street, walked to school together. Paco wondered if the lumberyard boss had always looked down on Chico, ordered him around. There was a pecking order in every group. Maybe Claudio had always been the top rooster. Now he had plenty of money and power.

"No importa," he concluded. "I'd rather be like Don Chico any day. He doesn't look down on anybody. He even had time for somebody like me." This last thought required so much attention that his hands stopped working momentarily.

"Somebody like me. Somebody like Lito." He wouldn't be so hard on the new guy when he got back. Who knows what he'd been through. He thought about how Don Chico gave him honest work to do and treated him with respect even when he made mistakes. He could do that much for Lito.

It had been a long time since Lito drove a motorcycle, but it was impossible to drive fast on the bumpy, dusty roads between the lumberyard and the shop, so he refreshed his memory as he went along. Within minutes he was wheeling into the familiar workspace. Only Don Chico was still there, and he immediately walked out of his tiny office.

"So, what's wrong with the truck?" he asked, wiping his hands on a rag that didn't look as if it could hold one more drop of black grease.

"The starter," Lito replied obediently. "Paco wants to know if you have something we can use. He's taking the old one out."

Don Chico frowned. He didn't usually have spare parts, even used ones, for big trucks like that, and it was too late to go to one of the parts stores.

"Did Paco tell Claudio that he needs a new starter?"

"I don't think so. I don't think he likes talking to Don Claudio."

Chico's smile returned, albeit a wry one.

"Who does?" he remarked with little feeling. He seemed to be elsewhere for a few moments, and then suddenly he was back on the job.

"Come on, let's go," he said with energy. "I'll drive." The older man mounted the bike easily and waited for Lito to slip on behind him.

"I'm a mechanic, not a magician," Chico mumbled as he turned the bike towards the street. It was after eight now, and he couldn't help thinking that if he *were* a magician he'd conjure himself up a big plate of *arroz con pollo*. And he wouldn't share it with the bitter man waiting to hear the bad news about his precious cargo of lumber.

Chapter Twenty-One

Although the pulperia owner had emphasized the negative aspects of Tania's appearance, she had a natural beauty which could not be hidden by the lovelessness of her upbringing. And as Lito had pointed out, she looked very much like her birthmother, so as Juanita and Julio picked their way carefully down the steps towards Dona Marta's house and nearly ran into Tania who was trotting off to see her friend Anita, Juanita immediately knew that she had located the lost baby. She was startled, however, and as Tania ran past without the least bit of curiosity, Anita's gate opened and closed, and the girl was enveloped before the search-and-rescue team could respond.

"That was her!" Juanita hissed at her brother.

"Yeah! Anybody who knows Santita could see that! Wow, she looks just like her!"

"Hmm," Juanita mumbled. "What do we do now? Maybe we should see if Dona Marta is home and get some information before we try to talk with Tania."

"Good idea," Julio answered. "We don't even know whose house that is, and it would look strange to be talking directly to a child."

"OK, let's go then. We'll look for the place with the sign about the used clothes."

Within minutes they were standing in front of Dona Marta's *choza*. Their eyes met with a look of apprehension combined with determination, and Juanita rapped on the door.

"Who is it?" an irritable voice responded.

"My name is Juanita Palma. I'm with an NGO."

"What do you want?" The voice was a bit closer to the door.

"We're interviewing families with girls between the ages of six and nine. We were told that you have a little girl that age. We might be able to help with a scholarship."

"Who told you about Tania?"

"A woman in the pulperia." Juanita felt a bit strange holding an interview through a closed door, but she was determined to get some answers.

"Tania isn't here."

"It isn't necessary to see her today. We just need some information from you," Juanita responded patiently. "We need to know if she qualifies for the scholarship program, and if you are interested in participating."

A latch was pulled from inside, and the door cracked open slightly. Marta peered out, obviously suspicious.

"What's the name of your NGO?" she asked.

"Step Forward for Women," Juanita answered. She was glad she had done her homework. Julio's eyebrows were raised. He was impressed with his sister's ingenuity and courage.

"All right," Marta finally succumbed. "Come in. You look legitimate. At least you're not dressed in police uniforms." All three smiled at this little joke. Thieves often dressed as policemen to get inside homes.

Marta was scrounging around for something to sit on. She dusted off an old stool and pointed to two ancient plastic chairs.

"Sit down," she ordered. "Now, what do we have to do to get a scholarship for Tania? I'm not going to any classes, so forget that. Tania makes good grades, though, and behaves herself, so if that's good enough, then she qualifies."

"What grade is Tania in?" Julio took the initiative and pulled out his notebook.

"Second. She hasn't failed at all. She's a smart little thing."

"Does she have anybody helping her financially other than you?" Juanita queried.

"No," Marta said emphatically. Well, it was true. Lito rarely left money.

"The pulperia owner told us that you are the girl's grandmother. Can you tell us anything about her parents?" Although Juanita's heart was pumping, she tried to sound businesslike and disinterested.

"I can tell you that her mother has never done one thing for her. In fact, she tried to sell her when she was a baby, but I got in the middle of that! I wasn't going to let a spoiled teenager hand over my grandchild to *proxenetas!*" Marta spoke triumphantly. She was proud of the day she had faced down the child traffickers.

"So Tania's father is your grandson? And does he help with her expenses?"

"He tries to help, but he doesn't have much education and his job pays hardly anything. He brings food every now and then, but can't leave money."

"We were told that he has a drug problem."

"Who told you that?! That old gossip at the pulperia up the hill? She doesn't know anything about Lito!"

"So he doesn't have a drug problem?" Juanita was open to hearing some good news.

"He did for awhile," Marta admitted, "But he got into a rehab program and got a job. Now he's doing fine, but he's just a mechanic's helper so he doesn't make much money."

"Does he see Tania?"

"He comes by about once a week," Marta assured them. "He brings food."

"That's good to hear," Juanita smiled.   "Children need to know that their parents care about them even if they don't have much to give them."

"He cares about her," Marta grumbled. "But I'm the one who takes care of her. I'm the only one who was there for her when she was a baby."

"She is very fortunate, then, to have you as her grandmother," Juanita said reassuringly. "I'm sure she loves you very much."

At this last comment, a shadow passed across Marta's face. She wasn't so sure that Tania loved her, or even that she loved Tania. She hadn't had any experience with love. But she had saved the little girl, hadn't she? And fed and clothed her and sent her to school! What was loved compared to that?

"Now," Juanita said authoritatively, recognizing Marta's discomfort, "We would like to tell you a little about our scholarship program, and then if possible, we'd like to meet Tania."

"She's visiting a neighbor," Marta agreed. "She likes to watch cartoons, and our telly is broken, but I can go get her when it's time." She was beginning to relax with these two amiable strangers. She would play along and see if they were offering anything worth taking.

Juanita had sized up Dona Marta as a hard, crafty woman who would do anything to survive. Having grown up in a similar neighborhood, she was familiar with *interesados* and sympathetic to the environment which nurtured such brittle selfishness. She would have to be very careful not to offend the grandmother or she would never see Tania. Julio was playing his part perfectly, pen in hand, seemingly taking note of every bit of information offered. Juanita forged ahead, describing the nonexistent scholarship program as if it were the inspired salvation of thousands of little girls living in poverty. As a Christian, she felt guilty about weaving such a lie, but hoped that the end justified the means. She was sure that God wanted Tania to have a better life, and now that she had met Dona Marta she was even more convinced that an honest, straightforward approach would never work. She finished her presentation with a hopeful smile and asked Dona Marta if she had any questions.

"You haven't said how much the scholarship pays," the old woman remarked flatly.

178

"Right now we're trying to find potential recipients," Juanita responded evasively. "Once we have an idea of the costs, and how many qualified girls there are in this neighborhood, we will be able to talk more specifically about the exact amount of the scholarship."

"So, you don't have any money?" the woman sneered. "You're just asking a bunch of questions with no money to back them up?"

Julio couldn't help hiding his anxiety at this point. He looked at his sister with real concern.

Juanita just laughed. "You know how these organizations are: paperwork, paperwork, paperwork! I wish things were easier and faster, but it never works that way. I would be interested, however, in hearing from you how much you think the scholarship should pay. You are the one paying for everything, right? What would you consider a good monthly amount for Tania's education?"

By turning the tables on Marta, the tension was diffused. Marta wrinkled her face to think.

"Let's see . . . uniforms, notebooks, pencils, snacks . . . " She was counting off the items on her long thin fingers. "And the school asks for money for the cleaning woman and the guard, too, and water, and sometimes for special celebrations." Marta didn't mention that she rarely complied with these requests. She often kept Tania home on special days so that she wouldn't have to pay the extra costs.

"It really adds up," Juanita offered sympathetically.

"I think a scholarship should pay at least five hundred lempiras," the woman concluded, "And I think you should give the children backpacks and school supplies when classes start."

"Are you writing this down?" Juanita asked her brother. "We don't want to forget any of these details." She seemed genuinely thankful for Marta's ideas.

"I wonder if we could meet Tania," she added. "We need a few photos of children who would be eligible for the scholarship program, and after hearing so much about Tania, we'd enjoy meeting her in person."

Marta stood slowly and walked towards the door.

"Why don't you come with me?" she said. She had never left strangers alone in her house. They would just walk up to Anita's, meet Tania, and they could go on their way.

"That's fine," agreed Juanita. She was glad for a stretch and the opportunity to leave this tiny, stuffy house. "We'll just follow you."

Marta let the two young people through the door first so that she could lock up.

"You can't be too careful around here," she remarked.

"I'm sure," Juanita agreed heartily. "Everybody told us to be careful."

"They found another *muerto* in the river last night," Marta said grimly. "The gangs are wanting everybody with businesses to pay a war tax, and if they don't . . . " She drew a line across her throat. "The dead man owned a taxi. He barely made enough for his family. The tax would have been a burden, but now his family has nothing. Last week they killed a woman who owned a little beauty salon."

"That's terrible," Juanita said, and she meant it. The gangs were running her neighborhood, too. It hardly seemed fair that those who were already living in poverty were being targeted by gangs. She had read on the internet that Central America was more dangerous than places like Afghanistan where wars were going on. Drugs, arms and human trafficking had turned the beautiful little countries into combat zones.

By now they had reached Anita's house and Marta was knocking on the gate and calling to her neighbor.

"Anita, it's me, Marta. Open up!"

Within moments the gate was open and a cheerful face appeared.

"Tania is watching cartoons," she offered warmly, and then she saw Juanita and Julio and her face became immediately suspicious and cold.

"They're all right," Marta assured her. "They want to give Tania a scholarship. We've been talking. They want to meet Tania. Tania!"

As they waited for the little girl to emerge, Juanita felt a surge of emotion. She wished she were wearing a little hidden camera so that Santita could share this moment. It didn't seem right that she was going to be able to talk with little Tania while Santita waited anxiously at home. She would take a photo and memorize every gesture and word for her friend. Anita had gone to get the child who was reluctant to leave her cartoons. As

Juanita fished around in her bag for the camera, they came out holding hands.

"Here's Tania," Anita said, obviously not yet convinced that these intruders were friends.

Tania bowed her head. She was naturally shy, and although Anita had told her that they had guests who wanted to meet her, she felt embarrassed to be the center of attention.

"Hello there," Juanita said gently. She drew near to Tania and squatted to her level. "We've been getting to know your grandmother, and she was such a big help that we just had to meet her, too."

"Say hello," Marta ordered.

"*Hola*," was the obedient, quiet response.

"We want to take your picture." Juanita showed her the camera. "I hope you'll hold up your head and let us see your beautiful eyes." Just like your mother's, she was thinking, trying hard to keep the tears from her own eyes.

Tania reluctantly raised her head, and as she looked into Juanita's sympathetic face, gained a bit of confidence. The tiniest hint of a smile appeared.

"That's better!" enthused Juanita. "Now . . . one, two, three!" As the camera clicked and everyone in the small group stared at the timid child, a young woman named Santita was on her knees pleading with God, and a young man named Lito was paying precious money for yet another DVD filled with pornographic images. Oblivious to everything except this moment of happiness, Tania took Juanita's hand and their eyes met with such feeling that both hearts were struck with painful joy. Juanita wanted to gather the girl into her arms and never let her go, but that particular blessing belonged to another. For now she would be content to carry messages of hope to her friend.

"Bye-bye, Tania," she said with feeling. "We'll see you again before long!"

A slight nod was the only response. Juanita and Julio walked up the stairs in silence. There were no words for their feelings, no audible expression for what was in their minds and hearts. Julio's right arm linked with the left arm of his sister. They were strangely altered by a tempered exhilaration. They must see Santita as soon as possible. As they left Flor del Campo on a new *rapidito*, the tears flowed freely down Juanita's soft cheeks.

Chapter Twenty-Two

Tania had seen the yearly *feria* from the window of a bus: the ferris wheel rising high in the sky, the rollercoaster ambling across a quarter of the field, lights and music, vehicles and people jostling for position. She never dreamed of actually going there. Dona Marta rarely allowed her to participate in the customary celebrations at school. Even birthdays came and went at their house without fanfare. Theirs was a cheerless life with days blending into one another without distinction. Entertainment, parties, and celebrations were for other people. She had grown up with the understanding that she wasn't worthy of such occasions. No explanation was given, and she knew other children whose lives were much the same, but she was a child, and children love color and light. She told Anita about the fair.

"It comes every year," was the dull reply. "It comes and it goes, and good riddance. A lot of hard-earned money spent on nothing."

Tania sighed. She loved Anita, but she was like Dona Marta in some ways, resigned to a life without the slightest evidence of fun or celebration.

"It's very pretty," Tania offered softly.

Something about the melancholy statement moved Anita's heart. A memory stirred of a time long ago when she had begged her mother to take her to the fair. She realized with a bitter start that her words to Tania were an echo of her mother's words to her so long ago. Unlike Tania, she had protested and stomped her feet – and had been dragged outside by her hair and given a sound beating. She had never asked again.

"I think we should go," she announced suddenly. She felt as if someone else were talking. "Yes! Let's go to the fair!"

"Really?!" Tania was on her feet. "Really?! When? Now? I have to change my clothes and put on shoes!" She ran to her plump friend and tried to reach her arms around her middle. Anita laughed. She felt fifty pounds lighter. Were they really going to the fair? She laughed again. Why not? She had a little money under the mattress.

"Go change your clothes and tell your grandmother where we're going," she instructed. "Try not to invite her. She'll spoil our fun." She laughed again. And again. She felt like a small child on Christmas.

"I'll be right back! *Abuela* won't want to go. She hates fun. I'll be very quick, you'll see!" The excited child burst through the gate and out of sight. She was back, as promised, in ten minutes.

"*Abuela* wants to know if you've lost your mind!" she announced. "She says if you have money to throw away, throw it into her pockets!" They both laughed. They were making a break from their prison of hopelessness for a few hours and were like a couple of drunken sailors.

"Well, come on before I change my mind!" Anita grabbed Tania's hand, but it was the girl who did the pulling and tugging.

"Hurry up, Tia Anita! Hurry up!" She knew instinctively how fragile the woman's determination could be. They had to get there quickly before somebody talked sense into Anita.

But Anita couldn't stop laughing. She laughed all the way up the stairs, down the street to the bus stop, on the bus to the fair. Smiling, chuckling, laughing outright. Going to the fair! She, Anita Carcamo, was going to the fair. Imagine. She hoped her miserable mother was turning over in her grave.

As they approached El Prado and the fair came into view, Tania began to jump up and down.

"There it is! There it is! Can we ride the big wheel? Can we go on all the rides?"

Anita started to feel a little queasy. She had never actually been to a fair and had no actual experience with ferris wheels and rollercoasters.

"I don't know, *mi amor*," she said. "We'll have to see how much everything costs, but we'll do as much as we can, I promise."

The bus stopped and the two adventurers trotted across the street to the clearly marked *"Entrada."* Anita was relieved to see that the entrance fees were less than she expected.

"How much are the rides?" she asked the tired ticket keeper.

"They have different prices. Go in and see for yourself."

"Come on, Tia Anita!" Tania was dragging her along again, but she was catching the excitement. Stuffing her money inside her brassiere, she hurried alongside her little friend into the wonder of *"La Feria de Maravillas."*

Since it was early afternoon, not many people had arrived yet. Young people preferred to go to the fair at night. The earlier hours were for young children accompanied by adults, and the busiest sections were the kiddie rides. There were food booths everywhere advertising French fries, cotton candy, candied apples, pizza, enchiladas and tacos, popcorn, soft drinks, hamburgers and hotdogs. But the food would have to wait; Tania was pulling her towards the merry-go-round.

"*Los caballos! Los caballos!*" she screamed excitedly. "Let's ride the *caballitos!*"

There were, in fact, horses and elephants and tigers and even giraffes on the merry-go-round. Anita bought two tickets and they joined the short line. Other excited children in the line were picking out the animal they would ride. Anita couldn't help noticing Tania's drab, wan appearance compared to these brightly-dressed, healthy children. She was rarely this close to children outside of their social class, and she realized that she was accustomed to thin children in worn clothing.

"Never mind," she thought. "For today, Tania will be just like them! She'll have fun and eat ice cream. We'll make some happy memories."

The merry-go-round stopped and they moved forward with the group to find an animal to mount. Tania chose a zebra, and Anita sat down in the kangaroo booth next to it. She was thankful that her seat would not be going up and down. Tania, on the other hand, was bouncing in the saddle, ready to gallop to the music. Anita had never seen her face so bright and joyful, and she felt the joy of the giver. She was poor, but in this moment she was able to share an unforgettable moment with a precious child whom she truly loved.

The ride was over quickly and Tania was dragging her to another one. She was dismayed to see cars swinging high in the air on thin cables, the occupants screaming hysterically. It looked positively nauseating.

"This one! This one, Anita!" Tania had already taken a place in line. "Come on! Then we'll go on the rollercoaster!" There was no turning back now. Anita said a few Hail Marys as they moved towards the battered cars. Tania made her selection and jumped in. As Anita pulled herself aboard and allowed the bar to be lowered, it seemed to her that the little strap across their laps was completely inadequate for the dangerous spinning she had witnessed from the ground. Tania had twisted a tiny arm into her friend's fleshy one and was talking non-stop.

"I'm so scared, aren't you? Don't let go of me! I hope I don't throw up! Oh, no, we're moving! Hold on, here we go!"

Anita wanted to scream, but she found the experience paralyzing. Tania's screaming was shrill and hilarious, and her fingernails were digging into Anita's goosebumps. They went higher and higher, dipping and rising while circling a giant tilted airplane, until the entire fair was blurring below them. She had *begged* to do this, she wondered? She could only thank God they hadn't eaten anything yet; her stomach was flipping and bobbing like their aerial prison. Barely conscious, she heard Tania's disappointment.

"Oh, we're going down already! I wanted to go on and on and on! Can we ride it again, Tia Anita? *Please!*"

A scrubby young man was disconnecting the bar and Tania was tugging at her sleeve, but she was strangely heavy.

"Come on!" the overly excited child was saying. "Let's go to the rollercoaster!"

Anita forced herself out of the metal container. She was sure that she was about to fall face first into the smashed straws and popcorn kernels in the ground at her feet.

"What's wrong?" Tania was concerned now. "Your face looks funny."

With tremendous effort, the shaken woman assured the anxious child that she was fine. "Let's just walk for a minute," she murmured. "I'm a little dizzy, that's all."

Tania lovingly took her hand and led her into the fairway.

"Don't worry," she said. "I'll take care of you. Do you want something to drink?"

Anita was touched by the child's concern. A bit of water would do her good. They bought a small bag and Anita nursed a corner of it until she began to feel more normal. Suddenly Tania shrieked.

"Valentina! Valentina!" Another girl about Tania's age was running towards them. Anita recognized her from La Cantera. The mother was hurrying behind, dragging a smaller boy.

"Thank God!" the woman, whose name was Karol, sighed. "I was praying we'd run into somebody we knew. Valentina wants to ride *everything*, but I can't go with her. I have to hang onto Ronaldo. I was just about to give up and go home when we spotted Tania."

As the woman spilled out her story, Anita also sighed with relief. Valentine and Tania would be able to sit together on the rides while she waited with her feet planted firmly on the ground. The two little girls were holding hands and talking excitedly.

Anita's eyes met Karol's, and the two women smiled happily.

"So, which ride is next?" they practically said in unison. The girls put their heads together and ran off towards the rollercoaster.

"Saved!" announced Anita, pulling a wrinkled rag from a deep pocket and wiping her brow.

"Saved!" agreed Karol with a big rolling laugh. "I wasn't going to let Valentina talk me into coming, but she wore me down. These creaky old rides scare me to death!"

"You might not believe this," Anita rejoined, "But this is my very first time at the fair. All my life I've dreamed about the fair, and now that I'm finally here I'm nauseous and dizzy after just one ride with Tania!"

"Some things are best accomplished while young," Karol smiled. "You were very brave to bring Tania, but I can certainly understand why you wanted to give her a bit of joy."

"Yes," Anita answered. "Marta is very poor."

"We're all poor," the younger woman retorted. "But every child needs love. That old crone never has a kind word for anybody, and poor Tania has to *live* with her. I don't know anybody who doesn't feel sorry for the little creature. Nobody should have to swim in another's bitterness day and night."

Anita was sorry to hear such hard words about her neighbor and friend, but she knew they were true. She often felt reluctant to send Tania home: she could see the misery in the girl's eyes as she marched like an exhausted soldier through the gate.

"But today we're having fun!" Karol announced, realizing that she had very nearly spoiled the occasion for Anita. She put an arm around the older woman's shoulders and pulled her towards the roller coaster.

"Yes!" Anita replied, remembering why she had come to the fair. "Let's get some cotton candy and watch the girls have the time of their lives!"

Chapter Twenty-Three

Santita was waiting anxiously at the same coffee shop in which she and Juanita had hatched the plan which had led to the visit to La Cantera under false pretenses. Just an hour before she had received a breathless phone call from her friend:

"We found her! We saw her! Meet me at the coffee shop in the mall! I'm getting into a *colectivo*--see you there!"

Santita had practically raced to the bus stop and less than an hour later was breathlessly hoping that Juanita would be waiting for her at their usual table in the coffee shop.

"I went to the camera shop first to get this photo developed!" Juanita cried as she rushed to Santita. "You're not going to believe how much she looks like you!"

Santita took the photo with trembling hands. Seven long years had passed, but in her mind Tania was still a chubby baby. She had not even though what she might look like now, but she had no trouble recognizing the eyes staring back into her own. In one glance she absorbed the shy, beautiful, thin child in the photo. Her daughter. She felt faint. Juanita grabbed her arm and led her to a table.

"Sit down," she ordered. "I'll get us some coffee."

As Santita lowered herself into a chair, her eyes never left the picture. She longed for the child to speak, to reach out to her and call her 'mama.' She began to murmur softly: "My baby. My baby. I'm so sorry . . ."

Juanita was watching her friend anxiously as she placed the order, and quickly realized that she had made a mistake by arranging this meeting in a public place. She saw Santita's lips moving, the tears falling, body trembling.

"Oh, dear!" she said to nobody and then realized that everyone in the shop was looking at Santita who was now moaning softly and rocking, the photo held against her chest. As Juanita hurried to her side, she heard the words of lament:

"*Perdoname, perdoname, perdoname,*" she chanted over and over, as if waiting for the child's image to respond with words of forgiveness, a hug of reconciliation.

"Santita!" Juanita whispered loudly. "Santita!" She put a hand on either side of the wet face and attempted to force the eyes to focus on her own concerned expression.

"Santita!" This time she spoke loudly and with desperation, and her friend seemed to hear her name being called as if from a long distance.

"Here I am," she said. "Here I am. I won't leave you again. I promise. We'll always be together. You'll see. We'll start a new life together, and I'll take care of you."

"Santita!" Juanita was frightened now, and a small crowd was beginning to gather. She put her arms underneath Santita's and practically lifted her from the chair.

"Let's go," she urged. "Let's get out of here." The awkward movement caused the table to jerk, and coffee spilled everywhere. Juanita pulled her friend away from the hot liquid and towards the causeway of the mall. As they moved towards the entrance like a pair of soldiers on the battlefield, Santita began to recover from the shock of the photo.   Her shoulders heaved as she took a deep breath and ran her free hand across her eyes as if to order the tears back inside.   Suddenly she straightened and grabbed Juanita.

"Stop!" she cried. "Stop! I have to know everything! Tell me!   Tell me!"   She was grasping Juanita so hard that her fingernails were digging into her upper arms.   Now she was the one pulling, and she dragged her distressed companion to a nearby bench and demanded to be told every detail.

"Don't leave anything out!" she ordered.   "I have to know every single thing you saw."

"OK, OK," Juanita responded, thankful at least that Santita was making sense again.   "I was planning to do just that.   That's why I went, you know."   Tears appeared in her eyes, and Santita realized that she was not the only one who was suffering.

"Oh, Juanita," she said, putting her arm around the sweet girl's neck.   "I'm so sorry!   I don't know what happened back there!   Forgive me?"

"Of course I do!" was the quick reply.   "I was just worried, that's all.   I didn't know what to do when you broke down back there.   Here we are, two nurses, and neither of us knows what to do!"   The laughter was good for them; they exchanged a quick hug and then Santita waited eagerly to hear the story.

Juanita began with the visit at the pulperia: "Nasty old gossip, but she told us what needed to know.   Your daughter's name is Tania."   She described how they had glimpsed their target running down the path, and that she and Julio had both gasped to see how much she looked like her mother.   At this bit of information, Santita jerked as if she had been stuck with a pin.

Juanita moved on quickly to the visit with Dona Marta: "A hard one, that woman, but she took us straight to Tania. The other *senora* – what was her name? Anita I think – she seemed nice enough, very protective of Tania.   I was afraid they wouldn't let us take a picture, but in the end they did!" At the mention of the photo, Santita's eyes moved from the storyteller's face to the precious picture in her hands.

"When I looked at her, something broke inside of me," she said softly, still focused on the image. "Those eyes--it's almost like looking into a mirror. It's more than a memory. I don't know how to describe it.   All these years of wondering and imagining, and here she is! Flesh and blood! Oh my God, Juanita, what are we going to do now? I can't just walk in there and take her. She probably hates me. I don't have a job or a house.   Dona Marta sounds as hard and mean as everybody says she is. I feel helpless, Juanita.   With all my heart I want to take care of Tania, but I just can't see a way to make it happen!" The tears were falling freely now.

"Don't say that!" Juanita commanded. "We just found her.   Now we have to figure out how to get her out of there. God will show us how to do it.   I can't believe He wants her to stay in that horrible place with that mean old woman.   We'll just pray and ask the Lord to show us what to do next." With that she began a fervent prayer right there in the mall:

"Lord Jesus, You love Tania even more than Santita does. You've been watching over her all these years.   And you see how much Santita wants to take care of her little girl.   Please show us what to do.   Protect little Tania from anything and anybody who wants to hurt her. Help her to know somehow that her mother is here and wants to be with her. Open a way, dear Lord, for Tania and Santita to be together forever. In Jesus' Name. Amen."

"Amen," Santita whispered. "I feel Him here with us, Juanita. I think He wants me to have hope, and to trust Him to work things out. Tomorrow I'm going all over Tegucigalpa looking for a job! I won't stop until I find one. Lord, please help me find a job! For Tania and me."

"That's the spirit!" proclaimed Juanita. "We can't give up. Tania needs us, and we can't give up. We *won't* give up!"

Santita threw both arms around the neck of this courageous, faithful friend.

"Thank you, Juanita! You're the best friend ever!"

Juanita held Santita tight for a moment and then gave her a short sermon:

"Just remember that God has forgiven you for leaving Tania all those years ago. Forget about that. Focus on right now. Focus on getting a job and a home for the two of you.   No more dark thoughts. Once Tania meets you, she'll jump into your arms and go wherever you want to take her. God is in control."

"Yes!" Santita smiled. "All we have to do is *hope and believe*."

Chapter Twenty-Four

"So they took her picture and said they'd let us know about the scholarship," Dona Marta concluded triumphantly. She was sure that Lito would be happy to hear of Tania's good luck.

"How do you know they were for real?" Lito asked. "Did they have any identification or anything? Did they leave any information about their agency?" He was naturally suspicious, and was growing increasingly possessive of Tania.

"They said they were just getting started," Marta replied. "They were just doing interviews. They said they would be back when everything was in place." Although she, too, had been reluctant to open her door to the strangers, she had become convinced of their reliability.

"Did they give you an address or a phone number?" Lito challenged.

"No," the woman snapped. "They didn't give me *anything*, I'm telling you, but they wrote down information about Tania and took her picture."

Lito sneered. He had replaced the drugs with pornography and had a preference for the kind that featured young children.

"That doesn't mean anything," he said drily. "They might want her for something entirely different. Not everybody out there is trying to *help* children, you know, and Tania is very pretty."

"What are you suggesting?" Marta did not like the direction this conversation was taking. "Nobody is doing anything with Tania without my permission. You might recall that I'm the one who saved her in the first place!"

Lito cringed under this accusation. He was never allowed to forget that he had been the coward and his grandmother the hero.

"I'm just saying that it seems strange that they didn't leave one single piece of paper behind. You don't even know the name of the organization. And anyway, I can pay for Tania's schooling. I got a raise. I'm a mechanic now, and Don Chico says I can stay on at the *taller*."

"That's great news!" Dona Marta responded with real happiness. "Let's stop talking about unpleasant things and start celebrating. I'll get lunch going. Why don't you run up to Anita's and bring Tania home?"

"I don't know why I always have to go up there and get her!" Lito responded hotly. "She knows I'm here! Why doesn't she just come back?"

"She's just a child," Marta said soothingly. "She likes to watch TV. Don't get so worked up. I'll go get her if you want. I just thought you might be hungry."

"I'll get her," was the impatient reply. With a slam of the gate, he was gone. Marta turned quickly to the bag of groceries and concentrated her energies on organizing the contents. What could she do about her short-tempered grandson? At least he was responsible these days. She would do her part to see that Tania returned his attention.

Lito walked quickly to Anita's house, angrier by the moment. Nobody appreciated him. Nobody saw how hard he worked for his meager pay. Nobody cared that he spent more than he needed to on groceries for Marta and Tania. Most of the guys spent their pay on beer and cigarettes. They had also introduced him to black market pornography. It was plentiful and cheap, and before long he was addicted. He told himself that it was normal for men to look at pornography, and that it was less harmful than drugs. Once he had a woman, he wouldn't want or need it anymore. Besides, it was just paper. Just pictures. Who cared? He even imagined sometimes that these weren't real children. They didn't have mothers or houses or schools. They were some kind of imaginary children, maybe a photography trick. And anyway he paid for the pictures, right? They probably gave the money to the imaginary children.

As he knocked on Anita's gate, his anger took control.

"Hurry up!" he shouted. "Tania! Come out of there!"

Inside, Tania jumped anxiously from the sofa and ran behind the curtain where Anita slept.

"It's him!" she whimpered. "I don't want to go. Please don't make me go."

"Now don't worry," Anita said worriedly. "Your grandmother is home. You'll be just fine."

"But he's very mad," Tania pleaded from behind the thin drape.

"Get out here right now!" Lito thundered. "I'll kick this door down!"

At that Anita felt her temperature rising and she moved quickly towards the gate that separated her from real and perceived neighborhood dangers.

"You do and I'll call the police!" she warned. "You don't have to act like that!"

"Then open up," was the slightly calmer reply. "I've come for Tania, and I want her right now, not tomorrow."

"All right, all right," Anita acquiesced reluctantly. As she unlatched the gate, Lito pushed through. His dark face looked ready to burst, and his eyes belied the absence of reason.

"Tania! Let's go!" he ordered. When the little girl did not immediately appear, he stomped into the house. "I said let's go, and I mean right now!"

"I'm scared," Tania wept. "Why are you so mad? Are you going to hurt me?"

The plaintive question seemed to confuse Lito. He reached for her arm, but she slipped quickly behind the curtain.

"I'm scared, Tia Anita! Please don't let him take me!"

The poor woman was intimidated herself by Lito's bullying. She didn't want to give him the child, but she was afraid not to.

"Could you calm down?" she queried. "She won't be so afraid if you would just calm down a little."

"I'm calm," Lito retorted. "I just don't know why I have to go looking for my own daughter every single time I come over! She should be at home! She should respect me and be *grateful*!" He made this last statement with forceful self-righteous indignation. No one could imagine how often he had lain his bed staring at the photos of naked children in grotesque positions, imagining his own daughter that way.

"I'm her father," he emphasized, "And I'm taking her with me."

Anita felt that she had to pry the child off the curtain and surrender her to this raging bull. She had always felt helpless against male rage. Her cowardice shamed her, but she tried to console Tania as she betrayed her trust.

"Your grandmother is fixing lunch, *mi amor*," she soothed. "And your father only comes to visit once a week. He wants to see you and spend time with you. Go on now. Don't be afraid. Nothing is going to happen." As she placed the weeping child into Lito's oil-stained hands, her heart broke with a silent shame.

"Come back later," she invited. "I'll be here waiting."

Lito lifted the girl like a doll onto one shoulder and carried his prize through the gate. Anita slumped to the sofa and wept softly. She was a liar, a coward and a traitor. She was a poor woman of the barrio, obviously abandoned by God to her luckless fate. Even as this thought crossed her mind, she grasped the crucifix around her neck and mumbled, "Mother Mary, watch over Tania."

Lito carried the crying child like a sack of corn back to his grandmother's house. At the sight, Martha's words erupted like a pierced boil.

"What are you doing? Why are you carrying her like that? What will the neighbors think?" She wanted to slap her nephew soundly as she had so many times when he was small.

"She didn't want to come," Lito grumbled loudly. "I didn't have any choice. She can't just do whatever she wants. You've spoiled her."

"*Spoiled* her?!" was the vociferous reply. "Look at her! Does she look *spoiled*?" As Tania stood there helplessly, thin and pale, with silent tears running onto her ragged, stained shirt and spilling onto the dirt floor around her bare feet, she bore witness to the truth of Marta's words.

"Nobody in this house is *spoiled*," the old woman sneered. "But we are also not accustomed to being treated like animals."

"All right. All right." Lito was tired now, tired of everything. What was he hoping for anyway? Why did he even come here on Thursdays? He had better things to do. He knew Tania didn't want to see him, so what was the point?

The point, said a dark voice deep inside, is that you want her. You want her, so just take her. She's yours, you know. Take her where you can do what you want with her. You don't have to listen to this old woman.

"Now go sit down and wait for lunch," said Martha, oblivious to Lito's inner struggle. She was facing the little stove now, stirring the soup. "Tania, go wash up and stop crying. You can go back to Anita's later on once Lito is gone. Everything is just fine, and we are going to have a delicious lunch, thanks to your father."

You are her father. She should be living with you, the voice continued. You are the one paying the bills. You shouldn't be begging for time with her.

"Tell me about your conversation with Don Chico," Martha said, trying to draw Lito into conversation again. "What did he say exactly?"

Make a plan. Come back with a present for the little girl. Find a place to live where you can keep her with you.

"Lito," Martha cajoled. "Come on, talk to me. I only get to see you once a week. Tell me about work. Or maybe you have a girlfriend? Let's have some news."

Tania wandered back in, tears washed but her face still somber. Lito had sat down on the water barrel. Neither spoke.

"It's a good thing the food is ready!" Martha exclaimed. The silence upset her. A roaring brawl was better than this! "Come to the table, you two, and make up."

Another day, said the voice. *Very soon she will be in your hands.*

The bowls and spoons clanked noisily as the family uneasily shared a common meal.

Chapter Twenty-Five

Amos had continued to visit Lito at the shop, and of course he saw him at the rehab center, too. The director had spoken to him earlier in the morning about the young man.

"He's coming up on six months here, you know. Time for him to move on."

"He isn't really where he needs to be with God," Amos had protested gently. "He's still wandering."

"But he's off drugs and working, and there are other people who need his space here."

"I know, I know," Amos had sighed. There was so much need in the neighborhood, and people were always asking for a place to stay and help to get off drugs and away from the gangs who controlled them.

"You'd better tell him," the director had urged gently. "Tell him he can stay two more weeks, but that's it."

"I will. I'll talk to him and help him find a place to live." As Amos walked out of the conversation and onto the street, he took a long deep breath and began to pray.

"Lord Jesus, you and I both know that Lito doesn't know you yet. He hasn't given his life to you. You helped him get off drugs and You got him that job, even though he hasn't asked You himself or thanked You for anything. Forgive him, Lord. He just hasn't been able to believe in Your love. Help me talk with him today. Show him how much You love him. And help us find him a place to live that's near some of Your children. Amen."

As Amos prayed, he walked along the dusty, familiar streets of his "church," this unpredictable community of some fifty thousand people crammed onto a hillside. In a sense he felt that for now this neighborhood was God's bride for him, a little like Hosea's Gomer: *"Go take for yourself a wife of whoredom and have children of whoredom, for the land commits great whoredom by forsaking the Lord,"* God had said to Hosea. And Hosea had done it. And even though Gomer had betrayed him time and again, he kept seeking her out and taking her home.

"Give me Your heart," Amos said aloud. "Give me Your heart, Jesus. I want to love the people around me like You do."

"Hey, Amos!" The shout drew the young prophet out of his inner conversation.

"Hi there, Walter!"

The children loved Amos. He always had time for a game of soccer, and if he was blessed with a few lempira in his pocket, he took them to the *pulperia* for a treat.

"Come play marbles with us," the dirty child smiled invitingly. "Do you have any marbles?"

"No marbles." Amos pulled out his empty pockets.

"That's OK. We can share." Walter was playing with two friends. They had about a dozen marbles between them, and had already drawn a circle in the dirt road. Amos knelt beside them and waited to be given a marble or two. That took some time as the boys were reluctant to give up their treasures.

"I won't keep them," Amos promised, seeing their struggle. "I'll just play for awhile and then you can have them back."

"We play for keeps," another boy named Samuel announced. "It's no fun if it isn't for keeps."

"I could just watch then," Amos offered.

"No, you can have two of mine," Walter insisted. "I'm going to win anyway, and then I'll have all of them!" He and Amos laughed.

"It won't be hard beating me," Amos assured him. "I haven't played marbles in a long time."

"Well, you aren't going to beat *me*," Samuel snarled. "We'll see who ends up with everything!" The third boy, Jesse, suddenly stood up.

"I have to go home," he stated flatly.

"Chicken," Samuel teased. "He knows he's the worst."

"Stay and play," Amos urged. "It'll be fun."

"No. These are my brother's marbles, and if I lose them he'll kill me," the child said, almost crying now. "I didn't know it was for keeps."

"We don't have to play for keeps," Walter interjected. "Let's just play for fun. It's better with four."

"No!" Samuel was angry now. "We're playing for keeps or we're not playing at all!"

"Come on," Amos soothed. "It's just a game, and we're all friends. Let's just play for awhile and see how it goes."

"Forget it! You're a bunch of pansies," Samuel accused. "And my mom told me to stay away from you anyway," he directed to Amos. "She says you're probably some kind of pervert or something."

Amos had heard this charge before. A lot of people didn't understand his life. Walking around the neighborhood talking and playing wasn't real work in their minds. He seemed harmless enough, but why didn't he get a job? Why didn't he have a woman? The gossip followed him like raucous ducklings. He tried to ignore it, but Samuel's comment hurt and he would have to respond.

"I'm sorry your mom feels that way," Amos said with real feeling. "God knows that I just want to love everybody and tell them about Him."

"Then why aren't you a pastor or a priest?" Samuel rejoined. "And how come you aren't married? Everybody says you're weird, helping people all the time without charging anything. And you're always playing with us boys or hanging out with people who do drugs. Why don't you get a job?"

"Shut up," Walter stated abruptly. "Amos is my friend. I don't think bad things about him, and neither does my mom."

"That's OK," Amos said, feeling a little tired. "You don't have to take up for me, Walter. The Bible says that if we follow Jesus, He will be our defender. He asked me to love this neighborhood and everybody in it, *especially* the lost sheep: the people who don't know Him yet. So that's what I'm trying to do."

"I'm outta here." Samuel stood up and brushed off the dirt. "I'm hungry anyway. When you want to play for keeps, come find me." He put his marbles in his pocket and ran off.

"Still wanna play?" Walter asked Jesse and Amos.

"Sure," said Jesse smiling, "If it isn't for keeps."

As the two boys and Amos knelt again to their game, Amos breathed a word to his Boss: "If they only knew what it means to *live* for keeps, Lord. If they only knew."

Chapter Twenty-Six

Lito was still brooding. The rest of his visit with Marta and Tania had been peaceful, but that voice continued to play in his head: "She's yours. Go get her. She's *yours*." He had looked around at his room at the center when he returned, and he knew that Tania couldn't live with him there. Some of the single women at the center had their children with them, but there were no single fathers. And anyway there was only one bed, and he would have to see that she got to school and was fed properly. He had no idea how to do all of that and little desire to learn. He went to bed troubled and woke up in a black humor.

As he mulled, he walked towards the shop. He wished he could get Tania off his mind. He wished his thoughts were more fatherly. Wishes, wishes . . what was that his grandmother used to say: "If wishes were horses, beggars would ride." He was sure she wasn't talking about *this* type of wish! And yet, how could he do it? He shook his head as if to shake water from his hair. Work would take his mind off this problem. He'd go out for a beer with the guys afterwards, and forget all about Tania.

As he turned the corner, his heart sank. Amos! He was the *last* person he wanted to see! Just what he needed right now: a conscience. But Amos was hanging around in front of the shop, obviously waiting for him. The other guys greeted them as they entered the lot filled with sick vehicles awaiting their greasy nursing. Lito gave a half-hearted hello.

"Hey, Amos."

"Hey, brother!" Amos grabbed him in a bear hug. Lito's arms remained limp and straight. "How's everything going?"

"Oh, great," was the response. "Don Chico says I can call myself a mechanic now, and he gave me a little raise."

"That's incredible, man!" Amos was genuinely excited. "God is so good! And I've got some great news for you, too!"

"Oh?"

"Yeah. I was talking with the director of the center this morning, and he says you're doing so well that it's time to transition out of rehab and into a place of your own. We don't have many people who get to that point, and you did it in less than a year. Praise the Lord!"

"You're making me leave?" Lito had not considered this possibility. He felt a pit in his stomach.

"Not right off or anything," Amos tried to say cheerfully. He could see that this bit of news was a blow to the young man. "We'll start looking around for a good place for you to live – maybe someplace near the shop. Maybe one of the guys knows of a place."

"I don't need your help," Lito said gruffly. "First you drag me there against my will, and now you're kicking me out. Some Christians." He tried to push by Amos.

"Now don't start talking like that," Amos responded sincerely, putting a hand on Lito's shoulder.

"Get out of my way," Lito said with his head down. "I guess since I didn't become a super Christian, you don't want me around there anymore. No problem. I'll get my stuff and get out."

"You've got it all wrong," Amos urged. "It's just that you're off drugs now and working, and the director has people knocking the door down for a place to stay."

"Why don't you give them *your* bed then? How long have *you* been there?"

Amos didn't have a ready reply.

"See? If I prayed and preached like you do, nobody would kick me out. But since I don't, you need to get somebody else in there!" Lito was getting worked up now. "I'm not good enough to live with you Christians, am I?"

Suddenly the answer came to Amos.

"You're right," he said gently. "You have more right to be there than I do. You can have my space. It's time I moved out." Again he attempted to place a hand on Lito's shoulder.

"I've been there long enough," he added. "Thank you for showing me that." There was no sarcasm in his voice, only love.

Lito felt his anger dissipating as it came face-to-face with this unashamed, naked humility.

"Hey, I can't take your place. Hell, *nobody* could take *your* place. You just caught me off-guard, that's all."

"But you're right just the same," Amos insisted. "The director said to tell you that he needs your space in two weeks, but I'll tell him to take mine instead. That makes a lot more

214

sense. I've been there longer than you have. It isn't fair for you to go before me."

Now Lito was really feeling the pain of his words. He couldn't imagine the rehab center without Amos. Amos' cheerfulness lifted people when they were down. Sometimes in the evenings Amos' strong, joyful voice could be heard all over the center as he belted out a praise song. He was always praying with people and sharing Scripture. He would bring anybody in from the cold, just like he did with Lito. Truth was, he didn't know if he wanted to stay at the center if Amos left. He didn't want to be like Amos, but he liked being around him. He couldn't explain it, but now he had created this dilemma and didn't know how to get out of it.

"Hey, let's talk about it later," he blurted. "I gotta get to work."

"OK," Amos agreed. There was a sadness in his voice. "Have a blessed day in Jesus!"

"Yeah, you too," Lito said dully, looking at the ground. He took Amos' outstretched hand for a moment, and then shuffled into the shop.

The unlikely prophet was left standing alone at the entrance to Don Chico's business. People walked past him to work, school, daily shopping. He didn't see any of them. Once again he had reached a turn in the road. While he knew that Lito's words were spiteful and hard, he also knew that God sometimes used those words to direct His people. Did God want him to leave the shelter? Where would he go? He began to breathe a prayer:

"Lord Jesus, were You talking to me through Lito? Is it time for me to move on? You know I want to be wherever You want me to be. Maybe You want me to be living out here in the neighborhood, or in another neighborhood. I really love the folks right here, but if you have something else for me to do, I'm ready. I'm so thankful for Your love, Father! Open my ears to hear Your voice clearly. Make Your will my will. Amen."

Chapter Twenty-Seven

A late October deluge that threatened never to exhaust itself emptied the heavens and ignored the banks of rivers and lakes, toppling latrines and oaks, sending defenseless homes into the weeds below as if they were abandoned paper mache projects. Schools began to fill with sodden refugees, and those who enjoyed the security of a dry house sallied out only to buy food or report to work. Most schools were closed, especially in the rural areas that depended upon commuting teachers and tended to be more like sieves than shelters. Farmers watched their livelihood drown, communities with fragile connections to paved roads became isolated as their toy bridges washed out, and the downtown Tegucigalpa marketplace flooded to waist-high levels. Garbage, merchandise, and an occasional body drifted toward the Choluteca river which was charging with a vengeance towards the southern bay, mounting low-lying edifices and scores of docks and boats on its surging back.

Tania picked her way carefully down the incline to her house. Marta had sent her to the pulperia for some coffee and sugar to take the edge off the chill in their bones caused by the gray days and steady rains. The sloppy walkway had become even more treacherous as debris and mud had loosened most of the rocks, making the steps indiscernable and every footfall risky. But the surefooted waif looked almost like a tiny ballerina as she cautiously but quickly tiptoed downwards, holding the coffee tightly in one fist. She was cold and soaked through, but Marta had lit a fire and she would soon be stripped down, wrapped like a mummy in an old blanket, sipping on steaming sweet coffee. Her stomach growled. Lito had not appeared on Thursday and

Marta had not sold any clothes lately, so their meals consisted primarily of tortillas and rice.   Still, although her grandmother complained when her grandson didn't arrive, Tania was relieved. She preferred hunger to his visits.   Anita sometimes invited her to share a pot of soup or beans and some conversation.   Lightning had knocked out a transformer three days earlier, so there was no electricity in La Cantera, but that was little hardship since they had only two lightbulbs on their property, one inside the house, and one above the back door to illuminate the path to the latrine. Marta and Anita cooked on woodstoves which were little more than adobe shells with a hole for the wood underneath and a space for the pots on top.   In fact, Tania had never seen an electric stove.   She had never flushed a toilet or taken a hot shower or warm bath.   At school a community worker would appear to give a talk about how important it was to boil water for drinking, and that during the cooler months of the year young children should be bathed in warm water.   But Dona Marta and most of her neighbors could not waste precious wood on such luxuries; water was only heated if it contained something edible. "Coffee socks" were used so that not a drop of water or grain of coffee was wasted.   Coffee was the Honduran's mainstay, a necessary ingredient of every meal, offered to guests, and consumed at all hours.   Strong and sweet was the preferred taste. Tania had been drinking coffee since she was a toddler.

As Tania tripped down to the waiting warmth, she passed a small stone duplex which belonged to a pair of sisters, Catalina and Serafina.   Both women were elderly by La Cantera standards, well into their sixties, and both suffered from diabetes.   Catalina had been widowed at a young age and had never borne children. Serafina had lived in *union libre* with a series of men, but had only two daughters living.   The rest had died in childbirth or earlier. They had raised the girls together.   Other family members lived

219

nearby. They were a hard, bitter group, the Fonseca family, known for their brawls and backbiting. Catalina, perhaps because she had no husband or children, or because she was small and sickly bore the brunt of everyone's wrath. She rarely tried to fight back, and because she was the only one who had steady employment, there was relentless competition to wrest from her the tiny salary she received from a neighborhood ministry. As Tania glanced at the shabby dwelling, she remembered a recent conversation between Marta and Anita.

"It was like a *velorio*," Anita had whispered loudly, as if frightened of arousing negative spirits. "They had her wrapped in a sheet and lying on a bed underneath a big crucifix with a rosary tied around her hand. *Except she wasn't dead.*"

"What?!" Marta exclaimed. "Where? Where did they have her?"

"In her own house!" Anita responded. "It's only two little rooms, you know. There was nothing in the front room except chairs against the walls and then there was Catalina lying under the crucifix. She wasn't moving. I thought she had died, but Serafina said she wasn't dead yet."

"Was it her diabetes?" Marta asked. "I didn't hear that she was sick."

"That's just it!" Anita's face was pale with the memory. "She wasn't sick. Some of the people from the ministry where she has worked all these years came to the house. Apparently Catalina resigned about six months ago. She had saved some money in the co-op, and they also gave her severance pay. Anyway, she told them she was going to open a little pulperia in her house with the money she'd saved."

"But she didn't," Marta remarked. "There's no pulperia there."

"No, that's just it," Anita interrupted. "The ministry people thought she was fine, and didn't know anything until somebody went to their office and told them Catalina was dying. They went to her house right away, and the family said that the doctors said she had a terrible stomach infection and there was nothing left to be done. But one of the Christians from the ministry asked to see the medical papers."

Marta was deeply engaged now. "And?" she said. "What did they say?"

"Serafina told them that the papers got lost."

"That woman is a witch!" Marta retorted.

"So the ministry guy went right up to Catalina. Catalina hadn't moved a muscle the whole time I was there. She looked like a mummy. But the man leaned down really close to her face and asked her if she wanted to see a doctor. He kind of shouted it. And Catalina just barely nodded her head."

"*Dios mio!* She could hear!" shouted Marta. "She knew everything that was going on! Poor Catalina!"

"The man took out his cell phone and called somebody, and within an hour the firemen came with an ambulance and carried her away."

"What did Serafina do?" Marta asked.

"Oh, she cried and carried on and said she hoped they could help her poor *viejita*, and that they had done everything a poor person can do.   Nobody paid her much mind.   Everybody hates her."

"Where is Catalina now?   Is she in the hospital?"

"No!" Marta smiled.   "At the clinic they ran some tests, and it turned out she didn't have *anything*.   She was dehydrated and anemic, but there wasn't any infection at all!   So the ministry took her somewhere to take care of her, and they say she's doing fine.   They're saying that the family was starving her to death because they had taken her money and wanted the house, too. They'd already divided up what little she had."

"*Malvados!*" pronounced Marta, as if she were the epitome of goodness.

"Serafina denies everything, of course, but there's talk that the ministry is going to help Catalina get her things back."

"Good for them!   Sometimes the Christians actually do some good," Marta complimented generously.   She had never been reluctant to accept gifts from God's people.   "I hope the whole family goes to jail or hell or both," she added, proving that the accompanying lessons about mercy and forgiveness had continued to miss their mark.

Tania had been watching television as this conversation began, but soon found her attention diverted to the plight of poor Catalina.   She sympathized with the helplessness of the old woman, and was almost moved to tears to hear of her dramatic rescue.   When, oh when, she wondered, would somebody rescue *her*?   Maybe if she stopped eating, they would wrap her in a sheet and put her on a table to die.   She doubted that the mother who had heartlessly given her away would come even then. Sometimes she couldn't tell if the pain in her heart when she

222

thought of her mother was love or hate; she only knew that it gnawed relentlessly, never allowing her a moment of contentment. She picked up the television remote and turned up the volume so that she couldn't hear the rest of Anita and Marta's conversation. Sadly, it did not silence the unheard cries of her loneliness nor the whimpering baby that still longed to be held possessively, protectively, passionately. Ignoring the clamor within, Tania turned her eyes to the noisy box on the ancient pine table. *"If wishes were horses, beggars would ride,"* Marta often mumbled. The little girl vowed that she would never wish or pray again, and the dark spaces deepened their hold on her battered heart.

Chapter Twenty-Eight

The constant rains seemed to have dampened even the job market. Santita felt that she had been to every hospital, clinic and doctor's office in Tegucigalpa. She had left dozens of resumes, asked hopefully at innumerable front desks, combed the newspapers and begged God. She had only been invited to two interviews and was beginning to believe that Dr. Pineda had followed through on his threat to make it impossible for her to find employment. Two weeks had gone by since she and Juanita had made their pact to hope and believe, and her spirits were waning. She couldn't get Tania out of her mind, especially at night. The central figure in her dreams was an ill-dressed, thin little girl tearfully calling, "Mami! Mami, where are you?" She often awoke in a sweat, crying herself. "I'm coming," she would mumble, still half asleep, "I'm coming, Tania. Hold on."

One morning after such a dream she decided to give in to the desperation, and instead of putting on her job application outfit, grabbed some jeans and a blouse, quickly laced her tennis shoes, and set off for the place called La Cantera.

The bus pulled into a side street next to a busy place called 'Pollo Vaquero,' and Santita stepped into the familiar mixture of smells: chicken, dust, sweat, smoke. Her own neighborhood was similar to this one, and she knew better than to stand around like the stranger she was. As soon as her soles hit the dirt, she walked briskly to the main drag, and following the description given by Juanita started walking deeper into the sprawling colony, downhill toward the river. After a couple of blocks she stopped a wiry boy carrying an empty plastic bin that had no doubt earlier been filled with tortillas to sell.

"Is this the way to La Cantera?" she asked.

"Straight ahead," he mumbled, hardling looking up. He had probably been wrested out of a makeshift bed at three a.m. to take corn to the mill. His mother and perhaps a sister or two would have had the fire ready at four o'clock or so to get the tortillas going in time for their regular customers' breakfast. It was still early when Santita arrived in Flor, and children were filling the road on their way to the seven o'clock classes. They would finish at noon and another group would attend the afternoon *jornada* until five o'clock. Santita hoped the tortilla boy was in this group, although she knew that many children did not attend school because the profits from selling tortillas barely provided food for the family table. There was nothing left over for study.

As Santita began the rocky, downhill path into La Cantera she thanked God that her parents had been able to provide her with an education, and even though she had not been able to find a job yet, she lacked nothing essential. She prayed that she would be able to do the same for her own little girl one day. At the thought of Tania, her heart began to beat quickly. She was filled with anxiety, and yet she could not live a day longer without confronting the fears that robbed her of sleep and peace of mind.

Once she was clearly inside La Cantera she approached a young woman who was sweeping the ground in front of a neatly kept house.

"A friend told me that there is a woman named Dona Marta who sells inexpensive used clothes. Would you happen to know where she lives?" She tried to act casual and friendly, and placed her sweating palms on her hips.

"Everybody knows old Marta," the woman said drily. "She lives right down there. You'll see a sign on the door about the clothes." As she talked her eyes traveled up and down Santita's body, taking in every detail of her clothes, shoes, hair and skin.

"Old Marta doesn't get a lot of business anymore, especially from outside right around here." The tone wasn't friendly. "Do you live in Flor?"

"Thank you for steering me in the right direction," Santita responded evasively. "Have a good day!"

In a matter of moments she was in front of the house. Tania's house. She was trembling. At that very moment her cell phone rang, and she gasped loudly. Sending a shaking hand into her pocket, she felt for the button that would silence the insistent melody.

"Who's out there?" demanded a voice on the other side of the door. Santita was sure the voice belonged to Dona Marta, and although she had expected rejection, the icy tone set her nerves even more on edge.

"I want to talk with Dona Marta," she ventured. In her own ears her voice sounded weak and shrill. She was quite sure that the old woman would eat her alive.

"For what?" Good question, Santita thought. For what, indeed. Her desperation to see Tania had not waned, but she had no courage and no plan.

"Can I talk to you, please?" she blurted, and immediately realized her mistake. The truth would never get her an audience with Tania's bitter guardian. Santita felt suddenly weary and her head began to spin. She leaned against the rotten wall and began to weep.

"Who are you?" On the other side of the door Marta was struggling with fear and curiosity. The voice was that of a stranger, and she never opened the door to a stranger without a full explanation of the visit. But she could hear the sobs of the visitor, and her curiosity was driving her to unlock the fragile door and solve the mystery.

"Tell me who you are and I'll unlock the door!" she commanded.

Santita was unable to respond. Seven years of emotion were washing over her as she struggled to remain erect, and words would not take shape in her mind. She breathed deeply in an effort to control the tears. She heard the latch on the gate click. Through a tiny opening the voice spoke again.

"Speak up, girl! I'm Dona Marta! What do you want?"

"I'm Tania's mother," she whispered. "I have to see her."

This time it was the old woman who gasped. Tania's mother! She had long ago stopped wondering if Santita would ever come looking for the baby. In her mind the girl had handed over Tania and never looked back. But here she was, wanting to see the daughter that Marta had fed and clothed all these years. Marta felt a rage building inside her. She slammed the gate as fear and bitterness surged upwards.

"You will *never* see her!" shrieked the old woman. "*Never!!* Do you hear me?"

Santita slid to the ground in a daze. Isn't this exactly what she had expected?

"If you ever come around here again, I'll have your throat cut!" The venom in this threat was palpable. Santita felt a cold, invisible knife against her neck.

"I curse you! I curse you! Curses on your family! Curses on your womb! Go to the devil!" The witch was rising now, her voice rhythmically chanting the *maldicciones.* "The fires of hell on your house! Poison and death! Sickness and suffering!"

As the wailing rose into the morning mist, Santita stumbled off and away from the horrible stench of Marta's encantations. She could see nothing clearly, and her body seemed to be moving at someone else's command. She never knew how she reached the bus again, but as it rocketed down Blvd. Fuerzas Armadas, she let her head fall back against the hard metal of the seat support, and stared through the window at nothing at all.

Chapter Twenty-Nine

"She was *here*, I'm telling you!"

Lito had come for his weekly visit, and Marta was diving into her news immediately so that they could discuss it before Tania got home from school.

"But it's been seven years," Lito protested. "Why would she wait so long? Are you sure it was her?"

"She said so herself," was the retort. "She said she wanted to see Tania."

"Well what did you do?" Lito asked. "What did Tania do?"

"Tania had already gone to school," Marta replied flatly. "She wasn't even here. And I didn't open the gate. I told her to go away or I'd cut her throat. And she did. She's never had any backbone. She ran off like an injured dog."

"What if she comes back?" Lito was concerned now. He had not considered the possibility that Santita would return looking for Tania. He did not want her interfering. The sexual fantasies had become obsessive, and he had no intention of letting Tania get away.

"I don't know," responded Marta. "What if she shows up at Tania's school? What if she just decides to snatch her? She knows where we live, and she seems desperate. I've been walking with Tania to school and back since Monday when she showed up here, but we don't have any place to go. She could come back with more people and just take her."

"Tania will have to come with me," Lito announced suddenly. His blood was rising at the thought of having the girl all to himself. "I'll get my own place. They want me to move out of the safehouse anyway. Santita doesn't know where I live, and she'll never find us."

"And what will she do about school? Who will take care of her? You work all day every day."

"She practically takes care of herself anyway," Lito charged. "She knows how to cook. I can put her in school where I live. She'll be fine."

"You'll need two beds. A father can't share a bed with his daughter," Marta snapped.

"I'll get something," Lito blurted. "I'll get those beds that fold up. I can buy stuff along and along. It's time I got my own place."

"Well, I don't want to let her go. I'm used to having her here. But that Santita could come back around any day, and if Tania sees her and knows who she is, who can tell what she will do? I guess it's the only solution, at least for now."

Lito was trying hard to mask his excitement about sharing a home with Tania. He had seen her face on the bodies of the photos he kept hidden under his mattress. She was often the object of his sexual fantasies.

"You know you'll have to get a transfer from her school to one in your neighborhood," Marta instructed. "And you'll have to make sure her uniform is washed and ready every day, and make her a snack. Hey! Are you listening to me?"

"Of course," Lito rejoined. "School, uniform, snack. I can do all that. Don't worry. You'll see. I'll go right now and find a *cuartito*. The sooner she's out of here, the better."

"You haven't even had lunch! Or seen Tania!"

"I only get one day off, *Abuela*. I have to get moving so I can be ready to take Tania as soon as possible."

"I guess you're right," Marta sighed. "Go on then! Try to find a place with women nearby and not a bunch of drunkards. Someplace *sano*. She's going to be by herself sometimes, and you know how a lot of men are – they don't care how old or how young."

"I'll take good care of her. You can come and see for yourself." Lito's hand was on the door, his mind racing. *You see? I told you she'd be yours one day!*

As Lito pulled the door open, Tania raced inside. Although she had obviously been excited about something, the sight of Lito stopped her short and the smile disappeared from her face.

"There you are!" Lito said cheerfully. "We've been talking about you!"

Tania moved close to Marta and mumbled a pathetic hello.

"Don't you even have a hug for your father?" Marta said, shoving her towards Lito. "He has to leave early today, so go give him a proper greeting."

The wary child shuffled across the short distance to Lito and let her arm reach his shoulder as he bent down to hug her.

"That wasn't much of a hug," he protested, "But that's all right. I have to go anyway. See you soon. Your grandmother will tell you everything."

Once alone, Marta turned to stir the soup which had been left forgotten on the burner.

"What happened?" she queried. "You looked like you had something to say when you came in the door."

"We're having a special program at school," Tania answered quickly. "And the teacher asked me to be in it."

"That's nice, but you won't be able to do it."

"Why not? It won't cost anything."

"Because you're not going to that school anymore."

"What? I'm not going to school? Why?"

"Because you're moving, that's why. You'll be in a different school in a different neighborhood."

"Where are we going?" Tania was truly concerned now. She had never lived anywhere else, and although she had few happy memories from La Cantera, she knew everyone and how to survive.

"*We*'re not going anywhere. *You* are." Marta said these words without turning around. Although she had agreed with Lito on the move, she was feeling unexpectedly emotional about sending Tania away with him.

Tania had come over to the stove and was trying to look into Marta's face.

"What are you talking about? I don't understand."

"Your father is getting his own place. He has a good job. He can take better care of you than I can, so you're going to live with him. It's all settled."

Tania felt dizzy. It's all *settled*?

"When?" she murmured.

"As soon as possible. Maybe this weekend. We'll start getting your things together."

"I don't want to go." The words were weak yet firm.

"I know you don't," Marta assured her. "But it's the best thing."

"I don't want to go." Tania was pulling on Marta's blouse, trying to get her to look into her eyes. "Please, *abuela*. Don't send me away."

At this Marta's rusty heart creaked ever so slightly. She knew the pain of being left behind, and suspected that it was very much like the pain of being sent away.

"I'll come visit you," she said, placing a bony hand on the girl's head. "You'll be fine. You'll see. Lito wants to take care of you now."

Silent tears were falling on the dirt floor. It was *settled*.

"Why don't you run over and watch television with Anita for awhile?" Marta suggested. Tania's grief was unsettling, and she didn't know how to respond.

"Yes. All right." As Tania walked heavily and slowly out of the room, Marta sank into a chair and sighed. She would be all alone again. All of her thoughts were on her own life of misery and loss. Why did that Santita have to come looking for Tania and spoil everything? She knew that entrusting Lito with the girl was unwise, even reckless, but what other choice did she have? Choices belonged to the rich, not poor old women like her. As she sank deeper and deeper into the chasm of self-pity, a shrill voice startled her.

"Open up right now or I'll know this door down!" a very familiar voice was shouting. It was Anita, and Marta had never imagined her in such a state.

"I'm coming!" she shouted back. "Stop screaming!"

She had barely pulled the latch back when Anita burst through the entrance, pushing the door with one hand and dragging a tearful Tania with the other.

"What do you mean sending this poor child to live with that demon?!?" she demanded. "Have you lost your mind?!?"

"He isn't a demon. He's her father," Marta replied sharply. "It's for her own good and it's none of your business!"

"None of my business!?" Anita face was inflamed with rage, and beads of sweating were forming at her brow. "She's like family to me! Where do you think she comes when she can't stand it anymore? And with good reason – her own grandmother turning her over to a drug addict and pervert! I won't allow it! You hear? I won't allow it!"

"You won't allow it?!" Now Marta was enraged. "And how exactly do you plan to stop me? You're a coward, Anita Perdomo! You're spineless, a nothing and a nobody!"

While the two women exchanged insults, Tania stood still and wept quietly. She knew that her grandmother would win, and she had already begun to retreat even further inside herself. She had no other protection, only whatever emotional walls she could erect herself.

"But why?" Anita finally asked, beginning to weep. "She's fine here with us. *Why* are you sending her away?"

"Because Lito has a job. He can buy her things. He can feed her properly and send her to school in a decent uniform and pair of shoes."

"That's it?" Anita was truly incredulous. "You're sending her to *him* because he can buy nicer shoes?"

"*Callase!*" Marta hissed. "Shut up and go home! My head hurts. It's all settled, and there's nothing anybody can do about it. Go home. Tania, go to your room." Marta had her hand on Anita's hip and was pressuring her towards the street.

"I don't understand," Anita murmured. "I've always known you were a hard woman, but *this*." She shook her head and let herself be shoved firmly out the door. "May God forgive you for this, Marta."

"What does God have to do with it?" Marta snapped. "When has He ever done anything for Tania since the day I snatched her from those baby-stealers! He's turned his back on us, so all that's left is to do the best we can."

By now Anita was in the corridor of stairs, but instead of turning toward her house she spun around and looked Marta directly in the eyes.

"You are a wicked woman without an ounce of love in your wretched heart. May God forgive you because I don't think I ever will."

Marta blanched as the heartfelt words penetrated the remnant of conscience in her dark soul. As tears threatened to come into the light of day, she cursed suddenly and spat in Anita's stricken face.

"Go away. Go away and *never* speak to me or Tania again. You are dead to us."

Anita dug an ancient rag out of her apron pocket and wiped the venom and tears from her cheeks. Without looking back, she trudged the short distance to her home, Tania's refuge.

"Lord, have mercy," she whispered. "Good Lord in Heaven, have mercy on us all."

Chapter Thirty

A heavy fog had settled over the Parque Central, and although there was no breeze and it was still eighty degrees, people pulled caps over their ears and sweaters across their shoulders.   December had just begun, and with it the slightly lower temperatures and holiday atmosphere.   The stores were decorated for Christmas, and shoppers crowded the park, streets, and businesses.   Juanita and her mother were ferreting bargains, entering store after store negotiating the lowest prices, enjoying the cheerful chaos of the season.   Juanita had not heard from Santita in several days, and assumed that she was continuing her job search, something she herself planned to begin immediately after Christmas.

"I wish I could help you, Mom," she offered plaintively as her mother made another purchase.   "I should be working.   I've been out of school for months now!"

"You'll be working soon enough," was the soothing response.   "And then I'll have to make an appointment to see you! Let's just enjoy these last few weeks together.   The grind of a job will come soon enough, you'll see."

Juanita sighed and put both arms around the ample waist of this dear soul who had sacrificed so much for the family she adored.

"I love you, mami," she whispered into one ear.

"I love you, too, *mi amor*."

"And I love you even more now that you don't make those awful dresses and skirts for me to wear!"

Both women laughed aloud. They often thanked God for liberating them from the legalism which had demanded discomfort and even shame. Not that they never wore dresses-- today they had each bought a special dress for Christmas. But they had also looked at pants, shirts, tennis shoes, high heels, makeup--everything except bikinis! Their God looked at the heart, not the outward appearance, and He had given them permission to expand their wardrobe.

"Isn't it time for lunch yet?" Juanita queried. "All this shopping has given me a huge appetite!"

"What do you feel like eating?" her mother asked, wading her hands through stacks of jeans on a sale table.

"Let's go to the bakery," Juanita suggested. "We can get *empanadas* and fruit custard, and then buy some rolls to take home."

"Good idea! Come on, let's get out of here before I spend our lunch money."

As they moved towards the open door of the shop, both women automatically tightened their hold on their handbags, sliding them firmly under one arm, and wrapping the straps around their wrists. Thieves were rampant in Tegucigalpa every day, but during Christmas one had to be extra careful. Even in broad daylight on a busy street a cry would ring out as someone was surprised by the sudden strike of a delinquent. Juanita clutched her bag under one arm and took her mother's arm with the other. They steeled their faces and readied themselves for the open sidewalk.

Despite the dangers, Tegucigalpa was charming during the Christmas season. Music blared from the stores, mostly Christmas music this time of year, some of it a disco version, all of it too loud and with plenty of static. Still, the music and the decorations and the general cheer of the populace lifted Juanita's spirits. As they approached their favorite bakery, the smell of fresh bread wafted out to welcome them, and their stomachs rumbled a friendly response. Juanita noticed a dirty boy leaning against the window as they went in and made a mental note to buy an extra piece of pastry to give him on the way out.

It didn't take long to place their order. They had been here many times before and knew what they liked. They settled into a familiar table near the sweetbreads, placed their purchases carefully under the table between their legs, and sipped their sodas through straws as they waited for their lunch. Within moments a young girl placed steaming chicken turnovers and large fruit custards in front of them. After a quick prayer, the two women turned their attention to the midday meal. Juanita noticed that the boy was staring at them hungrily.

"I'm going to get something for that little boy at the door," she said, rising from the table and walking towards the cashier. She purchased a large *pan con frijoles* and carried it to the malnourished child.

"*Gracias,*" he said with feeling, and in three bites he had devoured the entire sandwich. Juanita had not even returned to her chair as he gulped down the final bite.

"Did you see that?" she asked her mother. "He must be starving! Poor little guy."

"At least he's begging instead of stealing," responded the kind woman between bites. "Have you noticed how many children are on the streets this year? I'm sure there are many more than last year. Lots of people are out of work, and their children are hungry."

"I wish I could do more to help," Juanita sighed. "Giving one little boy a piece of bread doesn't seem like much at all."

"Someone else will give him another piece of bread," her mother smiled. "If we each do our part, then fewer children will suffer. Nobody can do everything for everybody, even somebody with a heart as big as yours."

"Can we take him to one of the used clothing stores and get him a change of clothes?" Juanita asked. "It wouldn't cost much. Look at those rags he's wearing! And barefoot, too!"

"Wonderful idea, *hija*!" Mother and daughter were gathering their bags already in anticipation of this change in plans. "Just don't tell your father! He'll say we're dressing up Tegucigalpa's delinquents!" While the order was given with a twinkle in her eyes, the good wife knew her husband well, and she hoped that Juanita would keep their secret.

At the door Juanita was explaining to the young beggar their plan. He nodded his head vigorously and grabbed her hand. At this show of affection, her heart melted even more. One day, she promised herself, she would do something to help more children in need. Surely God would help her. She knew that He loved these precious children.

"Come on!" she said cheerfully. "I know a great place!"

The bakery was located in a popular part of the city directly in front of the national cathedral. It was a wide pedestrian walkway filled with street vendors and holiday shoppers. As they strolled towards the clothing store, Juanita asked the boy his name.

"Miguel," he said shyly, his hand nervously squeezing hers.

Juanita decided not to ask him the questions that were burning in her mind about his home and parents. How did a handsome guy like this end up on the streets? He seemed so innocent and timid. Many of her friends were afraid of street children, but how could anybody fear this small, tattered boy?

They were passing a camera shop where huge speakers had been placed outside the front door. Disco holiday music blared, and a skinny Santa was dancing along for the amusement of the shoppers. Juanita and her mother tried to move away from the performance, but instead were pushed even closer by people who wanted a better look. Suddenly Juanita heard a cry and realized that Miguel's hand was no longer in hers. To her horror, she saw that he had been grabbed by the disco Santa who was clutching the boy's shirt with one hand and boxing his ears with the other.

"Chico maldito!" accused the evil Santa, who sneered while smacking the boy brutally. "Where have you been?" Juanita and her mom were paralyzed until Miguel was swung around at an angle which allowed them to get a glimpse of his pained, tear-streaked face.

"Hey, you!" Juanita heard herself yelling. "Let him go!"

"Yeah, let him go!" somebody else shouted, and the crowd started moving towards the fake Santa, who had been so intent on his punishment that he'd forgotten that he was surrounded. He lifted his hand for another punch when Miguel wriggled out of the fragile shirt and scooted quickly behind Juanita.

"Give him back!" the moldy Santa ordered. "He's mine!" But as he bolted toward Juanita, a strong hand grabbed his collar from behind. An obese security guard who had been passively watching the encounter had suddenly intervened.

"You're on the clock, remember? Start dancing or you're fired!"

The two men began to exchange words, but Juanita had put her arm around Miguel's shoulder and was leading him quickly down the peatonal. Her mother had the boy's other hand. As soon as they were safely away, they sat on a public bench to catch their breaths.

"Who *was* that?" Juanita asked Miguel.

"My *padrastro*," he whimpered. "He moved in with my mother. He's always hitting her and us." The tears began again. "I hate him."

"Why doesn't your mother tell him to go away?" asked Juanita's mother. "Surely she doesn't want him hurting you."

"She just screams and cries," the boy explained. "And then after he goes out she says she can't make him leave or we won't have any food."

"So that's why you're begging," Juanita added. "You're afraid to stay home, and you want to take food home so that your mom will tell that awful man to leave."

Miguel just nodded.   Juanita pulled him close against her. He was too young to have so many complex problems, she thought. Not fair. She thought of Tania and wondered how God could allow children to suffer so.   But it wasn't God, she protested immediately to herself! *People* caused children to suffer! She was sure that God was very sad to see how His littlest lambs were treated.

"Well!" she announced cheerfully. "Let's go shopping!" She mopped Miguel's face with her blouse, took him possessively by the hand, and she and her mother marched him toward "Ropa Americana Javier" for an outward transformation.   How they would let him go back to the street after that she didn't know, but for the next hour they would turn their backs on his cruel reality and bury themselves in the temporary refuge offered by the local merchants.

Chapter Thirty-One

Lito had never been so focused. After leaving Marta's, he went straight to the auto shop and asked Don Chico and the other mechanics if they knew of a place he could rent. He didn't mention Tania. He told them that it was time for him to move out of the safehouse and into his own place, and that he wanted to live where his privacy would be respected, a decent place without drug addicts and gang members. Don Chico laughed and said there weren't many *cuarterias* like that in Flor del Campo, but he gave him a name and directions, admonishing him to slow down and take his time. But an almost supernatural energy impelled Lito, and he walked the neighborhood all afternoon and well into the evening. He looked at a dozen rooms, but none of them pleased him. The living quarters were too close together, the people nearly on top of one another sharing bathrooms and cookstoves. He wanted to be left alone to do as he pleased--with Tania.

He trudged up the stairs of the safehouse tired and discouraged. As usual Amos was waiting for him with a slap on his back and a big smile.

"How was your day, *hermanito*?" he asked joyfully. "God bless you!"

Lito responded by asking if there was anything to eat.

"I saved you a plate," Amos assured him. Lito never ceased to be amazed by Amos' thoughtfulness, rarely acknowledged and never returned.

"Thanks," he said without meaning it. He was hungry, but he almost wished that Amos would forget about him every now and then. Still, when the plate of beans and eggs was set in front of him, he ate with gusto. Amos took his usual seat across the table.

"I've been looking for a place to live," he said quietly. "You were right. It's time for me to get out of this place and move on."

"Guess that makes two of us," Lito responded without looking up. "I'm getting out of here, too."

"But you don't have to," Amos protested. "If I go, you can stay."

"I don't want to stay," Lito grumbled. "I want a place of my own and some privacy. I'm tired of being around people all day and all night, especially people who get into my business." These last words were spoken emphatically, and he glanced at Amos to see if he knew they were for him.

"It's not all bad to have people around," Amos remonstrated. "Especially people who care about you. When we're on our own, we don't always make the best decisions."

"I guess you're talking about how I was when you found me," Lito said, getting angry. "I'm different now! I have a job, and I'm not drinking or doing drugs anymore. Maybe I'm not the greatest Christian like you are, but I'm ready to get out from under the pressure here to be a saint and just live like a regular guy."

"Have you found a place to live?" Amos asked gently.

"Not yet," Lito admitted. "I went all over today, but I didn't find anything I like for what I can pay."

"It's not easy in a neighborhood like this," Amos acknowledged. "People are suspicious of single men, too. They'd rather have a family, or a single woman or single mother. We're considered either dangerous or strange."

"There's nothing strange about me!" Lito retorted. His emotional response surprised Amos, and troubled him.

"Nobody said you're strange," he offered.

Lito realized his mistake and controlled his discomfort. He always felt as if Amos were staring right through him seeing who he really was, reading his thoughts and judging them.

"Yeah, sorry," he said. "I'm just frustrated about coming up empty. I'm in a hurry to move."

"Why are you in a hurry?" Amos asked. "Nobody is pressuring you."

Lito was tempted to tell him about Tania, but that dark voice urged him to hold his tongue. Amos might discover his secret.

"I'm just ready, that's all. I'm sick of this place."

A sadness crept into Amos' face as Lito expressed his complete lack of gratitude for all that the safehouse family had done for him. Lito noticed the change in Amos, but wasn't in the mood to ask forgiveness. They had helped him because they wanted to; he had never asked for help. He was clean now and had a job. He could have done that on his own without their help, or God's either for that matter. He had never needed

248

Amos and had told him so dozens of times. It wasn't his fault that Amos was hurt. He was always setting himself up, thinking people felt the same way he did. Well, he didn't and he never would, and Amos would just have to accept that.

"Hey!" Amos suddenly brightened. "I've got an idea! Why don't we get a place together?"

The dark voice in Lito rose up almost palpably at these words.

"No way!" Lito rejoined, his face growing gray and ominous. "That's the *last* thing I want! I don't want you looking over my shoulder anymore! I want to get away from you, from this!"

Amos' tender soul was pounded by the bitterness in Lito's short speech, but he also had a Companion, and his Companion held his heart firmly and reminded him that he was loved by One who would never leave or forsake him.

"I'm sorry to hear that," he was able to say lovingly. "I consider you my brother and always will. Wherever you go, I'll be praying for you."

"Save your prayers for somebody else," Lito responded. "Prayers don't work for me."

"I'm going to pray that you find a place to live where there are true followers of Christ," Amos insisted. "People who will remind you of His love and encourage you to stay on His path."

"Enough!" Lito retorted. "Good night!" He threw his dirty plate in the sink for someone else to wash and started towards his room. "Go find somebody else to save," he called over his shoulder.   The dark voice laughed, and Lito threw his head back and congratulated himself on having the last word.   He knew what he wanted, and he would dedicate his heart, soul, mind and strength to getting it as soon as possible.

Chapter Thirty-Two

"You're doing *what!?!?*"

"Sssssssshhhhhhh! People are looking at us!"

"I don't care!" Juanita responded angrily, although she lowered her voice to a loud whisper. "What in the world are you thinking? You can't do that!"

"Why not? Hundreds of people do it every day," Santita replied stoically. "And for the same reason: to work and make money instead of sitting around unemployed in Honduras."

"It's dangerous," Juanita protested. "And what about Tania?"

Santita flinched. She knew that Juanita would try to talk her out of this idea.

"She's why I'm going," Santita said softly. "I can't find a job here. How can I help Tania if I don't have anything?"

"But she's living in a very risky situation," Juanita reminded her. "You can't just run off and leave her!"

"I'm not running off!" Santita said angrily. Hadn't she struggled with all of these questions herself? And what about her own pain? Her eyes filled with bitter tears.

"Ok, Ok," Juanita soothed. "I'm sorry I got so worked up. I'm just so surprised. I never thought would go to the States illegally."

"It's not as if I'm going to ride the train or anything. My father knows a *coyote* with really good connections. He can get me there safely and quickly. It costs more, but he'll get me a job, too, and then as soon as I pay him I can start saving money to come back for Tania. Maybe we could even live in the States together. The schools are so much better up there, and since she's doing so well in school, she should have a better opportunity."

As Santita talked, the bitterness melted from her face and she seemed to be elsewhere, living her dream in her mind, Juanita and Honduras forgotten. Juanita sighed deeply. She was going to miss her friend, but it was obvious that she had made up her mind. Tania was almost eight years old, and the process Santita was describing would take years, if ever, to become a reality. Juanita knew many people who had left for the States with the same dream, but they had ended up dragging themselves home broken and destitute. However, she also had neighbors whose family members sent money regularly for food, education, and a better house. Santita was hardworking and intelligent; maybe she would be one of the few whose dream came true.

"I'll be praying for you," she said stalwartly. "I'm going to miss you like crazy, you know. You're like a sister to me. I hope you won't go off and forget all about your *amiga loquita!*" Now it was her turn to cry. She couldn't hold back the loneliness she was already feeling.

Santita reached across the table and grabbed her hand.

"Hey, if I get settled, maybe you could come up and live with me!"

253

"No," Juanita said more with a shake of her hand than with her unsteady voice. "I'd miss my mom too much. I'm such a baby. I'm not brave like you."

"I don't feel brave," Santita replied quickly. "I feel desperate. I guess that's how most people feel who leave for the States. Desperate and hopeful. In Honduras it's easy to feel desperate and almost impossible to feel hopeful. I'm going to miss my family, too, but my father thinks it's worth a try. He said he'd go himself if he were younger."

"I hope he knows that *coyote* really well!" Juanita remarked strongly. "You and I both know that they are always making promises, and then they leave their people abandoned along the way, or even worse, they deliver them to brothels or sweatshops." Juanita's face grew dark. "Or they kidnap them, get money from their families, and then kill them."

"Stop!" Santita protested. "Everybody's heard those stories, and they're true, but none of that is going to happen to me. My dad has known this guy forever, and he trusts him. He's giving him a big deposit on the trip, but I'm going to pay him back once I start working. So stop worrying!"

"It's part of my DNA," Juanita laughed. "I live to worry. Don't take that away from me. I want to worry about you so much that it keeps me on my knees begging Jesus to take good care of you!"

"Thanks," Santita said, and she meant it. Juanita was a gift from God. She was going to feel lost without her strong shoulder to lean on.

"When are you leaving?" Juanita asked softly.

"Tomorrow night."

Juanita gasped. "So soon?"

"There was one space left for this trip, and I couldn't think of a good reason to wait for the next one. We can't take anything with us anyway. And if I don't leave quickly, I might change my mind. Hey, I wanted to ask you a favor."

"Anything," Juanita assured her.

"I wrote a letter to Tania," was the unexpected reply. "There's always a chance . . . If anything happens, could you make sure she gets this?" She passed a thick, small envelope to a trembling hand.

"Don't talk like that!" pleaded Juanita. "This letter will be right here unopened when you come back!"

Santita smiled. She had always loved Juanita's optimism and faithfulness.

"Want another cup of coffee?" she asked. "It might be our last one together for a very long time."

"Why not? I won't be able to sleep until I hear you're safe and sound on the other side of the border. Bring on the caffeine!"

With that the two young friends freshened their cups and began to talk of happier days in the past. Their laughter hid the sadness in their hearts, and as they left the coffee shop arm in arm each one silently prayed for the other, ending with the plea that God might allow them to be together again one day.

"You'll let me know when you get there?" Juanita asked as they reached the bus stop.

Santita suddenly pulled her close and began to sob into her sweater. The little courage she had felt yesterday when she had agreed to leave was gone now, and all she wanted was to be close to her family and friends.

"You're going to be fine," Juanita said, trying to soothe her fears. "Jesus will be with you every step of the way."

Santita pulled away just enough to look her friend directly in the eyes. "Thank you for loving me even after you found out about Tania and everything," she blurted out. "You'll never know how much that meant – how much it still means."

"Thank *you* for teaching me how to buy jeans!" Juanita replied. She wanted to lighten the conversation, but began to weep, too. She pulled Santita to her and held her tight.

"You're the sister I always wanted. I'll never have another friend like you."

Suddenly Santita's bus was there and she was gone. Juanita took off her sweater and used it as a giant handkerchief, but nothing could wipe away the sense of futility and abandonment she was experiencing in the depths of her soul. As she boarded her own bus, she went to the One in whom she had always been comforted, mumbling aloud, "The Lord is my Shepherd, I shall not want." There were no seats, so she grabbed the overhead rail and braced herself for the short journey home.

Chapter Thirty-Three

Santita and Tania left their homes on the same day. The *coyote* knocked softly at four a.m., and a quick silent farewell was Santita's only *despedida*. Both she and her mother saved their tears for later. Lito arrived at the little house in La Cantera in mid morning. Dona Marta had packed Tania's belongings in two plastic bags. Grandmother and granddaughter were stoic and pale. By binding themselves irrevocably to Lito, they were also bound to keep the secret of Tania's fate. The tiny remnant of conscience remaining to Marta reminded her of the many times she had claimed to be Tania's savior. What was she now? The dead pain in the little girl's eyes seemed to say 'traitor,' and even the old cold woman could not deny that she had joined league with Judas.

"Well, what of it!" she told herself bitterly. "At least she won't go hungry!"

Lito picked up the bags, took Tania's limp hand and pulled her up the stairs of La Cantera and into the wider street above.

"I got us a place." He who had known little cheer himself could hardly hope to encourage the heartbroken child.

"Nice people live there. There's a school close by, and my work."

No answer.

"We'll be fine. You'll see."

As they reached the bus stop, Tania ventured one last glance backwards. Was anyone running after her? In her quiet desperation she pretended to hear her name being called:

Tania! Tania! Come back! I love you!

But all she saw were curls of heat and puffs of blown sand, and the only noise was the diesel engine of the city bus and the voice of the *cobrador*: "Las Torres! Las Torres!"

Lito sighed, picked her up with one arm while hoisting the bags with the other, and they pushed into the crowd of passengers. As the bus began to move, Tania pressed her face into the backpack of a slightly older child in front of her and began to sob. Into the backpack went years of helplessness and hopelessness; she had known all along that no one would come, that no one cared. She felt more alone than ever.

Part Three:

Ages 9-11

"The snares of death encompassed me; the pangs of Sheol laid hold on me; I suffered distress and anguish. Then I called on the name of the LORD: 'O LORD, I pray, deliver my soul!'" **(Psalm 116: 3-4)**

"My first birthday cake was white with a pink princess on top. My father bought it for me when I was eight years old. We had been sharing a cuarto for almost one year. He said a big girl like you should forget about princesses and dolls, but he got me the cake anyway. I hated living with my father; he had his own bed and I had mine, but he wanted to do things with me that were dirty and bad and sometimes it hurt and I would cry, but he would hit me and tell me to be quiet because the neighbors would hear, and did I want them to know what kind of girl I was, a shameful girl who flirted with her own father and made him do things he shouldn't. Then he would reach under his bed and take out a magazine and show me a picture and say do that to me or I will tell everybody that you are a prostitute and I'll take you to social services and leave you there, and you know what they do to pretty girls over there. I would run back to my bed and hold Rosita tight and tell her how lonely I was and that I wanted to die or run away and where was my mami, and I didn't have anybody else to talk to. My grandmother hardly ever came, and papi didn't like to go to La Cantera because I would cry for Anita and beg to stay with her, so he stopped taking me and I didn't see Anita again. She was the only one who cared about me, but she couldn't do anything to stop the pain. I just wanted to stop the pain all day in school I wanted to shout what was happening in my house, but I was afraid because my father said he would make sure I never opened my mouth again.if I said anything to anybody ever."

Chapter Thirty-Three

Santita had been gone for more than a week when Juanita finally received a call from her. She was in a safehouse in Houston, but would soon be taken to Memphis to work with other illegal immigrants in a cleaning business. She sounded tired and lonely.

"How was the trip?" Juanita asked. "Are you OK?"

"I'm fine," Santita assured her. "Just missing home and you, and wondering if I'll ever see any of you again." Her voice tapered off, and Juanita felt sure her friend was trying to hide her desolation.

"Once you start working, you'll feel better," Juanita encouraged her. "You'll make friends and start saving money to get Tania up there. Everybody says there is so much to see and do in the United States! You're going to have a great time—you'll see."

"At least when we go to Memphis I can travel more openly," Santita offered. "You wouldn't believe what we had to do to get across the border and into Houston. I never thought a person could fit into such a tiny space!"

"Hey, guess what—I have a new little brother!" Juanita suddenly interjected, wanting to change the subject. She had heard plenty of stories about the trip north, and most of them gave her nightmares.

"Your mom had a baby? Isn't she kind of old for that?" Santita queried.

"No, silly! He isn't a baby. He's eight years old. My mom and I brought him home from central park."

"A *street* child? You'd better be careful. He's probably a thief or worse."

"His name is Miguel, and he's a good boy. At first my father was upset that we brought him home, but now it's as if he's always lived with us. He's so thankful to be in a safe place. I wish you could meet him. He's very small for his age."

"Like Tania," Santita murmured. "And the same age, too."

"I thought about that," Juanita replied softly, "When he told us his age. But Miguel has never been to school. Tania is way ahead of him in that regard.   We're going to put him in school this year. He's so excited—says he's going to be a famous doctor one day."

Juanita laughed.   Santita missed that laugh.   She wished she were still sitting in the coffee shop with her friend, or shopping for clothes in the *mercado*.   The trip north had been frightening and humiliating, and she had wondered if she would become another tragic statistic.   Although she would give anything to be back in Tegucigalpa, she knew she had to go forward.   Her father had emptied his savings to get her to the States, and she wouldn't let him down.   She would work hard, pay him back, and then start her own savings account for her future with Tania.   After all, Tania would soon be eight years old!

"Hey!" Juanita insisted. "Are you still there?"

"Sorry," Santita murmured.   "I was just thinking.   And I have to hang up. It's too expensive to talk from here."

"I want to get back over to La Cantera to see how Tania is doing," Juanita offered. "I'll let you know. Hey – I'm praying for you. You're not alone!"

"Thanks," Santita replied with feeling. "You're a good friend. I have to go. Take care."

"I miss you!" Juanita called out, but the line was already dead. "Come home soon," she added quietly. "Go with God." Although she couldn't know that months would pass before she heard from Santita again, she felt the heaviness of every mile between them, but she knew that her friend needed faithful prayer more than sentimentality. She took a moment to ask the Lord to hold the lonely young woman in His arms and give her the strength she needed for the next stage of her journey.

"Who was that?" Juanita's mother had entered her room. She rarely saw anxiety on her daughter's face.

"Santita," replied Juanita quietly. "She made it to the States."

"That sounds like good news! Why the sad face?"

"She sounds lonely, and I miss her. She doesn't know anybody up there, and I can't help thinking of every terrible story I've heard about what could happen."

"Let's pray for her right now then: Lord Jesus, you love Santita. You have been with her every step of the way, and you won't leave her now. You have said that you will never forsake us, and we ask you to be very real to Santita as she begins her new life in the States. Bring people into her path who can encourage her and remind her how much you love her. Keep her safe and healthy. In your Name we pray. Amen."

"Amen. Thanks, Mom." The prayer comforted Juanita, and she determined to pray for her friend every day, and to do her best to keep an eye on Tania.

"Hey! Juanita! Let's go to the *pulpería!*" Now Miguel was in her room, too. He was waving lempiras in the air excitedly.

"Papi gave me some money! Come on! I'll treat you to a *churro!*"

Although Juanita didn't feel much like going on an outing with an excited little boy, she smiled to hear Miguel say *'papi'* so naturally. Obviously her dad had finally bonded with her new little brother.

"All right, all right! Who could refuse a date with such a handsome young gentleman?"

Miguel blushed. *Guapo?* Him? He was still unaccustomed to the constant love he received from his adoptive family. Sometimes he missed his mom and little sisters, but the nightmares from his stepfather's beatings and insults continued, and although he often awoke in the morning trembling and tired, when he opened his eyes to his new reality, he breathed a sigh of relief.

Juanita kissed him on the top of the head. Her conversation with Santita had filled her with sentimentality. She wished she could hold Tania and tell her how much her mother loved her and wanted to have her back. Santita was risking her life for a daughter who hardly knew she existed. It didn't seem fair, and yet she knew that her friend's decision years ago had led to these terrible consequences. Even a sincere, deep repentance could not turn back the clock or easily restore order and happiness. Juanita breathed deeply, wishing she could somehow accelerate the time so that Santita could be stable enough to be reunited with little Tania.

Miguel was pulling her out the door now. Her mother was laughing. There had always been so much love and joy in her own home. Somehow they had avoided tragedy and despair, and now their gratitude was spilling into the wounded soul of a small boy who had thought that no one cared.

"I want a *paleta*," Juanita informed her benefactor. "Do you have enough money for that and your *churro*, too?"

"Let's get *charramuscas!*" Miguel responded. "It's so hot today! We can bring them back and eat them in the hammock."

"Sounds good," Juanita agreed, taking his small hand in her plump one. "But later I have to go out and leave some more resumes around. I need a job. I can't depend on you and *papi* forever."

"Can I go with you?" Miguel queried. Being with Juanita was like bathing in cool water on a sweltering day. Her love was patching his heart.

"Oh, I don't think so, as much as I'd enjoy the company. I can go faster and cheaper by myself. Besides, *mami* might need some help here at the house. She loves being with you, too."

"OK." There was disappointment in the boy's voice, but staying home was hardly a punishment. Juanita's mom gave him a few light chores and then let him play with some old toys that had belonged to Julio. Julio was teaching him how to play marbles and checkers, and his new dad sometimes let him watch him work on the car. Saturdays were busy but peaceful – no more begging for food and money, and no more beatings if he came back empty-handed. Although he had never been inside a church before joining Juanita's family, he had quickly learned to give thanks to God. Who else could have given him this miracle?

"You're the man with the money. Are you going to order?" Juanita pulled Miguel out of his daydreaming. They had quickly arrived at the nearest neighborhood store.

"*Dos charramuscas de tamarindo,*" Miguel announced to the pulperia owner.

"Still with you, I see," she responded sourly, addressing Juanita. "I thought your parents had better sense. These creatures bring nothing but trouble, mark my words."

Juanita smiled. Several of their neighbors had felt compelled to warn them of the folly of their decision to keep Miguel. She put an arm around the boy's shoulders. The woman's words had destroyed his cheer immediately.

"*Dos charramuscas, por favor,*" she repeated, taking the money from Miguel's hand and pushing it through the window. "My parents and my brother and I are thankful to God for bringing Miguel to our house. He's part of our family now."

The grumpy vendor pushed the frozen treats under the barred window and grasped the payment irritably.

"Don't say nobody warned you when he burns your house down," she mumbled spitefully.

Juanita laughed out loud. The thought of such a thing was so fantastic that she found it humorous in the extreme. Miguel had been hanging his head and gripping her hand tightly, but when she laughed, he looked up at her in amazement.

"Well!" she expostulated. "I'd better post the number of the *bomberos* in every room then! Thank you for your concern." Still chuckling, she pulled Miguel away from the dark opening. Biting the corner off the plastic bag holding her homemade popsicle, she filled her mouth with icy sweetness, shaking her head and smiling.

"Go on, eat your *charramusca*," she urged Miguel, who was still bending under the burden of unjust criticism. "Don't pay any attention to that old witch. She's as sour as the lemons she sells and never has a nice word for anybody. We'll go to the other *pulperia* next time."

As she talked, she pulled Miguel closer to her and ruffled his hair.

"Never forget that God loves you and has a great plan for your life! You are precious to Him, and you are part of the Torres family now. We don't care what other people think. You belong to us now."

Miguel bit into his icy snack with tears in his eyes. He knew he didn't deserve this family's confidence and love, but he made a vow in his heart that he would never let them down.

Juanita sucked on the bag and mumbled as she walked, "Burn the house down! *Dios mio!*" No wonder there were so many lonely children in the world; they seemed to be met with indifference, criticism and abuse at every turn. She, too, made a silent vow: she would live her life for these children, by God's grace and with His help. With fresh resolve and a clarified vision for the future, she stepped into her home and determined to seek a job which would make her divine pact a reality. Miguel and Tania had led her to a special calling, and she knew that her time of rest had ended and her life's work had begun.

Chapter Thirty-Four

Interstate.   So that was what they called these endless miles of highway!   Santita was amazed by the speed of the vehicles, the absence of holes in the road, and the good behavior of the drivers in the United States.   Those who navigated Honduran highways were continually confronted with all sorts of dangers: broken-down vehicles left abandoned on curves, cracks and *baches* in the pavement, reckless drivers who ignored all traffic regulations, and the absence of policemen.   There were only a few police cars in the country, and they responded primarily to crime calls in the cities.   Except for the regular checkpoints, there was no law enforcement on the outlying highways, which made for very aggressive driving.   The relative orderliness of the interstate traffic and the long stretches of uninteresting scenery soon put Santita to sleep.

"Mami! Mami! Where are you? Why did you leave me? Don't you love me? Don't you love me?"

Rough shaking released Santita from the vivid image of a tattered girl reaching out for her and weeping.   Mumbling, sweating, trembling, she returned confusedly to the overcrowded van and unfamiliar landscape.

"Que pasa?"   The girl next to her was concerned, but also determined to restore Santita to the present.

"Nada. Una pesadilla."   Santita turned her face to the window, unwilling to share the nightmare and the tears.   Why had she come here?   Her little girl needed *her*, not American dollars.   But she couldn't turn back now; she had to pay her

270

father back.   She would work hard, pay off the debt, and return to Honduras as quickly as possible.

"Hey!   We're getting off the highway," someone said softly.

"Finally!" a weary voice enjoined. "I was wondering if we were going all the way to Memphis without food, water or a chance to go to the bathroom."

"I doubt they're thinking of *us*," the first voice responded. "We probably need gas."

But the van passed several gas stations and restaurants and headed towards a large truck stop.   Once there, the driver ignored the convenience store, restrooms and filling station, and instead drove the vehicle behind a nondescript building situated near a grove of trees.   Some of the girls began to murmur uneasily when the door slid open and a well-dressed, dark-skinned man leaned inside and saying nothing, began to look closely at each passenger.   The group went silent.   A huge gold necklace dangled from the stranger's open shirt.

"Now you can start paying for your trip."   His words were spoken carefully and dangerously.   A gasp was heard from the rear of the van, and another girl cried out.   Santita was confused. Pay for the trip?   Her father had paid the *coyote* to take her to Memphis to work in a factory.   What was this guy talking about? She was carrying very little cash, and doubted the other girls had money, either.   The bus driver had slipped off when the bus stopped, and the unknown man was standing next to his seat, his right hand touching a pistol in his waistband, his left pointing towards the frightened girls.

"Don't worry.   We don't need *all* of you.   Only four customers tonight.   You got lucky.   You four right here in the front two seats follow me, and don't give me any trouble.   The rest of you can thank them later.   You'll have your chance, though, to say thank you for this nice ride."

The selected girls were protesting and crying, but the pistol was drawn now, so they allowed themselves to be brusquely escorted from the bus.   The young woman next to Santita who had been so concerned about her nightmare began to weep.   Santita took her hand, although she, too, was trembling.

"Why don't we pray?" she offered quietly.   "Would you like that?"   She could hardly believe she was attempting to comfort someone else when she felt so frightened herself, but in the medical clinic she had also found this particular strength.   She knew it was a gift from God.   When the sobbing girl next to her nodded awkwardly, Santita began.

"Lord Jesus, we're very scared.   We are in the hands of bad people, and we need Your protection.   Please show us how to stay out of danger.   We are putting our trust in You because we know that You love us and you will never abandon us.   Help us, dear Jesus.   We have only You.   Please be our hiding place. Amen."

As Santita finished the prayer, she was aware of a new sound outside the van: a police siren.   It was so loud that the bus vibrated, and then shouting and shooting joined the harsh shrill. Hardly aware of what she was doing, Santita grabbed the hand of her seatmate and pulled her to her feet.

"Come on!" she urged. "Run!" She was dragging the terrified girl towards the door when a bullet shattered one of the windows.

"Let's go!" another woman shouted. "We have to get out of here!"

There was a wild rush now for the exit, and as Santita and her companion fell into the chaos taking place outside, she could only think of one thing: a hiding place. The last phrase of her prayer was now an urgent reality, and she struggled to get her bearings in the strange surroundings of the truck stop. Most of the girls were running towards the store, but Santita had a sense that safety did not await them there. Living for years in a dangerous neighborhood had developed strong survival instincts; she looked for the darkest place within easy running distance. Just behind the building in front of them was a wooded area which appeared to be completely unlit. Santita headed for the trees with her traumatized friend in tow. The police, traffickers and clients were in a deathly confrontation, so nobody could turn attention to the girls just yet. However, shortly after feeling the crunch of grass under her feet, Santita heard the cry go up.

"Find the illegals! Don't let them get away!"

By now she and her partner were several yards into the forested area, and Santita knew she had to take charge.

"Ssshh!" she ordered. "Be very quiet. If they find us, they'll take us to jail and deport us." She pulled the shaking woman into a cluster of thick bushes, and yanked her to the ground. Putting both arms around her now quiet companion, she held her tightly and prayed silently. She could only see lights through the small openings in the branches, and it looked to her as if every police car in the United States had arrived. She heard women screaming, but the shooting was over, and the desperate shrieks were mixed with authoritative shouts encouraging the hunted illegals to submit to peaceful arrest. It seemed to go on forever, so much so that Santita closed her eyes and tried to retreat more fully into her true Hiding Place. Her friend had wrapped her arms around Santita as well, perhaps lifting up her own pleas to God. To Santita it seemed as if they were a tiny ball of humanity held firmly in the mighty hand of Christ. She was surprised to realize that a peace had settled over her. If Juanita could see her now! And with that thought came another: Juanita is praying for me. I'm not alone. We are not alone.

"Thank you, God. Thank you for Juanita, for my family. Thank you for bringing us to this safe place. I feel Your presence, Your strong arm of protection," she whispered, ever so softly.

"Yes, thank you, Lord," responded the young woman clutching her tightly. "Thank you, thank you, thank you." The tears began to come again, and this time Santita wept, too. The Lord had His eye on these two lost lambs, and He would not let them down. As the girls' tears ran together into the forest floor, the police cars drove slowly away. The criminals would be taken to prison and the *mojados* placed in another type of jail for illegal immigrants.

"What's your name?" Santita whispered to her clinging friend.

"Pamela . . . and yours?"

"Santita. Well, Pamela, it looks as if we are traveling companions now."

"Thank you for dragging me off the bus and into the woods," the quiet voice responded sincerely. "I'd be in one of those police cars right now if you hadn't taken me with you."

"We aren't safe yet," Santita reminded her. "We don't even know where we are, and I don't know about you, but I don't know anybody in the States. We need help."

"I have family in Memphis," Pamela answered. "They know I'm on my way, but I don't have a cell phone, just their number. They told me to call them when I got there."

"I guess the first thing to do is to find out exactly where we are," said Santita. "But how? I don't speak English, and anyway the police might be looking for us."

"Let's try to get to one of those restaurants down the road," Pamela offered. "I'm dying of thirst, and hungry, too. I can speak a little English. I've been in the States before. Most people up here don't like to get involved in other people's problems. As long as we pay for our food and mind our own business, we'll probably be all right."

"I don't have much money," Santita confessed. "I wonder how much it will cost to get the rest of way to Memphis. Well, first things first: we'll sit down and eat and have some coffee. God has gotten this far, and He won't let us down now!"

"You have a lot of faith," Pamela responded. "I used to go to church, but I haven't been walking with God much lately. I guess He decided to have mercy on me anyway!" Both girls laughed, and as they disentangled themselves from one another and the bushes, they felt hope returning.

"Two are better than one, because if one falls, the other can pick him up," Pamela recited with real feeling. "I remember that from Sunday School. I think it's in Proverbs. Hey, thanks for picking me up!"

"You're welcome," replied Santita, "But it's going to take both us now to find a way to get to Memphis."

The two young women stayed in the shadows as they picked their way back down the highway towards the fast food places. They agreed that it would be best not to be seen walking. When they reached the nearest restaurant, they kept outside the lights until they were near enough to a vehicle to appear that they had parked their car and were going inside for a bite to eat. Once inside, Santita let Pamela take the lead. She appeared to feel perfectly at home as she walked up to the counter and ordered two meals in what appeared to be perfectly understandable English. They selected a table near a window, smiled across the table at one another, and attempted to eat without revealing their ravenous hunger. Santita couldn't help commenting on the inferior quality of the coffee. After all, Honduran coffee was the best in the world. Did all coffee in the States taste as weak and watery as this? She hoped not. Over hamburgers, Santita learned that Pamela was from San Pedro Sula, that she had lived in the States for three years before being deported, but after two years of trying to live on Honduras' minimum wage, had decided to try to get back to Memphis. Santita told her a little about her family, but didn't mention Tania. She shared her frustrating experience of looking for a nursing job.

"You won't be able to work as a nurse up here, you know," Pamela said between bites. "Lots of professional people from Central America work as maids and laborers in the States. I worked with a cleaning business. We went into office buildings after hours and vacuumed the carpet, scrubbed the bathrooms, and left everything ready for the next day of work. They paid us cash so they wouldn't have to give us benefits, but we still made more in one day than a person makes in a whole backbreaking week in Honduras."

"Do you think we'll be able to get a job like that when we get there?" Santita queried. "I don't care about the kind of work; I just want to make enough money to pay my father back and then save enough to get back to Honduras."

"You're already planning to go back? Why? A young single woman like you could make a good life here. I sent money home to my parents and still had enough to pay my own bills and even go out sometimes. There is nothing for us in Honduras."

Santita's vivid dream on the bus rushed into her mind. A lonely, tattered child was counting on her, but she decided not to open her heart to Pamela just yet.

"You're right," she agreed instead. "Let's focus on getting to Memphis and finding work. I'm just homesick, that's all. It's been quite a trip."

"*Hola! Bienvenidos a Texarkana!* We don't see many latins around here. Where did you come from?"

Pamela and Santita had been so engrossed in their conversation that they had failed to notice the large black woman who had been studying them from another table, and who was now staring down at them across a huge bosom.

"Oh, we're driving from Houston to Memphis," Pamela offered hastily. "In fact, we've never made this drive before, and we were just wondering how much further we have to go."

"That a fact? You from Houston? City girls!" The big woman suddenly plopped down on the seat next to Santita. "You see all those police cars up the road awhile ago? Broke up some bad stuff and took a whole load of illegal immigrants away."

Santita and Pamela obviously failed to hide their uneasiness, but their new tablemate quickly put them at ease.

"Don't you worry, though. I didn't come over here to shake you up. You might want to step into the restroom with me and get that grass out of your hair and clean up a bit. You don't look like you've been driving, if you know what I mean."

The girls exchanged a frightened glance. Should they trust this person?

"Come on," was the motherly command. "I know everybody around here, and right now you're all right, but like I said, it wouldn't hurt to freshen up a little. You never know who might walk in. My name is Nora, by the way."

They had no choice except to follow the matronly hostess to the ladies' room. Once inside, Santita glanced in the mirror and gasped. Pamela burst out laughing.

"*Caramba!* We looked like we just crawled out from under a rock!"

"How could we not notice?" Santita commented with astonishment. "I mean, you can see me and I can see you, but somehow we didn't see *this*!"

278

"Don't waste time chattering," the black woman interrupted. "The police might have already figured out that two women are missing, and they might just come back looking for you."

Her old friend, fear, sent a quake through Santita's body.

"We need to get to Memphis," Pamela said brusquely.

"First things first," replied Nora. "Wash your face and comb your hair. My car is in the lot, and we can go to my house and make a plan. But first we need to get you clear of this neighborhood."

Again the girls had no idea in whom they were trusting, but the Bible story about Peter's miraculous deliverance from prison flashed into Santita's mind. Had the Lord sent an angel to lead them to a safer place?

"Are you an angel?" she asked Nora.

A huge smile broke across the huge face.

"Not exactly," she said. "But right now I'm going to act like one. You girls stay close to me."

With that, Pamela took one fleshy arm and Santita took the other. The trio walked out of the restaurant without incident and climbed into an old sedan. After a couple of cranks, the reluctant antique shivered and started, and Nora pulled slowly out of the parking lot and onto the highway. In the back seat, the exhausted girls joined hands and silently gave thanks for this unlikely rescuer.

"We're all right now!" Nora announced jubilantly. "Glory to God, we're all right now!" She began to hum an old gospel tune, and before the junket had gone one mile, both rescued lambs were sound asleep.

Chapter Thirty-Five

Tania would be eight years old in one week, but her birthdays had always been just like any other day, so she was speechless when her father came home, plopped into a chair and asked, "What do you want for your birthday?"

Although she had very few personal possessions, the first wishes that came to mind were not things that her father could buy her. She wanted to be with Anita watching cartoons. She wanted her mother to come and take her away from this man whom she was learning to hate. She wanted to be older so that she could pack her things and leave. She wanted money so that she could get on a bus and go far away. Money! Should she ask for money?

"Well! There must be *something* you want. Let's hear it. Clothes? Toys?" Lito was always short and impatient with his daughter. He felt guilty about what he made her do, but at the same time wanted to please her somehow. He had no idea why he was so perverted in his thinking and behavior, but he knew that what he was doing was very wrong. Being with Tania soothed his loneliness, but the guilt made it impossible for him to speak to her without an edge in his voice.

"I don't know," Tania replied timidly. "Nobody ever asked me that before."

"I can imagine," Lito replied sarcastically. "That old witch of a grandmother only thinks about herself. And you don't have anybody else except me. Don't you forget that!"

"Can I go see Anita?" the small girl ventured, almost with a whisper.

"No! You are *never* going back to La Cantera! *Never!*" Lito was roaring now. He suddenly stood up and threw the plastic chair across the room.

"What is the matter with you? I give you everything, and all you can think about is two old women in shacks down by the stinking river! Never mind! Maybe we'll just let your birthday go by like it always has! Get out of my sight!" And with that, he turned on the TV, opened a beer, and slumped onto a slovenly armchair he'd found by the side of the road.

Tania slipped gratefully into her tiny space, picked up Rosita, and began to hum a song she had learned in a Bible class nearby. A man named Amos had invited her one day as she was walking home from school. Since Lito never got home from work before six or seven in the evening, she was left to herself all afternoon. School was out at noon, so she would walk the six blocks to their *cuarteria*, make a simple lunch, and then she would do homework, play with other children in the group of apartments, or just sit in her room and chat with Rosita. The now worn doll never tired of listening to the lonely child share the events of the day and dreams for the future. On one of her walks home from school, she had noticed a small group of children gathered around a scruffy man with a big smile. Remembering her father's warnings to go straight home and not to talk with strangers, she looked at the ground and tried to loop around the group. As she was passing by, however, she heard the man say, "And we'll color pictures and learn about Jesus."

Color pictures! Tania loved all sorts of arts and crafts, and more than one person had remarked that she had talent, but she had no materials at home.   She slowed her steps.

"We're going to meet on Thursday afternoons after school over by the soccer field. It won't last more than an hour or so, so you can eat lunch afterwards. We'll play games, too. Be sure to ask your parents' permission."

There was no doubt in Tania's mind that her father would never give permission. He had only bitter and sarcastic things to say about God and the Bible.   They didn't go to church. In fact, Tania had never gone to church. Anita had offered to take her a few times, but Marta would just laugh and say, "What has God ever done for us?   It's better not to fill her head with that silliness."   Anita would tell her stories from the Bible, though, and encourage her to pray to Jesus and Mary.

"Jesus loved the children," she would say. "He put them on his lap and blessed them. And Mary is praying for us, too." She would take out her rosary and teach Tania how to pray with it.

"If He loves me so much, why doesn't He send my mother to get me?" Tania asked one day. A deep sadness came over Anita's kind face.

"I've had a lot of questions like that in my life," she sighed. "I wish I knew why we have to suffer so much. But He *does* love us."   Running her hands through Tania's lice-filled hair, she encouraged her earnestly, "He loves you, dear. He sees you. Don't ever give up hope."

What was hope? Tania had no idea. Hope, like cars and vacations and new clothes, was for rich children with parents.

She was a poor girl who had been abandoned by her own mother, living with a father who abused her. What could she possibly hope for?

She went to Amos' Bible club without telling Lito. She wanted to color pictures, and if she had to listen to stories about Jesus in order to do that, then so be it. She was sure that part would be boring, and she didn't enjoy children's games much, either, but maybe she would be able to slip a crayon or two into her pocket and take them home. She and Rosita could draw some pictures to hang in her space.

As it turned out, the club wasn't boring at all! Tania looked forward to Thursdays and was often the first child to arrive. Amos greeted all of the children with a boundless joy, as if he had been waiting all his life for their arrival. He taught them songs, told Bible stories, gave them sheets to color, and sometimes even brought them a piece of fruit. After just one club he knew all their names. He had written them on a slip of paper and said that he prayed for each club member every day. One week some teenagers came to the club to do a puppet show, and another week one of the neighborhood churches sent juice and cookies. The children grew attached to Amos, who was infinitely patient and forever happy. One week he announced to the group that he wanted to visit each of their homes.

"I want to meet your parents," he said, "And see where you live."

Tania's heart had skipped a beat. If Lito found out that she was going to the club, he would forbid her to return. As the children made a line to give Amos directions to their homes, she made sure she was last. She would have to tell her new friend the truth and hope that he wouldn't insist on a visit. After a long wait, it was finally her turn.

"You were very patient to wait until the end," Amos smiled. "I have to tell you that you are one of the best students in the class. I wonder if your parents know how smart you are."

"I like the class," Tania answered shyly. She had received few compliments in her life, and was especially touched by these generous words from her beloved Bible teacher.

"So, where do you live? And what is a good time to visit?" Amos queried, pencil in hand.

"You can't visit me," replied Tania, head down. "I live with my father, and he doesn't know that I come to the class. He wouldn't like it if he did. He doesn't like God."

Amos was silent for a moment. For the first time since Tania had known him, he looked sad.

"I see," he said quietly. "Does your father work? Maybe I could visit him at work. He wouldn't have to know about the Bible class. I would like to talk with him about the love of Jesus."

"You wouldn't tell him that you know me?" Tania asked hopefully.

"Not at all," Amos assured her. "People in the neighborhood are used to my preaching and evangelism. I'll just act as if I don't know who he is, and we'll see if he wants to listen to the Good News. Now, where does he work?"

As Tania began to explain the location of the car repair shop, Amos' eyebrows moved upwards, and when she mentioned Lito's name, he gasped.

"Lito is your father?" he blurted out incredulously.

"Do you know him?" Tania asked.

"Yes, I do." Amos had quickly calmed himself, although he was truly shocked to learn that this beautiful, sensitive child belonged to Lito.

"But not to worry," he added quickly. "The club will be our little secret for now. How long have you been living with your father?"

"Just a few months." Tania was uneasy now. She knew that if Amos pried, she would be hard pressed not to reveal the dark secret she carried day and night, the heavy weight that often threatened to suffocate her.

But Amos seemed distracted. Memories of experiences and conversations with Lito were flooding his heart and mind.

"I'll visit him at work," he said finally. He determined to fast and pray before the visit. This little girl needed a father who loved Jesus. He had left Lito alone long enough. Another precious life was at stake. He would return to the battle for his friend's soul.

"I have to go," Tania said, urging him out of his thoughts. "It's getting late."

"God bless you, child," Amos responded, placing a big hand on her small head. "And remember: *No one* is outside of God's reach. We'll pray for your father and just see what Jesus can do." Laughter rushed out as he repeated loudly, "We'll just see what Jesus can do!"

After that conversation, Tania had waited anxiously for Lito to mention a visit from Amos at work, but he had said nothing and of course she couldn't ask.   Almost an entire week had gone by.   Maybe Amos was visiting the other families first.   She had been last in line, after all.   She wondered if God really could change her father.   She had always been so focused on finding her mother that she had never really prayed for Lito.   For a long time she hadn't prayed about anything, but the Bible club was opening her heart again to hope.   She had remembered Anita's admonition not to give up, and Amos' faith was contagious.   He believed that God could do *anything*.   She decided to try a simple prayer.

"Father God, I'm going to try to talk to my father again about my birthday.   Please help him not to yell at me.   And please keep him from calling me to his room tonight.   Amen."

"*Bueno*, Rosita, we'll see if God was listening!"   With that she placed the beloved doll on her bed and walked slowly and quietly the short distance back into the television area.

"*Papi*," she said quietly.   There was no answer from the chair. Only Lito's long legs were visible.   Tania stepped a bit closer.

"*Papi*, I've been thinking about my birthday."   Still no response.   The small girl walked around the chair and saw that her father was sound asleep.   His empty beer can was on the floor, and an excited announcer followed a soccer game on television.

Tania smiled.   "Amos says that sometimes God answers our prayers in unexpected ways."   She trotted softly back to her sanctuary and gave Rosita a big kiss.   "No yelling and no bad stuff!

God *does* hear us!"   She was so comforted that she decided to pray every day: "I know the answer isn't always *yes,*" she thought, "But it feels good to know that He's listening."   She pulled a worn cover over her thin frame and in a few moments was sound asleep.

A few blocks away, Amos was kneeling by his own bed. His stomach was growling from the beginning of his fast, but the young man was focused on an earnest prayer:

"Lord Jesus, in less than three days I'm going to visit Lito. Please open his heart to hear Your voice."   His supplications joined with those of a suffering girl and entered the heavenly realm where faith and hope reign.   Lito would soon be confronted again by the spirit of the living God.

"In the Name of the Father, Son and Holy Spirit. Amen."

Chapter Thirty-Six

Nora lived in a trailer park. She was still humming as she wound her way past mostly dark, run-down metal boxes filled to overflowing with families who had not yet experienced the American dream. She had lived in this park for six years, having escaped from an abusive alcoholic husband in Houston. Her job as a waitress in the restaurant at the truck stop paid the bills, and her ongoing inner conversation with the Holy Spirit fueled her soul and spirit. She pulled in front of a rusted trailer surrounded by a multitude of potted plants, none blooming at this time of year, and gently encouraged the sleepy passengers into her home and her own bed. She curled up on a small sofa, and all slept peacefully until mid-morning.

Santita awoke to the smell of frying bacon. She was alone in the bed, and for a moment could not orient herself. Then the events of the night before charged into her mind, and her heart raced until it recalled Nora's appearance. She looked around the tiny room at the spattering of photos and a wooden plaque that read, "The Lord is My Shepherd." Muttering a quick word of thanks to that very Lord, she sidled around the bed and into the kitchen. Nora was at the stove, and Pamela was sitting at the table with a cup of coffee. The women were having an animated conversation.

"How did you know who we were?" Pamela asked. "And why did you help us?"

"You might say I got mixed up in it," replied Nora, "Only God knows how, but I knew I had to do something about some men who were following a big dude with a fancy necklace."

Seeing Santita's puzzled look, Pamela began to translate the conversation both ways.

"You mean you knew about the guy with the gold chain? How?"

Juanita poured herself a cup of coffee and joined the story.

"I guess most people eating in restaurants think their waitresses are deaf and dumb!" Nora laughed loudly, and her whole body shook. "Sometimes what they talk about is so silly I want to stuff cotton in my ears, but last night I knew the good Lord was giving me good ears to hear what that man was saying. He was at one of my tables."

"The man with the chain?"

"Yeah, that one. Another guy came in and sat across the table from him. He didn't order, just leaned across the table and said something real low. I was pouring coffee for the gold chain man. He got this ugly look on his face and said, 'They'll be here any minute. Hold on to your pants.' The way he said it gave me one of the worst feelings I ever had!"

A plate filled with crispy bacon and eggs was set on the table between the two women, along with a stack of toast, a jar of jam, and a stick of margarine. Nora said a short blessing, eager to continue the tale. Nobody touched the steaming food.

"I wasn't even back to the counter, and all of a sudden your man shouted at me, 'Bring me the check, girl! Hurry up!' He had his phone in his ear and was calling them guys to come on. I was still writing up the bill but he come up to me, shoved a twenty into my hand and said, 'Never mind. Keep the change.' And those four guys – no, *five* -- hustled out of there."

"They must have been the clients!" Pamela offered. "Remember the man on the bus said there were four."

"Is that something that goes on all the time at your restaurant, Nora?" Santita queried. "I mean, how did you know what was happening?"

As Pamela translated the question, and to the girls' surprise, Nora's eyes filled with tears.

"I didn't know *anything'*," she said quietly. "I mean, I wouldn't have known anything except for God. He knows *everything*." Tears began to roll down her face, and Santita and Pamela became aware of a Presence in that beaten up trailer that made it seem like a little piece of heaven. The momentary silence was sacred.

"He said, 'Nora, honey, those men are *bad business*.'"

Pamela and Santita's eyes joined as their hearts pounded.

"What did you do?" Santita whispered.

"I ran to the bathroom, shut the door, and called 911."

"What did you say?" Pamela insisted. "I mean, you didn't really know what they were planning to do, did you?"

"No, ma'am, I didn't. So I just said, 'There's a man with a gun at Frankie's Truck Stop, and he seems like he's going to use it on somebody.' It wasn't a lie; I saw a gun bulging under the shirt of your man."

"That's *it*?" Santita responded incredulously. "And they sent all those police cars?"

"Well, you might remember they sent just one at first. But when he shined the flashlight into your van and saw all those girls, he called his friends!   And that's when the shooting started!"

"You were watching?"

"Sure was," Nora smiled. "I sneaked out back. Told my boss I was taking a smoke. I guess she clean forgot I don't touch cigarettes!"   Another belly laugh erupted.   "I saw the whole thing. Even saw you two running for the woods!"

"If *you* could see us, how come nobody else did?"

"That was God," Nora declared.   "He opens our eyes to what He wants us to see. He opens our ears to what He wants us to hear. And then He tells us what to do."

Santita couldn't help thinking that it took most preachers about an hour to make a less powerful point. She smiled.

"I couldn't stay out there all night," Nora continued, "But when the shooting started, everybody in the diner ran out anyway, so there wasn't any work.   I was outside just long enough to see you two start walking over to the hamburger place. And that voice said, 'Go get'em, Nora. Go get'em.'   So I did, and here you are!"

Pamela jumped from her chair and put her arms around the big, soft waist of their guardian angel. "Thank you, Nora!" said her muffled voice from the deep chest where her face was buried.

"Yes," Santita added earnestly. "Who knows what would have happened to us if you hadn't listened and obeyed." Her coffee had grown cold, forgotten as the story unfolded. She lifted the cup in the air, smiled, and offered a toast:

"To our angel, Nora!" she declared. "May God lead her to many more women with grass in their hair!" All three women laughed with real joy as Santita left the cup on the table and joined the hug.

"Now!" Nora admonished. "We're going to eat big and talk about what we're going to do next!"

Unraveling themselves obediently, Pamela and Santita sat down to the meal before them, and the three women began to plan their trip to Memphis.

Chapter Thirty-Seven

Fasting was never easy, but Amos sometimes felt as if he could physically feel the spiritual war waging around him. There were strong forces at work in Lito's life, and after a day of prayer for his meeting with the young man, Amos had gone to his church to ask for others to join him in the battle. He had learned that he could not serve God alone, and although the church was far from perfect, he clung to it with determination and love. Every day a small group of women gathered there to pray, so he stopped by on the second morning of his fast to present his petition for Lito. As he spoke of Tania, he felt real sympathy among the women for the defenseless child, and they all agreed to support him spiritually.

"We want to hear what happens," one *anciana* urged quietly. As she looked into Amos' eyes, a tremor went through his soul. This woman had 'tarried in the temple' for many years, and emitted a powerful sense of God's presence.

"Of course," Amos assured her. "Thank you so much for praying."

"Have we ever told you how pleased God is with your life?" the old woman asked with a smile. She took Amos' two large hands into her tiny, wrinkled ones, squeezed them tightly, and added, "You are a good shepherd."

Amos blushed, but the warmth he felt was not limited to his face; it surged through his entire being.

"I just want to say thank you to Jesus with my life," he murmured, eyes on the floor.

A small hand gently lifted his chin.   Looking into his eyes once again, the old prophetess loving admonished him.

"You are beloved of God, dear son.   Never doubt that. And, by the way, the Lord will soon bring someone into your life who will become as one with you in your calling."

Amos' heart nearly stopped, and the shock must have shown on his face because all of the women laughed.

"Yes!" the ancient prayer warrior continued.   "Although you are willing to walk alone, the Lord desires that you take a wife.   Very soon you will meet her.   Now, go and seek God's face, and then do whatever He puts in your heart."

No further words were spoken.   Amos walked quietly out of the tiny church, and the intercessors returned to their daily work.

Not two blocks away, Lito was hurrying to the shop.   He had not heard Tania get up for school.   For some reason he had not been able to sleep until the early morning hours.   He had wanted to call Tania to him, but some unseen force seemed to hold him to his bed, so he had tried looking at his porn magazines, but they only seemed to increase his anxiety.   He had finally drifted off to a restless and then profound sleep.   When he had finally opened his eyes, the brightness of the sun streaming through his window had alerted him to the lateness of the hour. Don Chico was not sympathetic to late sleepers; the shop was filled with cars, and Lito would have to work late to make up the time.

Tania was accustomed to getting herself ready for school, and although she was surprised that her father had not stirred from his room before she left, she was thankful, too.   He called her to his room nearly every night now, but he had not spoken to her at all the night before.   She quickly prepared a burrito, stuffed it into her worn *mochila*, and hurried out of the *cuarteria*. For the first morning in many moons, she left for school feeling relatively unsullied.   It was Thursday, too, so she had Amos' group to look forward to.   All in all, her day was looking better than she had remembered in a long, long time.

In another part of Tegucigalpa, Juanita was stretching in her bed, yawning contentedly, and reaching for her Bible.   She really should get a job, she told herself again.   She should be dressed and out of the house, earning a wage to support her family.   She had left resumes in several places, but had not followed up with a visit.   Today she would make some calls, she told herself.   Later.   After coffee and prayer.   And a short reading lesson with Miguelito.   And she needed to ask her mom if there were any errands that needed doing.   And she had also been planning a return trip to La Cantera to check on Tania.   Oh, dear. Work would interrupt so many things!   How would she be able to do the things she truly enjoyed if she had to go to a job every day? She slipped to the floor and began to try to sort it all out in the best way possible: on her knees.

A few thousand miles away, Santita was becoming acquainted with Greyhound buses.   Even if Nora's car had been able to get them to Memphis, just putting gas in the old clunker would have cost more than three bus trips, besides the fact that Nora had to work swing shift all week.   She had tearfully put Pamela and Santita on a bus, pressing hard-earned bills into their hands, and whispering prayers of blessing and protection in their ears.   The two travelers longed to stay with this gentle soul, but had to agree that the sooner they were settled and working, the better.   As Santita breathed the stale, nauseous air and tried not to look at the dizzying landscape flying by her window, her thoughts returned to Honduras.   It seemed further away than ever.

Chapter Thirty-Eight

By the time Juanita struggled from her knees to the bathroom, the trip to La Cantera had risen to the top of the list. She felt an urgency to see Tania. Everything else, including the job, would have to wait. She took a quick, very cold shower, pulled on some clothes, borrowed a few *lemps* from her mother, and caught a bus to Flor del Campo. This time she barely looked at the businesses, homes and other pedestrians as she retraced her steps to Dona Marta's house. As she entered La Cantera, she realized that Tania would be in school already. Maybe she would avoid old Marta altogether and try to see Tania at school. There were plenty of children around, so Juanita simply asked one of them to direct her to the nearest public elementary school. After a short walk, she stood in front of a tall metal gate covered with graffiti, her view completely blocked from the multitude of noisy children on the other side. She pounded loudly and waited. Nothing. She pounded again.

"If you're wanting the guard, you'll have to wait," remarked a droll woman who was selling candy a few feet away. "He's over there having his breakfast." She pointed with her mouth to a streetside food vendor across the dusty road. The rumpled, uniformed guard was chewing slowly on a *baleada*, one hand on a plastic coffee mug. The vendor, a plump girl in a stained apron, re-filled his cup while relating a bit of news which seemed to interest neither. Juanita sighed and leaned against the wall of the school. Little could be accomplished in her impoverished country without patience. After what seemed a very long time indeed, the guard ambled back to his post.

"Excuse me," Juanita ventured. "I would like to speak with the director of the school."

"She isn't here," was the blunt response.

"How about the subdirector?" Juanita insisted. "Or anybody in the office. Is the secretary here?"

"All right, all right. Your name? I'll see if anybody wants to let you in. It's better to come after school lets out."

"I'm sorry to be a bother." Juanita tried to mask her frustration. "I can't come later because of work. I would be really grateful if somebody could see me now."

"I'll ask." As the guard moved off, Juanita breathed a silent prayer. Nothing was easy when it came to Tania.

After a few moments, the dingy watchman returned. "It's down there at the end. The secretary is Carolina."

"Thanks!" Juanita responded gratefully. As she walked briskly toward the office, she studied the children playing outside, hoping to catch a glance of Tania. Once inside with the secretary, she moved quickly through the necessary greetings and then got to the point.

"I'm looking for a little girl named Tania Maria Rivera Ramirez. She's in second grade. Could I speak with her?"

The secretary had the lined, passive face of most government employees in Honduras. She was chewing gum with parted lips, and seemed to be slowly processing the request.

"Tania Rivera. Second grade. And who are you?"

Juanita repeated the story of the fabricated non-profit offering scholarships to impoverished children. She would need to see Tania in her school environment, she said, and talk briefly with her teacher.

"Too bad," the secretary responded without feeling. "She was a smart little thing, but she isn't here anymore."

Juanita's heart sank. Not here?

"Do you have any idea where I could find her?" she asked, attempting to belie her very personal interest."

"No. Her grandmother came in a few months ago and asked for her papers. Said she was going to live with another family member someplace else. She could be in Choluteca or Yoro for all I know."

"Oh." Something about the tone of Juanita's voice seemed to rouse a bit of conscience in the secretary.

"Her teacher might know more. You can talk to her if you want. Profesora Candy. Room 14."

Juanita took her leave quickly, eager to question the teacher. She had not expected that Tania would leave La Cantera! How would she be able to tell Santita that the child had disappeared? She found Room 14 easily enough. There were about forty boys and girls crammed into the small space, some of them sitting on the floor, as there were not enough desks to go around. Profesora Candy was shouting above the chaos, chalk in hand, pointing to a math problem on the board. A few of the distracted children saw Juanita hovering in the doorway and began to shout at the teacher.

"Visitor! Visitor! Profesora Candy!" They were gesturing wildly towards the door while shouting at the harried instructor, who finally caught sight of Juanita. She seemed relieved by the interruption and walked outside the classroom to attend to the welcome visitor.

"What can I do for you?" she asked not unkindly.

"I'm looking for Tania Rivera," Juanita answered. "The secretary says she isn't in this school anymore. Do you have any idea where I might find her?"

A shadow crossed the teacher's face when Tania's name was mentioned.

"She was a good student," the teacher replied. "Quiet and shy. Always did her homework. I was sorry to hear that she was going to live with her father."

"With her *father*?" Juanita forgot to be businesslike and nearly shouted the question.

"Yes," Profa. Candy confirmed. She seemed troubled by Juanita's emotional response. "Is something wrong? The grandmother said that he had a good job and wanted to give her a better life."

Juanita had quickly realized her mistake and attempted to calm the teacher's fears.

"No, nothing," she said reassuringly. "It's just that our organization had approved Tania for a scholarship, and now we don't know where she is. I'll need to talk with her father. Do you have any idea where he lives?"

"No," said Candy, "But I don't think Tania left Tegucigalpa. The grandmother said something about being able to visit her as often as she liked. Does that help?"

Not really, thought Juanita, as there were multitudes of neighborhoods in the capital city, and Dona Marta might not want to tell her where Tania was living, but she would have to try. She needed Julio and the camera and notebook. She berated herself for not returning sooner. Tania was with Lito! Unless he had changed considerably for the better, he was not a suitable father for the little girl. It was time to go undercover again and ferret out the whereabouts of the poor child. Juanita was beginning to think that she should have become a private investigator instead of a nurse. She thanked the teacher and began the trip home to fetch her brother, forming in her mind the conversation which would extract the necessary information from Dona Marta. Today. There wasn't a moment to lose.

Chapter Thirty-Nine

As Tania headed towards the meeting place for the Bible Club, she suddenly remembered that she was about to turn eight years old. The following day was her birthday! Not that anyone had ever celebrated it, of course, but she would sing to herself and Rosita, and try not to think about her loneliness and suffering. Lito was angry, and she did not expect her grandmother to visit. Anita would have bought two *rosquillas con miel*, and placing them in a pair of chipped saucers, would have sung her *las mananitas* and given her a hug. How she missed Anita! Maybe she would tell Amos. He liked to pray for children on their birthdays, and although she was not yet convinced that God was paying attention to her life, she would enjoy feeling Amos' strong hand on her small head as he prayed. She had never heard anyone pray like Amos. He sounded as if he and God were having a personal conversation, face-to-face. She wondered what it was like to know God so well.

"Tania! Wait! I want to walk with you!" The friendly shout startled Tania from her thoughts. It was Sindy, another member of the Bible Club, running to catch up with her distracted friend. Sindy was a sociable fifth grader who knew and liked everybody. She threw an arm around Tania's thin shoulder and let out a huge gasp of air.

"I've been calling to you for a whole block!" she admonished. "What's the big rush?" But she was laughing, and soon moved on to another topic.

"Guess what – my birthday is on Sunday! We're having a piñata. Want to come?"

Tania thought of her own birthday the very next day. There would be no piñata.

"Oh, I don't know," Tania mumbled. "I don't think my father will let me."

"Bring him!" cried Sindy. "We live on Calle San Ignacio. It's a pink house. The party starts at 3:00. You don't have to bring a present or anything. I really want you to come."

Tania was moved by the other girl's sincere invitation. She couldn't remember if she had ever been invited to a birthday party.

"Maybe I'll come," she said, knowing she wouldn't. "I'll ask my dad," she added, but of course she couldn't.

"Hello, girls," Amos interrupted. Tania hadn't noticed that he had arrived.

"It's good to see you together. The Bible says that two are better than one, because if one falls, the other can pick him up." How did Amos know so much about the Bible? She seriously doubted that she would be able to pick up a fallen Sindy.

"I was just inviting Tania to my birthday party on Sunday afternoon!" Sindy announced cheerfully. "You can come, too. You already know where we live. Will you come?"

"Oh, I don't know," Amos replied teasingly. "Is Tania going? If Tania says yes, maybe I will, too." He lightly touched Tania on the arm. He longed to draw the girl out of her quiet world, sensing that dark thoughts held her captive.

Tania looked into Amos' eyes, and for a moment Amos felt as if she were drinking from the depths of his very being. He felt her thirst for love and acceptance, her desperate loneliness . . . and something more. He knew that something dreadful needed to be revealed. He had one more day of fasting before visiting Lito on Saturday, and he prayed that both he and Lito would be ready for the encounter. As his eyes locked with those of Tania, he silently communicated to her his understanding and friendship. Her head dropped suddenly. Sindy had seen nothing.

"Tania says she's going to ask her father," Sindy informed Amos. "But you'll come, won't you? *Please!*"

"Yes, I'll come, silly girl," Amos laughed. "Especially if there will be food!"

"*Arroz con pollo!*" Sindy assured him. "And cake!"

Tania felt the old resentments surfacing as her excited friend described the birthday party she could only dream about. She had tried very hard to die to hopes and dreams, but her own birthday was imminent, and she struggled to control the feelings of jealousy and disappointment.

Other children were arriving by now, so Amos and Sindy left the conversation about the birthday party, and the club activities began. Tania participated bodily, but her mind and heart were dead to the liveliness of the group. The idea of telling Amos about her own birthday so that he would pray for her had left her mind entirely. She longed to curl up on her bed, clutching Rosita and wishing to be gone from the earth. She hated her life. She hated Lito and Marta and even Anita, who had abandoned her. She hated her mother, whoever she was, and she would hate everybody until she was delivered from the interminable sickness which was her pitiful life.

Amos pretended not to notice Tania's dark humor, but his sensitive spirit had connected with that of Tania in the moment their eyes met. He would wait until the club ended and then try to talk with her. He didn't want her to go home so desperately sad. Somehow he would have to convince her to let him pray for her, as only God could free her from such grasping bondage.

It seemed to Tania that the club lasted longer than usual that day. She was too shy to draw attention to herself by leaving early, but when the snacks were served, she wriggled to the front of the line to get hers quickly and take it home. Amos was too quick for her, though, and as she headed for the street, he called out.

"Tania! I want to talk to you!" A subtle voice in the little girl urged her to keep walking, but instead she froze. For the second time that afternoon someone was calling her name, an occurrence so unusual that she did not know how to respond.

Amos reached her in a moment and put a hand on her shoulder. Tania flinched.

"I want to pray for you," he blurted, not intending to be so blunt. "I *need* to pray for you."

Now the subtle voice was more insistent. 'Say no,' it urged. 'Go home.'

"I need to get home," Tania murmured, wanting more than anything to stay.

"I won't keep you very long," Amos insisted. He knew more about this kind of inner battle than he wanted to admit, and he would not let the darkness pull her away.

"Well, all right," Tania conceded. "I was going to ask you anyway. Tomorrow is my birthday."

The girl made the pronouncement as if it were a death sentence rather than a celebration. The pain in her voice struck a chord deep in the heart of the young man, and without further conversation, he placed a hand on Tania's head and began to pray:

"Lord Jesus, Tania's life is in Your hands. You have a beautiful plan for her. You know her disappointments and pain, and you long to turn her sadness into joy. I pray, Holy Father, that you free her from all evil spirits that take away her hope. In the powerful Name of Jesus, I command these spirits to be gone forever! Set Tania free to love and worship you, Lord God. Give her new life in your Spirit. Fill her with faith and love and joy!"

He would have gone on, but the pale object of his intercession crumpled to the ground.

As Amos knelt beside the still girl, a few children ran over to see what had happened. His first impulse was to shoo them away, but then he remembered the words he had spoken a short time earlier: "Two are better than one."

"Come, children, let's pray for Tania. She isn't feeling well."

Several boys and girls quickly dropped to the ground and placed innocent hands on their friend.

"Help Tania," one said.

"Jesus, please heal Tania," said another.

"Make her better," pleaded a small boy.

"Wake her up in the Name of Jesus!" declared Sindy, with the faith of Abraham.

As each girl and boy pleaded with God for their little friend, Amos continued to pray along silently.   Presently Tania began to stir, and the group responded with excitement and more encouragement.

"Wake up, Tania! It's us!   Are you OK? We were praying for you! Can you open your eyes? Here, we'll help you sit up!"

Amos sat on the ground and lifted Tania into his lap, holding her against his chest, continuing to pray fervently in his own spirit.   The children chattered and cajoled, and finally Tania opened her eyes to them.

"What happened?" she asked weakly.   In Amos' strong arms, she felt as if she were lashed to a mast in hurricane winds. A storm was raging inside her, and she did not want him to let go. He didn't.

"You fainted!" Sindy responded.   "Amos was praying for you, and you fell right over on the ground.   Sometimes that happens to people in my church.   Do you think it was because of the prayer, Amos?"

Amos smiled.   "I don't know," he said honestly. He would not pretend to understand the ways of God.   "But I think she's starting to feel better now, so you should all go home.   Your mothers will wonder where you are."

As the final phrase left Amos' lips, and the small group of Bible clubbers ran off in different directions, Tania began to weep. Her mother would not wonder where she was.   No one was waiting for her to come home, and when her father finally arrived home, he would have his dinner and then call her to his room. The bitter tears began to fall, and Amos could see that something had broken inside the little girl. He lifted her easily and walked the short distance to his own little church. As he entered the sanctuary, the same old prophetess who had reassured him the day before rose from her gnarled knees to greet her young brother and his light burden.

Before Amos could begin to explain, the old woman's hands were on Tania's head and heart, and she moaned softly.

"Such pain!" she cried, eyes closed tightly. "Such loneliness!" Amos stood very still as the intercessor began to pray in a language unknown to him. Tania's weeping stopped, and she began to wail, loud and long and piercing. It was more than a sound; it was something living, rising out of a very deep place in her soul, traveling through her mouth into the air, bewailing its eviction and causing even Amos to tremble. Then the wailing stopped, and Tania seemed to sleep.

"Hold her as if she were a baby," the woman instructed, and Amos obeyed. He pressed her head against his shoulder and began to rock gently, whispering a lullaby into the seemingly unconscious ear.

As Amos and Tania rocked, the old woman walked around them quietly, murmuring prayers of protection and covering. A deep peace settled over the surrogate father and his small charge. Time stopped as Tania's healing began.

Chapter Forty

When Julio heard Juanita's news about Tania, he was eager to help. Disguised once again as humanitarian workers, they boarded a bus for the neighborhood which was becoming more and more familiar to them.

"We'll tell Marta that our organization has approved a scholarship for Tania, and see what she says," Juanita instructed. "We'll pretend we don't know she doesn't live there anymore."

"Sounds good," Julio agreed. "The old witch! Packing her off to that druggie! If we find Tania, what are we going to do then?"

Juanita was silent for a moment. She didn't know what they could do to help Tania, assuming they found her. She had to admit that she was a little scared of both Marta and Lito. What did she know about rescuing children? Her experience with Miguel, though, had shown her that it was worthwhile to step out in faith.

"I don't know," she finally conceded in a soft voice. "Let's deal with Dona Marta first, and then trust God for the next step."

Julio looked admiringly at his older sister. She had always been an anchor in his life, but he was seeing maturity and courage which lifted both of them to a higher place.

"I'm with you," he said. "You just tell me what to do." They rode the last half mile to Flor del Campo hand in hand, their thoughts centered on one little girl, determined to break through the barriers which separated them from her.

This time they did not stop to talk with anyone, but walked purposefully to Marta's door and knocked loudly.

"Who is it?" the familiar, cranky voice queried.

"We're back, the representatives of the organization with a scholarship offer for Tania Ramirez." After a brief, uncertain wait, the sound of the latch being pulled back gratified their expectant ears. Marta peeked out.

"So you came back? Well, Tania doesn't live here anymore. She went to live with her father."

"I see," responded Juanita without emotion. "If her father lives nearby, perhaps we could talk with him about the scholarship. The scholarship is for Tania, and if she is still in need, it doesn't matter where she lives."

"He doesn't live in this neighborhood," Marta answered. "Can she still get the scholarship if she lives in another neighborhood?"

"Oh, yes," Juanita said assuringly. "Once a child has been approved -- and Tania has been approved -- the scholarship is given until the child completes sixth grade, regardless of change of address – unless, of course, they are living with a relative who has considerable financial means. Does Tania's father have considerable financial means?"

"Pah!" spat Marta. "He works, I'll grant him that, but he's poor just like the rest of us!" Her eyes darkened a bit. "He's not that reliable, either. You might want to send the money to me, and I'll make sure it gets to Tania."

"That's very kind of you, Dona Marta," Juanita responded. "But the scholarship isn't given in cash. Tania has to come to our office with her family member to pick up school supplies, clothes, shoes, milk and other donations that come in for our beneficiaries. Of course it would be perfectly fine for you to bring her instead of her father."

"I guess you realized from the form that tomorrow is her birthday," Marta suddenly interjected, with something like regret on her face. "She'll be eight years old. I was thinking about going over to Las Torres to see her. I could tell Lito – her faither – about the scholarship, and see what he wants to do."

Las Torres! A piece of the puzzle was already in place! Julio tried to control the smile sneaking its way onto his poker face.

"That would be fine," he heard his sister saying. "Here is my phone number. When you have decided how you want to manage the scholarship, please call me. I think you'll be glad you did. We provide considerable support for our children."

"May I take a photo of the outside of your house?" Julio asked. "Would you like to be in it? Our donors like to see pictures of the neighborhoods where the children live."

"Go ahead if you want, but I don't want to be in a picture." Juanita saw in that moment a side of Marta which she had not imagined existed: an insecure, even frightened, old woman.

"This ugly old face might break your camera," she said brusquely. When nobody laughed, she slammed the gate shut and disappeared.

"Las Torres," said Julio.

"Las Torres," answered Juanita.

Not bad for a couple of unpaid, untrained private detectives.

Chapter Forty One

Pamela and Santita reached Memphis without further problems other than motion sickness. As the big bus pulled into the final terminal, Pamela remarked that she hoped never to make another journey on a Greyhound. Santita could only nod in agreement; she was dizzy and nauseous. She had ridden many buses in Honduras, but the closed windows, bathroom odors, and greasy food on the Greyhounds had done more damage to her body than any number of dents and bumps in the Honduran highways.

"Let's find a phone," Pamela urged, grabbing Santita's hand. "We'll call my cousins. I hope they aren't too far from here and can come right away."

It was about eight o'clock in the evening. Santita had walked to the front door to seek some fresh air while Santita used a pay phone. The terminal was on a neglected, wide street which seemed to be devoted to small hotels, a large adult bookstore, and plenty of closed businesses.

"And people say Tegucigalpa is dreary!" thought the young woman, homesick and travel weary. "I would give anything to see it right now."

"Need a place to stay?" said a voice very near her ear. Startled, Santita scuttled quickly back inside the terminal door.

"Sorry I scared you." The voice belonged to a young woman in tight jeans and a skimpy shirt. "I should have introduced myself first. My name is Polly."

Without Pamela by her side to translate, Santita was at a loss. She wanted to be polite, but she also wanted to get away from this stranger.

"*Perdon*," she squeaked out, and turned to walk away.

"Oh, I get it. You don't speak English! *No hay problema. Espera.*" The familiar words stopped Santita in her tracks. Since she and Pamela had left the van at the truck stop, she had heard little Spanish.

"*Habla espanol?*" she asked a little too eagerly.

"*Un poco,*" replied the woman, smiling warmly through heavily painted lips.

Santita was about to say something else when Pamela came rushing over and grabbed her arm.

"Come on!" she said. The urgency in her voice frightened Santita.

"What's wrong?" she asked. "Can't your cousins come for us?"

"Never mind that," Pamela ordered. Santita had never heard such a bite in her voice. "Just come with me – *now*."

"What's the rush, girls?" queried the painted lady. "I'd be happy to show you around, buy you a drink, give you a place to stay for a few days."

"No, thanks," Pamela responded brusquely. "We don't need your help."

"Have it your way," shot back the young woman. "But if you change your mind, I'll be in the hotel across the street, the 'Wayfarer.' Just ask for Polly."

Pamela had already dragged Santita halfway across the terminal by then. When they reached the restrooms, Santita resisted. Her stomach couldn't bear another restroom just yet.

"Are you *crazy*?" Pamela almost shouted, very close to Santita's face. They were crammed into the corner outside the ladies' room.

"What is the matter with you?" Santita asked, truly confused. "What are you so mad about? I was just having a conversation with that woman. She speaks Spanish."

"Yes, and probably about ten other languages – or at least enough to get women like us over to that hotel."

"She seemed nice enough," Santita protested. "And I thought your cousins might not be able to come right away, and we'd need a place to stay tonight."

"You don't get it, do you?" Pamela asked in amazement. "This is a prostitution district. That woman is looking for hookers. The people she works for hang out at places like this bus terminal looking for women to lock up in little rooms and sell to men. If we walked over to that hotel, we would probably never come out again. And who would ever know – or care? Just two more dead illegals. Good riddance, the police would say."

As Pamela was talking, Santita began to feel faint -- first the incident at the bus stop, and now this. Was this country just one long trap laid for unsuspecting women? She had never felt as vulnerable in Honduras as she felt just then, except for the night with the *roqueros,* but she had known that Javier and his friends were bad. Since she had landed in the States, she had been deceived again and again. Friendly people were not to be trusted. Or maybe *nobody* could be trusted. Although she had saved Pamela at the bus stop, she would have to depend upon her now to teach her how to survive.

"I get it," Santita said softly, her head down. "I'm sorry. I don't understand anything about this country." The tears hit the floor silently, but Pamela saw them and instantly lowered her voice and put an arm around her friend.

"*No hay cuidado,*" she said as a sort of apology. "It just frightened me, that's all, seeing you chatting with that prostitute. I know girls who had no place to go, and these vultures took them and used them and threw them away. I don't want anything to happen to you. If it weren't for you, I might be in a brothel right now." The thought made her tremble visibly, and Santita grabbed her hand.

"Well!" she said, lifting her head. "If I'm not saving you, you're saving me! We are quite a pair!" Neither felt lighthearted enough for a real laugh, but they smiled and shared a hug, thankful for another narrow escape.

"So, what did your cousin say?" Santita asked.

"He's on his way," Pamela replied, and her smile was broader now. "My aunt answered the phone. She burst into tears when she heard my voice. I told her I was bringing a friend. She said she'd heat some leftovers. Very soon we'll have this nightmare of a trip behind us, and we can sleep easily and then get to work."

Within the hour, Francisco the cousin arrived, and as the girls threw their small bags into his car, Santita glanced across the street at the *Wayfarer*. Polly was standing outside, puffing on a cigarette and watching her prey escape. Santita could only feel pity for the woman. No one would willingly choose such a life. For a moment the two women stared across the street at one another, Polly cursing and Santita praying. It occurred to Santita that life was a very precarious business indeed, and that it was impossible to understand how some people were gathered into God's fold while others remained seemingly content outside of it, and still others suffered and died without knowing about Him at all. Had anyone told Polly about Jesus? She saw no church spires, and none of the people on the street carried Bibles. Probably the Christians were afraid to be in this part of the city, but wouldn't His light shine brightest where there was so much darkness? Pamela was calling her name again, so breathing a deep sigh, she asked the Good Shepherd to send someone for Polly, folded herself into Francisco's Volkswagen, and allowed herself to be driven to safety and a new life.

Chapter Forty Two

On the day of Tania's eighth birthday, Lito was out of bed earlier than usual, and had made coffee and swept out the little *cuartito* before Tania appeared in her school uniform.

"Feliz Cumpleanos!" he said, almost shyly.

"Gracias," Tania replied. She was still in a kind of afterglow from the attention and prayer she had received the day before, so much so that she had almost forgotten that it was her birthday. For two nights Lito had not called her to his room. She had gone to bed the night before happier than she had ever remembered. She could still feel Amos' arms around her, and when she had regained full consciousness in the church, he and the old woman had talked with her for a long time, drawing out of her the story of her motherless life, and finally the truth about Lito. A fire had come into Amos' eyes as she had blurted out her shame and terror. The prophetess had enfolded her in long, thin arms, saying nothing and yet accepting her fully on God's behalf. As Tania had walked home afterwards with Amos by her side, she had felt like a different person. Amos was reluctant to leave her when they arrived at the *cuarteria*, but Tania threw her arms around his waist, thanked him, and ran to tell Rosita everything that had happened that afternoon. When Lito came in from work, she made supper and served him a plate in front of the television. He had looked at her in surprise, but simply said thank you and returned to the soccer match. Somehow Tania knew that he would not call for her that night; she felt covered in an invisible shield. She had fallen asleep peacefully with Rosita in her arms, dreaming of a home with a mother *and* father who loved her, and had awakened to the smell of coffee and eggs.

She almost expected to open the curtain which served as a door to her room and find two smiling parents seated at the little table, arms open to receive their beloved daughter.   Only Lito was there, but she smiled anyway.

"I'm bringing home a cake tonight," Lito announced. "Do you want to invite anybody?"

"I don't know," Tania responded from her unseen bubble of happiness. "I'll think about it."

"See you later then," her father responded, his hand on the door latch.   "Maybe it's because of your birthday, but you seem different today somehow."

Tania smiled again, and Lito realized he had never seen a happy look on her face. A stab of guilt ran through him, but then he told himself that she had always been sad.   It was her mother's fault.   She had abandoned both of them.   That was probably what had turned him to pornography, too, he reasoned. Both he and Tania were victims of Santita's selfishness.   Fully justified, he turned the latch and walked the familiar road to the auto shop.   Tonight he would give Tania the first birthday cake she had ever had.   Maybe he wasn't perfect, but he was better than Santita.   He and Tania would continue to take care of each other without anybody's help or interference.   By the time he reached work, he was convinced of his own righteousness, and what better proof than the obvious happiness on his daughter's face that morning?   He made her happy.   His guilt fully dealt with, he marched towards a frowning client with a light step. This was going to be a good day.

In her dreamlike state, Tania had hardly heard her father's voice that morning --   something about a cake and that she looked different.   She certainly *felt* different.   She looked into the cracked mirror on her father's side of the curtain to see if anything had changed physically, but saw the familiar face staring back at her, except that it was *grinning*. She grinned back and then laughed out loud. The sight of her teeth reminded her that she had not yet brushed, and she ran out to the *pila* for some water.   Lito had said she could invite someone to her birthday celebration.   She would ask Amos if she could find him. As soon as school was out, she would look for him, maybe go by the church to say hello to the prophetess. Except for Anita, Tania had not known what it meant to be cared for. She was hungry to feel Amos' arms around her again.   Maybe he would invite Lito to church. She skipped all the way to school, hardly heard anything the teacher said all morning, and then skipped back out. She was saying goodbye to Sindy at the gate when she heard her name called.

"Tania Ramirez?"

Both Tania and Sindy turned to see who was speaking. Juanita and Julio had been waiting for the children to come out, and had immediately spotted Tania.

"Yes?" Tania asked cheerfully. She recognized Juana and Julio, and with so many people around and a lightness in her heart, she was not afraid. She couldn't help thinking how strange it was to be suddenly sought out by so many people in such a short time.   She was more accustomed to being ignored and neglected, even abused.   Having nice, friendly people call her name was a new experience.   It had ended nicely the day before, however, so she faced the two young people squarely and awaited their response.

"You might remember that we work for an organization that gives scholarships to needy children," Juanita explained. "We talked with your grandmother awhile back, and you have been approved for a scholarship."

"I don't live with her anymore," Tania replied simply.

"We know that. We saw her yesterday at her house in La Cantera. Oh, by the way, Happy Birthday! How does it feel to be eight years old?"

"It feels great," Tania replied with a smile. "How is my grandmother?"

"She seemed fine," Juanita responded. "She said she might come to see you today."

"Really?" Tania didn't know how she felt about that. She wasn't planning to go straight home, but what if Dona Marta was waiting for her? At that moment, Amos walked into the conversation.

"Happy Birthday, Tania!" he said, giving her a hug which lifted her completely off the ground.

"Thanks, Amos! I was just going to look for you! But then these people showed up, and then you showed up, too!"

Amos turned to look at the visitors. His eyes locked with Juanita's, and the words of the prophetess resounded in his mind. He felt a little weak in the legs. Juanita offered her hand and said, "Hello. I'm Juanita, and this is Julio. We were just telling Tania about our scholarship program. We hope she will accept our help."

"I'm Amos," replied the shaken young man. "Tania is in my Bible club. She's a very bright little girl. You couldn't have selected a better student for your scholarship program."

Tania blushed at the compliment.

"Thanks, Amos.

Juanita suddenly seemed uncharacteristically tongue-tied as well.

"Great!" announced Julio, silent until now, but no stranger to this particular brand of tension. "We'll be in touch then. Happy Birthday, Tania!" He had a hand on his sister's arm and gave a gentle squeeze.

"Yes, right!" Juanita nodded, still gazing at Amos. "Now that we know where to find Tania, we'll let you know as soon as everything is in order."

"Do you know how to get in touch with her? Do you have her father's phone number?" Amos queried. "Because I could, you know, give you my number, or we could exchange numbers or . . . "

"Great idea!" Juanita interrupted. Her heart was pumping, and she had all but forgotten about Tania in her sudden enthusiasm to stay connected somehow to -- what was his name – Amos. Julio was smiling and staring at something interesting at his feet so that no one could see his amusement. Amos and Juanita quickly exchanged cell numbers, but remained frozen in place, unwilling to part company.

"Come on, Amos," Tania urged, pulling on one of his big hands. "Let's go by the church, and then Lito is bringing a birthday cake, and he said I could invite somebody. You'll come, won't you? Please?"

"Yes, of course I'll come," Amos responded, forcing his eyes away from Juanita to focus on the excited little girl attached to his arm.

"We'll be going then," said Juanita. "But we'll be in touch soon."

"That will be just fine," Amos assured her. "I -- I mean *Tania*, will look forward to learning more about the scholarship."

Julio gave a tug this time, and he and his sister began their walk towards the bus stop in the opposite direction. Neither of them spoke for several minutes.

"Nice guy," Julio offered. But to his amazement, his normally loquacious sister said nothing – all the way home.

Meanwhile, Tania was dragging Amos towards the church, chattering with hardly a breath between sentences.

"I told Rosita *everything* that happened yesterday, about the church and the prayer, and then Lito came home and I fixed him supper and went to my room, and when Lito was tired of watching TV he went to bed and he didn't call me, and so I went to sleep, too, and then this morning when I woke up I felt so good, and Lito said I looked different. Do you think I look different? Because I looked in the mirror and the only thing different was that I was smiling really big, and I don't remember anything about school this morning because I couldn't wait until it was over to go look for you to tell you about the birthday cake, and I was thinking that maybe you could invite Lito to church because he really needs to meet the prophet lady, and . . ."

"Hey!" Amos laughed. "I didn't know you had so many words inside you! You're usually the quietest one around!"

Tania laughed, too.

"I know! It's like somebody unplugged me down deep inside and everything is running out!" She laughed, too.

"I know how that feels," Amos replied, remembering his own first experience with "the prophet lady."

"It feels *great*," Tania assured him. "I've never felt like this before. I don't ever want to go back to feeling the other way. Do you think Lito will really bring home a cake? I've never had a real bought cake on my birthday."

"I guess he will," Amos conceded. "If he said he would, then he will. In fact, there he is, cake in hand." He motioned with his free hand towards the young mechanic, who seemed happy until he saw whose hand his daughter was holding. A storm cloud quickly replaced the cheerful smile. Once again, Tania was oblivious to everything except her own joy.

"You got it! Look, Amos! He got it!"

"Yes, I got it. I said I would, didn't I? Where did you get *him*? What are you doing with my daughter, Amos?" The irritation was evolving into rage. Amos inwardly called upon the grace of God before answering.

"I was surprised, too, when I found out you were her father," he said easily. "I've known Tania for awhile. She comes to my Bible club. We're friends, right, Tania?"

"Amos is my *best* friend, and you said I could invite somebody to my birthday, so I invited Amos. Anyway, he says

330

you're his friend, too." Tania was now aware of Lito's darkening mood, and her old fears resurfaced.

"I guess I was thinking of some of your *school* friends," he smirked. "I didn't know that Amos hung out with little girls." The irony of the remark aroused a righteous indignation in the neighborhood missionary, and instead of backing down he seemed to grow taller and stronger.

"Careful, *hermanito,*" he responded firmly. "Tania and I have been having some talks, and it appears that you and I need to sit down and discuss your home life. What you have been doing to Tania is against man's law and God's law, and it has to stop."

Lito's face, which had been turning a deep red, now began to pale. Tania had moved closer to Amos, pressing her body into his leg and gripping his hand with both of hers. This confrontation had been completely unexpected, and she was certain that her father would take out his anger on her, as he had so many times before.

"I don't know what you're talking about, *no brother of mine,*" replied Lito, trying very hard not to lose control. "Tania can make up some big stories, can't you, *hija*? I don't know what she said, but our home is just fine, and we don't need any interference from you or anybody else. Come on, Tania, let's go home. We have a birthday to celebrate, don't we?"

But thoughts of a celebration were far from anyone's mind at this point. Tania was trembling, and she looked up at Amos for direction.

"Tania isn't going home with you, Lito." The words were spoken quietly, but with deep authority. "I wouldn't be God's friend, your friend, or her friend if I handed her over to you."

"I get it. You want her for yourself, right? Everybody around here knows you're a pervert. Tania, come with me right now or I'll call the police on your friend. They'll put him in jail, and you'll never see him again. Now let's go." He moved towards the terrified child, and held out his hand.

"No!" she screamed. "I'm not going with you! I'm staying with Amos! If you call the police, I'll tell them what you do to me when nobody's looking! I'll tell *everybody!*" Tania was shaking, but there was no mistaking the determination on her face. She meant what she said.

Lito threw the cake to the ground, and for a moment it seemed that he would lunge at Amos, Tania or both. Eyes wide and fists raised, he froze for a second in indecision and horror. Tania was peering at him from behind Amos, who seemed perfectly at peace, still as a sail in a windless sea.

Lito dropped his fists and ran. Tania began to weep. Amos let out a deep breath, gathered the child into his arms, and walked slowly towards the shelter. The cake remained on the dusty street, a sweet reminder of a sour love, soon devoured by mangy dogs who knew a little themselves of the indiscriminate cruelty of humans. Within a few minutes, the only remaining evidence of the cataclysmic drama was a tattered carton covered with ants. Although it had happened in a way completely unimagined by Tania, her prayer had finally been answered: someone had come for her because of love. That big empty place which had caused such desperate emotional hunger for all of her short life had started to fill.   She felt exhausted in her gratitude, and for the first time began to experience a new sensation: hope.

The bundle nestled against his heart had given Amos something which he had never identified as a personal need or desire, but which had already become his most important reason for putting one foot in front of another.   He had not planned to take responsibility for a little girl, but clearly that had been God's plan. He considered the necessary steps that needed to be taken: prayer with the prophetess, counsel with the shelter director, a phone call to a certain scholarship representative, a visit to Tania's school . . . but first they would get a bite to eat, wash off the day's filth, and worship with the community.   In God's kingdom there is always time for details once the way is committed to Him.

"Thank you, Lord," whispered the new father. "As always, make Your way mine." He climbed the stairs to the shelter door, his pulsing burden lighter with each prayer, their future unknown yet held firmly by the One they trusted most.

"Lord, have mercy," he spoke gently into Tania's ear.

"Lord, have mercy," prayed Juanita, kneeling by her bed, the faces of Santita, Tania, and mostly Amos rolling through her mind.

"Lord, have mercy," muttered Santita, finally at her destination, too tired for a longer conversation with her Father before sliding into a profound sleep.

Little Tania found no words for her new life.   Tears continued to fall, but the despair was gone.   Marta, Lito and the faceless mother were already supporting actors on her heart's stage.   Amos had stood in the breach for her, and he had won!

She knew with the innocence of her age that his love for her was sincere, and that she was safe. She felt that her whole being was a prayer of thanks to Amos and to God, so she ate the simple supper shared with others who had sought refuge from their own daily nightmare, then climbed quietly into a small bed and immediately fell into a deep, dreamless slumber. Rosita would hear no shameful secrets this night. Other children in the shelter cried anxiously, but not Tania. For now, in this moment, she was at peace.

Made in the USA
Charleston, SC
04 February 2014